Ascend

The Aurora Marellup Saga Book 1

Written By:

Serenity Rayne

Special thanks.

Thank you to my husband for believing in me and pushing me to do better.

Thank you most of all to my readers that have stuck by me through the years. Without you I never would have had the courage to keep going.

Adult Supervision Required

Reverse Harem Romance / Why choose?
True / Fated Mates
Medium—Fast Burn
Multiple Points of View
M/M
M/M/M
Wolf on Mate Action
Twin Sammich
Blood and Gore

Musical Inspiration Provided By

A x 7 – Hail to the King
Metallica – Sanitarium
Megadeth – She Wolf
Metallica – Of Wolf and Man
Shinedown – Devil

Contents

Prologue

Royal Fae Court Winter 500AD

This morning I have received word that the other four fae kings have arrived for today's council meeting. The Drow have entirely broken with the beliefs of our race under the leadership of Lolth. They have fled to Illythirr in the Underverse to escape prosecution for their countless crimes. Hundreds have died because of the insurrection that Lolth started, trying to overthrow our once stable government.

The crystalline viewing room is made from varying quartz shades since it harmonizes well with our natural powers. For what I wish to do, I need the other four kings to touch the viewing pool at the same time to harness its full potential. The viewing pool I'm using today is made of pure lapis lazuli, meant to amplify astral travel and clairvoyance. I need to see into the future to ascertain precisely how much trouble the Drow will cause in the future.

Pacing within the viewing chambers, my anxiety has hit an all-time high. My heart hammers within my chest as I wait for the others to join me. First to arrive is King Arathorn Chaephyra of the Woodland Fae. Majestic, as always, he stands tall and proud. His skin a similar hue to the bark of a tree, and his long hair a smokey gray in color. In the tradition of his people, his crown is constructed of dragonroot and bloodstone.

"Blessings and health to you, Arathorn," I say with a flourished bow.

"Blessings and health to you, Oberon. I hope today is productive. The concerns you raised are rather troublesome if they come to fruition," Arathorn states before bowing to me in return. His lithe hands adjust his sand-colored robes before he moves to stand before the leaf carved in the edge of the viewing pool. Slightly I bow my head to him just as the door opens again.

King Arlen Trazana, the most flamboyant of all of us, enters next. He flutters his sliver-blue swallowtail-like wings before folding them behind him. Arlen has short,cropped blue hair, exceptionally on point today; he must have stopped and got a trim on the way here. Bowing deeply, he smiles, looking up at me. "Greetings and health to you and your home, Oberon." His voice hits tones that make mine pale in comparison. If I had to imagine what Gaia's voice sounded like, I would imagine it is similar to his.

Gracefully I return the bow and flourish my hand in the direction of the viewing pool. "Greetings and health to you and yours, Arlen. Please join Arathorn at the pool, if you would be so kind." A soft smile graces my lips as I stand back up again. Before Arlen moves past me, I adjust his flowing, shimmering baby-blue robes so that his folded wings wouldn't get tangled.

"Thank you, brother," Arlen says on his way to his place at the pool. He looks for his wind symbol and traces it with a single finger, smiling all the while. I catch him admiring his own reflection in the waters of the pool, looking over his perfect pale skin and gray, almost silver, eyes.

King Tanyth Parona of the Moon Fae and King Narbeth Quivaris of the Sun Fae arrive simultaneously, still bickering over which clan makes the best weapons. Rolling my eyes, I move forward to garner their attention. Once I possess both kings' attention, I bow deeply and flourish my hand in the direction of the viewing pool. "Greetings and health to you and yours," I say to both kings at the same time, showing no favoritism to either clan.

The stark contrast between the kings is evident in appearance, manners, and tone of voice. Tanyth responds in a soft musical tone. His bright blue eyes are mesmerizing, contrasted with his iridescent silver hair and pale skin. Narbeth, on the other hand, lacks the musical quality to his voice that most Fae possess. His flame-red hair and sunkissed golden-brown skin sing of the days he spends in the bright sunlight. They both respond with the traditional greeting and move to their places on the viewing table.

As the King of the High Fae, it is my place to keep order of all known species within the realms. Unfortunately, with Lolth breaking away from his kin and taking all of the Drow with him, this poses a significant safety issue within the realm. Once everyone is in position, I place my hand upon my mark and the pool's surface begins to ripple.

The initial vision moves to Skaldi Nyx Atriox, otherwise known as the Blood Queen. "Our first creation seems to be doing well, is she not?" Narbeth questions as the pool focuses on her rending the flesh from the Orcs that had invaded the southern part of her territory. The Orcs were released from the Underverse by the Drow; thankfully, Skaldi is strong enough to handle it.

"Yes, she is, but we need to see what the future holds if we don't interfere," I state, and the other kings agree with me. I move the visions forward twelve-hundred years, and Skaldi is in decline. Her Grandson, Nicodeamus Tepish, rises to power next and rules for almost three hundred years before the Drow rise-up. Battle after battle, the species of old are slowly slaughtered to extinction. Next, the Drow begin to march on the Strigoi as well as the human settlements. Each skirmish brings about a higher death toll until the human race has no paranormal defenders left to protect them. In the end, the humans are slaves, and our settlements are burned to ash.

Arlen, the most peaceful of us all, stands there with his hands in fists and his teeth gritted so hard his jaw trembles. "I implore you to allow us to interfere yet again. We must create a defender that no Drow will ever be able to destroy." His gray eyes flash wildly as he looks to each of us, hoping to sway the verdict.

"I second the motion; there are many powerful bloodlines that we can mix. Perhaps create a hybrid similar to our cousins, the Lythari, that helped create the Lycan and Dire Wolf races." Arathorn shrugs his shoulders as he passes a hand over the pool to the point in time where Anca Marelup is forced to take her mates.

"What if we send Skaldi's grandson here, and he's a true mate of the last Marelup? We would have to send a special tincture to make sure the hybrid is created and survives gestation." Arathorn stands tall, knowing full well his plan so far is the most solid.

Leaning forward, waving my hand over the pool, the scene rewinds and then proceeds how Arathorn suggested. "Who shall we send with the tincture?" I question, looking directly at Arlen.

He rolls his eyes and huffs. "We can send my niece, Laurel, to deliver the tincture and make sure our plans are carried out to the letter." Arlen bows his head, having offered his niece's services for part of the plan.

"Excellent," is all I say before I wave my hand again, fast-forwarding through time. The Marelup Queen dies in labor, and our creation is born. Waving my hand again, moving time forward, we see our creation as a young child, shifting for the first time after being attacked by a cougar. She decimates her attacker and carries the head home. So far, so good. We leap through time again until she's about a hundred years old. Furrowing my brows, I study the tea the older woman keeps sending her. I rewind time to when the tea is packaged. Blood magic is at work, but to what end? Our creation's beast loves her protector's Bear; they're mates, but something in the tea is blocking the bond. "Should we interfere here and free their bond, so it flourishes?" I question the others.

"No," Tanyth states, then moves time forward and shows the importance of the stalled bond. We watch her battle time and time again, success after success. That is, until the Drow rise again. Hmm... She never took a dragon mate. Sebastian lives even after all of his deception.

"This blasphemy cannot be allowed to happen," Arlen says, then waves his hand over the water moving through time at a break-neck pace. He stops at a particular point and allows a Polar Bear to get involved. The course of history changes dramatically. Our creation takes an Ice Dragon – Gold Dragon hybrid as a mate. They birth twins, which is unheard of for Ice Dragons to do. The female has all the markers of Skaldi, plus the attributes of the Titanium and Silver dragons that had long since been extinct.

"Perfect," I say as I move time forward again, watching the hatchling mature and take her mate. Unexpectantly with the Drow's abduction, she ascends far younger than we had anticipated. The amount of power that child holds is staggering. Simultaneously we release our grips on the table and look at each other in shock. We may have just have figured out how to end the Drow once and for all. I stare down at the blank reflective surface of the pool in awe of what I had just seen. In my gut, I have a feeling this may be me signing my own death warrant.

All of this interference isn't natural; then again, neither are the Drow. I can only hope the Goddess keeps me safe over the centuries to come. The other kings bow and leave quickly to carry out their part of this plan. At sunrise tomorrow, I shall set my part in motion. After that, it's all just a matter of time.

CHAPTER 1

Anca

Moldavia, July 17, 1791

My ancestral home resides at the top of one of the most treach-
erous mountains in the Moldivian range. Winding narrow cliff-
side roads are the only way to ascend the mountain to my castle.
At the very peak, my family's castle sits. Tall, proud, white spires
reach towards the heavens, getting lost within the cloud cover.
The main gates are hand-forged wrought iron depicting a pair of
wolves locked in battle. The roadway leading up to the castle
doors are made of cobble stone; the clacking of the horses
hooves can be heard where I sit. I seek refuge within the castle's
library. So many centuries of knowledge are contained within
these walls. The shelves are a myriad of colors on every subject
you could imagine.

I'm stuck sitting here looking over the scrolls of the families
whom have sons of proper age that make a good mate for me.
The list feels never ending as I sort though the bloodlines, making
sure no one is related to me. It's such tedious work, and my father

wants a list of suitors I'm willing to meet. Gently I shake my head, looking over what seems like a mile-long list.

Out of all the females of my family, I am the oldest to ascend. None of the healers know why it took over a hundred and fifty years for it to happen. All of the mystics my family consulted had no answers as to why. I honestly don't care; I don't want to face the trials to select my mates. Whatever happened to falling in love naturally? instead of being forcibly brought together and hoping they click. I furrow my brows as I ponder my soon to be sealed fate. Today, hopefully, will pass quickly and without incident.

The click of the latch for the door echoes in the library, forcing my eyes to raise and watch to see who has come to disturb me. The high priestess of the clan enters without knocking, carrying a jug and cups.

"Have you made a decision, Princess?" the priestess states, a sneer crosses her lips as she narrows her eyes.

"No," I state as tersely as possible. I don't want to have to deal with the priestess at this moment.

"The king expects a list from you by sundown today. Otherwise, he will send for the males I've selected for you to meet." The priestess tilts her head, looking at me, waiting for some sort of a reaction she can complain to my father about.

If she wasn't warming my father's bed, I would have slit her throat from ear to ear years ago. I roll my eyes, then I finally answer, resigning myself to my fate. "Fine, you and Father pick the males I'm supposed to meet. It's not like my choice makes any difference; you'll get your way in the end." I stand and grab the scrolls I was looking over and walk over to the fireplace. Before the priestess can react, I toss the lists into the fire, watching them turn to ash. I turn triumphantly, smiling, placing both hands on the tabletop, and staring at the priestess.

"You wonder why we make all the decisions for you, Princess; you're brash and impulsive," she says, flailing her hands in the air. "You'll never make any male a good mate with the way you are." The priestess waves her hand dismissively in my direction. "You need Alpha males to put you in your proper place and guide you to make the best decisions." She bares her canines at me as she looks back at the ornate pitcher she brought with her.

The priestess pours two cups of the scented tea she has brought with her. With a flourish and a smile, she places my favorite flower-covered teacup in front of me, filled to the brim. Suspiciously, I look at the cup before me, staring at the dark amber fluid within; then over to the priestess, studying her features. The priestess makes a big deal out of sipping at the tea before her. I scrutinize every movement of every muscle in her face and throat, trying to discern if she actually drank the tea or not.

I have never liked the priestess and her bossy ways; the trust has never been there, she always seems to have ulterior motives. The priestess is very close to Grigore and his family. Every waking moment she's encouraging me to take Vladimir as my mate. I ponder as I look down at my tea. It smells okay, and it would be rude not to drink it. Several moments pass before I raise the glass to my lips and drink the sweet tea. The priestess's expression changes, and a wicked smile plays upon her lips. Fuck, she tricked me. Deep in the recesses of my mind, my wolf begins to howl and rage. Something is wrong; my fight-or-flight instinct kicks in. I find out quite quickly that I can't summon my beast anymore. Suddenly, the fight drains out of me, and I just don't seem to care anymore.

The priestess moves to my side and walks me out of the library. In the hallway, she hands me off to my handmaiden. "Dress her appropriately; she's meeting the mates her father has selected for her tonight." The tone of her voice chills me to the bone, the lack of emotion is frighting. I move, not of my own volition, following the handmaiden. The further I walk, the less I seem to care about what's happening; I'm numb to everything.

****The Priestess****

The handmaiden nods and moves off with Anca, heading to her suite. After handling things with her, I head towards the west wing and into a secret passageway; one no one seems to know about. Looking left then right, I slide the secret door open and walk through. The door moves slowly and closes on its own with a soft whoosh, sealing me inside. Several twists and turns later, I enter a large room in an older part of the castle. The smell of mildew and mold hangs heavily in the air as I push open the large oak door.

The room used to be the original war room. The walls are still covered with maps of the kingdoms along our borders. A small weapons rack still sits close to the desk loaded with rapiers and dirks. Several suits of armor are placed between the bookcases from different points in our kingdom's history. The man standing at the head of the table is Grigore, captain of the king's guard. "Did you succeed?" Grigore stands tall, broad shoulders back as he puffs his chest out, looking down at me.

"Yes, she drank the tea and herbs. I have the handmaiden preparing her to meet the mates you picked out for her, M'lord."

I make sure to bow deeply and gradually stand up to face him again.

"Good. Of my three sons, I only trust Vladimir to handle this unruly bitch." Grigore motions to Vladimir who's leaning against a bookcase not far from his father. His chiseled features scream predator and to run at the first chance you get. His eyes bore into you, hollow and filled with hatred. Grigore starts to speak again, snapping me out of my inner monologue.

"If we didn't need an heir from her to ascend to the throne, I'd say kill them all. Let the gods sort the bodies out." Grigore looks to his left, where his sons Vladimir, Josef, and Jacob sit together.

Vladimir is smug and almost a spitting image of his father, hatred and all. Josef and Jacob are twins, though much smaller than Vladimir. I glance back over Grigore's three sons then back to him quickly.

"I must take my leave before anyone goes looking for me." Carefully I start to back up, attempting to cut this meeting as short as humanly possible. It's probably the smartest move that I have made today. Never give a predator your back; you never know when they may strike.

"Oh, I forgot to inform you: you'll be teaching my daughters blood magic. They may need it in the future." A twisted smile plays upon Grigore's weathered lips as his yellowed teeth are exposed in a creepy manner. "A father only wants what's best for his daughters; they need to be able to handle any situation that may come up." He looks over to his daughters, Elena and the elder dame. *Grigore must be a lot older than I had initially thought, I say to myself.*

I lightly bow my head to Grigore and his children, then exit the room swiftly. I run down the stairs heading towards the dungeons. Just past the primary cells off to the side sits my private study as well as laboratory. Several books are thrown onto the table, most on blood magic as well as transmogrification.

A gentle knock sounds at the door which catches me off guard. I look up from the book I am reading, startled to see Laurel standing there wringing her hands together.

"Priestess… has it begun?" The beautiful, young elven woman stands there, several strands of her pink hair covering her eyes.

"Yes, my dear, it has." I finish writing on a scroll and hand it to Laurel.

"Take this directly to Oberon and then return." I stare down at the scroll as it leaves my hand. "I gave the unsuspecting mother the herbs mixed in with the blood magic I used. She will produce a hybrid at the cost of her own life." I try to show no remorse over my role in this event.

Laurel takes the scroll and holds it close to her chest. "I will deliver it straight away. Oberon will be most pleased with you." A quick bow of her head, and she is gone in a wisp of glimmering light.

"What have I done?" I lower my head into my hands; regret almost instantly begins to sink in. My stomach is in knots, knowing full well the magnitude of what I have done. Basically, I have assisted in assassinating the last pureblood Marelup. I'll be responsible for bringing an abomination into this world.

Later today, those two wicked daughters of Grigore will begin to learn blood magic. Tonight, poor Anca will be bound to four males undeserving of her. The last of a noble bloodline shall forever be tainted.

I stand off to the side, watching the gala in full swing as dignitaries from all around begin to gather to watch Anca accept her mates. On the other hand, Anca sits upon her throne with a blank expression on her face, devoid of any emotion. The king is off speaking to Grigore before the presentation begins. Vladimir, Josef, and Jacob all approach the throne heading directly towards Anca. Her dead eyes lock with Vladimir. Languidly she rises from her throne and moves to stand before him. Anca is easily five inches shorter than Vladimir and has to crane her neck to look up at him.

They stand there, staring at each other for several minutes. There's zero emotion betrayed on Anca's face. A sigh escapes her lips before she leans her neck off to the side. Submission to Vladimir is given without contention, and quickly he moves and bites her shoulder, sinking his canines in deep. My stomach churns with bile watching this mockery of a mating ceremony taking place. No pain or pleasure registers on Anca's face as she stares off over the crowd with dead eyes. Vladimir releases her shoulder and grips her neck to bring her mouth to his shoulder. Several attempts are made before Anca bites his shoulder in return. Cheers go up throughout the hall. Boldly, Vladimir moves to the king's throne and sits down. He's already assuming the mantle of king.

Anca is just a shell of herself as she sits upon her throne. She watches the party with unseeing eyes. The leader of the Great Bear Clan, Mikhail, arrives; Vladimir stands and greets him. With Mikhail is Dimitri Kovac, now assigned to be the queen's personal guard. Dimitri doesn't look thrilled with how Anca is acting. His eyes narrow, studying her closely.

Vladimir motions to Anca, and she stands only to move sluggishly to Vladimir's side. Vladimir passes Anca to Mikhail as if she holds no value to him. Her dead eyes look up to Mikhail, and Vladimir issues the order to submit once Dimitri has walked away. Gradually Anca tilts her head to the side and exposes her throat to Mikhail. He hesitates for a moment, then sinks his canines deep into her flesh. Anca shows no reaction to his bite, except a single tear that rolls down her cheek. Mikhail withdraws his canines and then presses Anca's mouth to his shoulder. Several seconds pass before Anca bites Mikhail's shoulder; she holds on for only a few moments before she heads back to her throne.

Even drugged, Anca's depression becomes evident. She's now bound to two males unworthy of her. The doors to the grand ballroom blow open, and with it the temperature begins to drop swiftly. Anca's head remains lowered as she stares at her wine glass, barely able to keep her thoughts straight. Frost on her glass catches her attention, and it's the first time this entire gala that her wolf has stirred.

Gradually she raises her head, and sees the beautiful man standing before her. I'm finally excited for her. This time, she appears to have some semblance of control over herself. His eyes churn like liquid mercury around his Dragon slits. His hair is as white as freshly fallen snow, and his skin is as smooth as fine china. Anca moves for the first time tonight of her own volition.

Without warning, her Lycan forces her shift and raises its head to howl her summoning call. All the Lycans within the great hall break free of their human bonds at her call, my own beast included. All eight feet of heavily-muscled Lycan stalks forward, toward the beautiful man.

"*Mine,*" her wolf says through the pack bond, and that is all Anca needs to hear.

Quickly her beast strikes, sinking her canines deep within the unknown male's shoulder. I watch Anca react to his fingers threading through her rough fur in soothing circles. Carefully she withdraws her canines and licks his wounds clean. Her pure-silver orbs stare down at his draconic eyes, while the beautiful man removes his cloak and wraps it around her beast's shoulders.

Anca shifts back to her human form quickly and stares up at the hunk of a man. His shoulders are broad and heavily muscled. He gently kisses Anca's forehead, then nuzzles her cheek and she willingly moves her head to the side. He finds an unmarked spot close to her throat and bites her. Anca wraps her hand around the back of the man's neck, holding his head to her shoulder. For the first time tonight, I see that Anca is actually smiling; this man's powerful blood has erased whatever spell she was under before. He gently cleans his bite and looks Anca in the eyes.

"My name is Nicodeamus Tepish, of the Ice Dragon court, first-born prince. You, my beautiful, fierce Anca, are my mate. I will love you forever and a day." He reaches down and lifts her hand to his lips, and kisses her knuckles.

I watch Vladimir standing off to the side, fuming while watching the event transpire. Anca's shift marks her true mate's arrival, thus lowering his chances of fathering the first child with her.

Suspiciously, he gathers those closest to him and begins to plot what to do next to secure his place on the throne. The representative from the Dire Wolves arrives tomorrow evening. All he has to do is drug Anca again and get her to accept the last fool to arrive. Her heat is due to start any day now, so in theory all he has to do is make sure he's the only one able to produce an heir.

CHAPTER 2

Dimitri

Moldavia, Romania

Night of the Wolf Celebration

November 30, 1791

Festivities are underway within the Lycan castle. Wolves and other shifters from surrounding clans are gathered for the celebrations. Queen Anca sits upon her gold and crimson dais, hand resting on her heavily pregnant belly. Her dark crimson gown hugs her generously. Within her womb is the heir to the Lycan Empire. Her gunmetal-gray eyes follow her mates' movements throughout the hall as they mingle with the various creatures gathered. I notice the mild contractions had begun almost a half-hour ago. It was still too soon to alert anyone to the impending birth. This child would be the first one born in about one hundred years. How fitting that the pup chose tonight to make its appearance.

I am a local Great Bear Shifter, tasked with the protection of the Queen and Heir. My hazel eyes lock onto the Queen's hands and her stomach; something has changed. My eyes churn, turning golden as my bear rises to the surface. Quickly I cut through the crowd and arrive at her side.

"My Queen, is it time?" I tilt my head to the side, eyes focused and muscles tensed, ready to spring into action. The Queen slowly turns her head to face me.

"Soon, my friend. Send Andre to gather the Elder Dame to my chambers. We will follow shortly." Anca's voice is strained as she tries to remain composed, watching the gala. I turn slowly and lock eyes with Andre; a simple short nod of the head sends him off to do his Queen's bidding. I then watch for the Queen's mates to look towards the dais; one by one, they are given the signal— only the Alpha King, Vladimir, approaches.

"Is it time, my love?" he speaks reverently to his mate. His tone, however, doesn't convey the affection his words suggest. He offers her his hand and helps her stand up. Anca nods her head slightly. Carefully and slowly, she stands. Vladimir and I flank her as we escort her to the birthing chambers. Several stops are made as the contractions increased in power. Poised and proper to a fault, Anca refuses to show pain or weakness. She clenches her jaw and lightly growls through the pain. Her eyes bleed to the liquid mercury of her she-wolf, both of them anxious to meet their pup.

Once within the chambers, the Elder Dame leads her to the bed and prepares her for the birthing. Vladimir paces the rooms anxiously, waiting for the arrival of his firstborn child. I move and take my post just outside of the chamber, but remain close enough if I need to get back quickly. The Queen's agonizing screams during labor makes even my big bear cringe. The tones she hits sounds like she is being murdered within her chambers.

A sudden pounding on the door startles me, making me turn and rip the door open. In the hallway, I find the Queen's second mate, Mikhail. His face and clothes are covered in blackened blood. "The Strigoi are attacking; we must evacuate Anca and the pup, now!" As soon as his statement leaves his bloody lips, I whip my head around, looking back towards the birthing chambers. Anca's blood-curdling screams pierce the night.

"I'll see to it myself, M'lord. Send Andre. Worst case scenario, he can fly off with the pup while we move your mate." I hope my words are what Mikhail wanted to hear. A swift nod was all he gave before he retreats and takes off running down the hallway. I double bolt and barricade the door before running to update my charges. Andre's Golden Eagle sits on the windowsill before dropping into the room to join the evacuation.

Anca screams and thrashes on the bed with each contraction. Unable to shift, she grips onto the sheets for dear life. The Elder Dame keeps passing different herb mixtures to Anca, but nothing is helping. Without warning, the sheets start staining red with blood. Way too much blood for it to be from labor alone. The Elder Dame draws back the drenched sheet to find tiny white talons ripping through Anca's flesh. Anca screams, her voice growing horse from effort. Nicodeamus's dragon calls back to her in the distance.

Several moments pass, and the partially-shifted little baby has clawed its way free of her mother's womb. The blood-drenched, hairless Lycan pup paws at the flesh of its mother as it drags itself free of her womb. Vladimir orders for his daughter to be cleaned immediately and tended to. He shows no concern for the Queen as she lies dying, bleeding out in her own bed. Her dying words whispered, begging for her Seraphina to be protected. I watch Anca as the life drains from her body, desperately wanting to save her but not sure how to. The internal damage to Anca's body is too significant. The Queen expires silently, her lifeless gray eyes looking in the direction of her daughter. I turn, watching the Alpha pace back and forth next to the bed. Vlad is deep in thought as the Elder Dame slowly covers Anca's lifeless body, as he gently rocks the tiny package in his arms, humming softly.

The Elder Dame brings forth the family crest—the blackened brand that all Marelup descendants were marked with. Andre and I stand shoulder to shoulder, watching the little bundle get marked. A shrill scream comes from the pup as the silver burns her flesh. The sounds of battle drift to us as the fight draws ever closer to the birthing chambers. Swords clashing, and the shrieks of the Strigoi draw closer. His back suddenly straightens, and his presence becomes commanding. "Take my daughter, Aurora! Please, protect her with your lives!"

The Elder Dame comes forth with a magical potion and a very sharp dagger. "I must bind her to one of you; otherwise, without a pack she will be amongst the lost ones—insane from the lack of a pack." Her eyes dart between Andre and I then settle on me. "You're a predator like she is; a beast. You will be the best candidate! Give me your arm, Dimitri!" Such authority from a little old woman almost frightens me. I hold out my left arm to her. She dips the blade into the magical elixir, then makes a swift cut across my forearm. The wound stings then turns to a warm tingle as the flesh begins to knit back together.

Her amber eyes turn to the pup still in Vlad's arms, pulling out her tiny left arm and repeating the process. Instantly I feel her like she's a part of me. I feel such a sense of wonder as I am handed the pup. This tiny cherub looks like a mini version of her mother, right down to the gunmetal-gray eyes and ruby lips. Hands grip my shoulders and turn me, snapping me out of my inner thoughts. "You must go!" the Elder Dame shouts at me, then pulls out a gnarly, twisted stick from her robe and flourishes it in the air. Energy explodes into the room as a rip in the fabric of reality opens before us.

"Go! My sister Elena will shelter you in the new world. Go now!" As soon as she finishes imploring us, a harsh pounding starts coming from the direction of the door. The cracking sound of the wooden door starting to give way dispels any hesitation we had. Without a second thought, Andre, the pup, and I venture into the unknown.

Vladimir

Wood splinters fly everywhere as a dozen Strigoi break into the room, remnants of the door littering the floor. The metallic tang of blood and the scent of spilled birthing fluid mixed with magic lie heavily in the air. The Elder Dame and I remain in the room, looking without fear at the monsters beginning to fill it.

The Strigoi are a vile bunch; ashen skin, long, pointed, bat-like ears, and dozens of needle-like teeth fill their mouths. Their noses are the most disturbing part of them. They are a larger version of a bat's flared and rippled nose. On the tips of their long, boney fingers, sharp, hooked claws glisten with the blood of my people. These horrid creatures reek of sulfur death and decay and look as if they had freshly risen from the grave. They stand there as Tomas moves through the gathered horde to stand before myself and the Elder Dame.

"You shouldn't have tried to exile us forever, Vladimir, we are many." He flourishes his boney, clawed hand towards the door.

"Your kind is dying off." I face off with the Strigoi Alpha showing no fear. Tomas's needle-like fangs glisten in the candlelight, fresh blood staining his chin and chest.

"Once our pets, now our wardens... Wardens no more! Now you are food for the horde." Tomas steps forward. Slender, clawed hands flexing as he tries to bait me.

"Your kin lay dead at the feet of my kind. Your allies run in fear and die before me. You are king no more." As he speaks, droplets of blood fall from his mouth and onto his chest. Tomas's black eyes drift to the sheet-covered body on the bed and smiles. "Shame, I wanted to dine on the blood of your pup."

That made my blood boil. That creature wanted my daughter, my only heir. We lost the pup's mother in childbirth. I would not let anything happen to alert the Strigoi that my daughter had survived. "You want the crown, come for it..." I know this fight could mean my death. My eyes drift to the Elder Dame, a slight nod tells me my precious cargo is safe. My last thoughts are of the daughter I would never get to know as I charge into what may be my final battle.

Nicodeamus

On the far side of the castle, I fall from the sky the moment my mate died. My chest feels as though the weight of a thousand worlds lay upon my heart, smashing it to dust. My dragon bellows his grief into the night; its mate is gone. Slowly, he releases his hold over me and allows me to return to my human form. By some miracle I feel the faint thread of life that is my child. Somehow, even though my mate had perished, she lived long enough to deliver our baby into this world. This small joy spurns me on to seek out what's left of my mate and my surviving child.

The battle wages on throughout the castle as I barrel through Strigoi and Dires alike. Reaching the demolished birthing chamber to find the Elder Dame in a magical sphere, where a lone Strigoi attempts to attack her. My hands shift into my taloned gauntlets, and without a second thought I cut the Strigoi's head free from his shoulders. A satisfying, wet thud resounds through the room when its body hits the floor.

My eyes drift to the blood-covered sheets before me. Slowly, walking to the edge of the bed, I lift the corner of the sheet. I have to see my Anca one last time. Her abdomen is shredded, a hole was created where it looked like something punched its way out. My eyes go wide, horrified at what's left of my beloved mate. Silent tears stream down my cheeks and drip onto the floor. My heart sinks further as I begin to mourn the death of not only my mate, but also my hatchling too. I turn slowly, looking at the destruction around me.

The Elder Dame approaches and squeezes my shoulder. "I couldn't do anything for Anca, M'lord. The baby was partially shifted during the birth and ripped her way out of her mother." The Elder dame moves forward and motions to the hole in Anca's abdomen. "She's a powerful one, the strongest I've seen in generations."

The Elder Dame lowers her head and sighs. "I sent the baby to my sister, where she will be safe. The Strigoi have yet to cross the ocean, so she will have time to grow strong. They won't be able to find her until she ascends." She lifts her eyes to lock with mine, hoping to give me some comfort.

I turn back to look at Anca; carefully, I close her eyes and kiss her lips one last time. Slowly I pull the sheet back up and over Anca's body before turning to the Elder Dame. "Leave now. I will cremate my love and send her to the great beyond." I wait for the Elder Dame to leave before breathing my frost flames upon my love. I watch as the bed ignites and begins to burn as I back into the hallway, watching the fire burn my beloved mate.

That was my fatal mistake; once outside the door, a broadsword comes down and lobs off my left arm. My remaining hand shoots up, burning white-hot to stop the bleeding and cauterize the wound. I whip around quickly to find the Dire's Beta, Lucian, holding the sword's point to my throat. "Surrender and live; fight, and I'll take your head where you stand." A sinister sneer crosses his thin lips as he stares at me. His cold, hazel-green eyes bore into me, challenging me to make a move against him.

For now, I have to bide my time and make sure to live long enough for my child to find me. Even though my dragon fights against my decision and wants to rage for what has been done. I must surrender so we could live to fight another day.

CHAPTER 3

Aurora

Present Day

Heavy tones ring out from my amplifier as I jam out on my guitar. The main riffs from Avenged Sevenfold's "Hail to the King" fill my room and probably most of the house and yard. The tones make the glass in the windows vibrate with each cord I hit. The song speaks to me about things to come, about things that could have been. Playing music is how I work through the vast span of time that I've lived through.

For the last two hundred and twenty-eight years, we've always been on the move. Never have I been able to call a house a home or a section of woods my territory. My wolf grows restless as time goes on, feeling more like a listless rogue than the Alpha I am meant to become. My guardians keep me isolated from most of the world for my own safety because of who I was born to be. I am the last Lycan Princess destined to reclaim my mother's throne from the Strigoi. No pressure, right? Music has always helped me work through all the anger that has built up over the past decades.

Why am I so angry? one may wonder. Well, let's see here. An ancient evil murdered my family, took over my kingdom, and because of that, I'm stuck in some fucked up witness protection program. The last hundred years have been the most difficult. Not only do I have dreams of battles I've never fought in, but I've also started dreaming of a man that looks like a Viking, who has been teaching me how to fight in my dreams.

The man in my dreams has long white hair as I do, and his eyes are the same steel-gray as mine. I believe him to be a relative or an ancestor of mine. His lessons are in images and actions; I never hear his voice, but instinctively I know what he's trying to convey. From the descriptions Dimitri has given me, I believe the man in my dreams is the lost Dragon King. But why would I be dreaming of him? The lessons I've learned are quite useful. Hell, I've used some of this new knowledge against Dimitri in some of our sparring sessions.

I stop playing as Andre drops off a new cup of tea from Elena. Something about this tea takes the edge off of everything. Sipping my tea slowly, I start thinking of Dimitri; I have a major crush on him. Like really bad. My wolf is convinced he's ours; though, I'm not so sure. Shouldn't I feel something towards him as well? I mean, I do love him, and that love has changed from father-figure to friend; and with the urging of my wolf, it's a little more than it used to be. If he were ours, he wouldn't go out to be intimate with other females.

Maybe it's just a first love crush that eventually I'll forget ever happened. Then again, I admit it; I'm jealous. Angry even... Though honestly, I'm not sure if it's just the mystical bond that makes me think I love him. It's probably because I'm always so lonely. Sighing deeply, I switch songs to something a little sad to fit my heartache.

My fingers trace the length of the scar that, over time, seems to have stretched as I grew. I find myself staring at this mystical lojack. What male in his right mind would want to be bound to a baby? Dimitri is kind of stuck with me because of the Elder Dame's magic that binds us. Dimitri's and Andre's lives are directly tied to mine, thus extending their lifespans far beyond what it should have been. Andre, I had found out, was attached to Dimitri because of their jobs. So when Dimitri was bound to me, Andre had been roped in—to a lesser extent. How fucked up is that?

I wonder what will happen to them when I choose my first mate and the bond is broken. Will they instantly die? Or will they slowly age like ordinary people? Lost within a sea of emotions, I almost miss feeling Dimitri coming closer before I see him. He must be sensing the turmoil within me at the moment. Sometimes I can't stand to look him in the eyes. I know he sneaks into town to take care of his needs, I *feel* it—probably the cruelest part of this binding. He gets to share my lifespan, and I get the eternal pain of knowing when he gets laid.

Speaking of the bear, there he is in the doorway; looking at me, sipping his tea, and trying to discern my mood. "Aurora, are you okay, love? You feel like a maelstrom of emotions." He tilts his head to the left and studies me more. His eyes glow a gold-tone, signs that his bear is flaring to the surface. Honestly, lately, I've enjoyed the bear's company more than his. Dimitri is a rather large man in stature in comparison to Andre. Think of the guys from the strongman competitions, and that's D. His honey-brown hair and matching hazel eyes make him appear as if he's very approachable. His current expression betrays his concern because of my mood.

The air shifts slightly, and a new scent is blown my way. Instantly my beast becomes a raging mess; it's another female in her territory. I sit my guitar down and stand up. Slowly, stalking towards him, sniffing the air. Panic streaks across his face; he knows what I smell, and a deep guttural growl escapes my curled lips.

My wolf makes her presence known as my canines lengthen while I assess him. I see Andre coming over his shoulder, running towards us before he skids to a stop halfway down the hallway. Slowly, turning my attention back to Dimitri. I find myself not even a foot away from him, my nostrils flaring.

"How dare you!" Baring my canines at him, "Entering my den smelling of some whore!" I growl. I am literally shaking, trying to keep from ripping him apart. My snow-white fur ripples up and down my arms as my beast demands retribution. "It's bad enough I fucking *feel* every time you get off. I don't need to smell her too,"

I seethed through clenched teeth. "My wolf wants her head and her blood on our talons. You may have signed that slut's death warrant just 'cause you wanted to get your dick wet," I snarl and feel my hands shift and lengthen into talons. Flexing my hands several times, my eyes are fixated on my talons' sharp planes, imagining them covered in blood. Raising my gaze slowly, I watch his face visibly pales as he takes several steps back with his hands up in a pacifying manner.

"I didn't know Aurora..." He gulps, eyes wide as saucers. "I didn't know you could feel that?" He looks honestly horrified and remorseful at his actions. Shaking his head slowly, a single tear breaks free from his left eye and rolls down his cheek. I've never seen a sign of weakness from the big guy. Hell, he's six foot five and over four hundred pounds of solid muscle. I've never seen him cry. Hell, I never in a million years thought I'd see him cry.

"I'd love to say it's fine, but it's not. I've been dealing with this for the last hundred years." I take a deep breath and push my wolf to the back of my mind as I turn and walk to the other side of my room.

"Please, leave... go shower, burn those clothes... Fuck... just please leave... I can't deal with this right now." My voice breaks as I utter the last half of the statement. My heart feels as if it's in a vice being crushed.

Fuck, *I* was ready to cry. I hate fucking crying. I wipe my eyes, trying to hide my pain. How many times can my heart get broken before my damned wolf will give up on the bear that honestly doesn't want us? After a few moments, I hear a sniffled "sorry" and listen to Dimitri walk off. I remain standing rigid, trying to show no signs of weakness even though I feel my world come down around me. A softer set of footsteps enter my den and slowly approach. I know it's Andre, and I lower my head in defeat and relax my stance considerably.

"Hi, Andre," escapes my lips far softer than I anticipated.

"Baby girl. I'm so sorry this is hurting you so badly." He hesitates as he starts to reach out to me, then stops himself. "Why didn't you say anything to him? Or to me?" He sighs softly. "I would have talked to him and let him know what you're going through." Andre was distraught; he's the best friend I could ever ask for. He slowly approaches me, his movements careful and calculated, making sure not to set my wolf off. His lithe hand gently rests on my shoulder and rubs softly, trying to comfort me.

"Why would I take away his freedom and his choice?" Raising my eyebrows, I open my eyes wide.

"I'm the one that must wait for my first heat to come into my full power." My emotions are a mess as tears freely roll down my cheeks in frustration.

"I'm the one who must wait until then to start choosing my mates and gaining power. No one needs to share my hell with me. No one needs to suffer as I do." Wrapping my arms tightly around my stomach, I slowly turn my head to look into his eyes; he seems just as sad as I feel.

"Baby girl, we are here for you. I am here for you," Andre says with so much conviction. "I'll talk to the big guy. Why don't you go hunting? You know that will make you feel better." Andre motions back to the kitchen. "Elena sent us another care package, I'll leave it for you to open later."

As usual, Andre is right. Hunting will clear my head, and I can take my aggression out on my dinner. "Okay, I'll be back by nightfall." Slowly, I turn fully and kiss him on his forehead. "You have been a wonderful father, Andre." I had to let him know how much I appreciate him. I smile weakly at him before moving off to get ready to hunt.

I start stripping off my clothes as I head out of my sliding glass door. As my feet hit the grass, the shift takes me quickly. My bones break and grow and shift alignment. My muscles stretch and gain in mass, my arms and legs elongate, and my knees break and bend backward. Thick, white fur covers my body as the final changes take place. Last to change are my fingernails that grow to look like long-hooked talons. Tiny, silver-white, scale-like growths surround them.

It seems that with each shift I go through as I get older, more and more white scales appear. My muzzle is longer and broader than the average Lycan. The boney prominence on my muzzle is raised, unlike any wolf I have ever seen. My skull is broader and thicker, with long pointed ears. Almost all eight feet of Lycan stretches out before I start moving towards the woods. Unlike other wolves, I'm bipedal—like the werewolves of horror movies, but bigger and scarier. I'm a freak, and I know it. I kind of like being unique; it makes me feel special. I would almost say I was an albino, but I tan every summer, so that thought is out of the question.

I haven't ever seen another Lycan like me. Then again, I've only ever seen one other. Our friend Elena is also Lycan, but her fur is black as night. She says that's the natural color for our species coat. It makes me wonder if the Alpha, my mother's first mate, was my father or if one of the other males is my sire. The shit you think about to distract you from heartache. Logically, the Alpha couldn't be. I mean, his fur was black like my mother's.

I take a running start and leap up into the air to sink my talons into the cliff-face and start climbing. The cliff's face is a vertical climb and so worth the strain to get to the top. I've been climbing this cliff for the last few years—to be honest, it's gotten relatively easy. The area I want to hunt in is on the other side of this divide. Reaching the top, I haul myself over and creep on all fours to look down into the valley below.

My liquid-mercury eyes lock onto a herd of deer in the distance, moving towards the lake. It's a good-sized herd for this time of year. There's a decent blend of old and young deer, which usually means the herd is healthy. Calculating the distance to the large oak tree, I take a running start and leap through the air flying towards my target.

Landing softly, my talons sink deeply into the tree's bark. I scan the perimeter and plan the next several jumps needed to be within striking distance. One last jump and I'm at a fork in the trail where the deer should cross. The wind is blowing from behind them into my face; the wind is perfect for my attack. A roar sounds in the distance, scaring the herd and sending them running. Okay, now I'm genuinely pissed off. There went my motherfucking hunt. Something is going to die, so help me.

I remain in the tree, talons digging into the bark, as I wait to see what just ruined my fun. Then it hits me; Dimitri, or should I say his bear. The big guy is upset with its human counterpart. Personally, I can't blame the furball. I'm not overjoyed with his human side at the moment either. Ever so slowly, the bear lumbers its way towards my hiding spot. His snout lifting slightly in the air as his nostrils flair, trying to catch my scent. By the looks of it, he has sensed me and starts looking around for me. Silly bear never looks up. When he's close enough, I release my grip and fall to the ground about ten feet in front of his nose.

Landing in a crouched position, I look up at Dimitri's bear, who is now standing on his hind legs. Quickly, I launch myself at him, my shoulder catching his bear right under his ribcage, knocking him off balance. My momentum causes him to fall backward, allowing me to pin him on his back. My canines lightly press into the bear's throat, and I let off a soft, non-threatening growl.

The bear releases its control of their body, and before I realize it, I have Dimitri's smooth human throat in my massive maw. I could quickly kill him at this moment, crush his throat like a grape. His fingertips begin to run through my coarse fur. He's calm, too calm; he trusts me, but right now, I don't trust me. I'm hurt and angry. Quickly, I release my grip on him and scoot back to see what he does next.

"Aurora, please shift back so we can talk," he says. I grumble and shake my head, my tail thrashing wildly against the ground. "Okay, but please listen to me. I didn't know you felt what I was doing; you never hinted that anything was bothering you." His eyes stare at the ground; his guilt and anxiety coming off him in waves.

I almost feel sorry for him. I growl a little bit more and grumble. Deep down, I'm still debating on hunting the whore down. It's not like there are many towns close to here; it should be easy. My wolf is calling for her blood; she believes that Dimitri is hers alone, and no other should touch him. She's too smug, too demanding. I'm mildly concerned she may try something at some point. I snap back to the present. I'm feeling Dimitri's pain now; his heart almost feels like it's breaking. Sensing his emotions, my damn wolf betrays me and forces me back to my human form. Of course, because it's not planned, I fall flat on my ass.

"Son of a bitch!" I stand up and rub my ass. Real fucking graceful. "Listen, Dimitri..." I never call him by his full first name, and the visible wince is evidence enough that I've gotten his attention. "You've done as nature intends. Your instincts and drive can't be silenced because you've been sentenced as my eternal babysitter. I'm sure being forced to be bound to a baby for life really wasn't high on your list of shit to do." I begin to pace, running my hands aggressively through my hair.

"I'm doing my best over here. My wolf still wants to hunt that female, she's jealous and has a sick idea that you and your bear belong to us." I scoff and scrunch my nose as I turn and swipe at a tree. Just before impact, my talons extend and cut through the tree like a hot knife through butter. I get ready to swipe at another tree, but a firm hand wraps around my wrist and stops me.

"I'm sorry I hurt you, my bear is furious at me. He forced the shift and dragged me out here, knowing that this is your favorite hunting ground." He releases my wrist and starts wringing his

41

hands together. "I'm not trapped as your babysitter. It was, and is, a great honor to protect you. Now, you quite honestly don't need my protection. I've half been waiting for you to tell me to move on, that you've outgrown wanting me around." His eyes are sincere, and yet there's fear behind them. He's afraid I'll do away with him.

"I haven't outgrown wanting you around, D. It's my damn wolf, she's got it in her thick skull that you and your bear are hers." I look down and away after admitting that. "I don't know what to think or do anymore. I should be ascending soon. I feel the change coming. My wolf is anxious and becoming more aggressive. We may need to sedate me, as Elena suggested." I didn't like that idea at all, but what was I to do? Risk hurting others? It wasn't worth it. I didn't give him a chance to speak his mind on the matter. Honestly, I didn't want the answer. I start walking back the way I came. "Come on, D, up the cliff face we go. Time to head home."

My shift comes quicker than usual, bones pop and realign to take on the form of my Lycan. She turns her head to look at Dimitri then motions for him to climb on. Dimitri isn't all that heavy to me in this form. His thick arms wrap around my beast's neck and his legs wrap around my waistline, holding on tightly. When I was absolutely sure he was secure, I leap up and sink my talons into the rock and clay of the cliff face and start my climb. The bear is afraid of heights, so part of me revels in the fact that he's worried. The climb that would typically be over swiftly, stretches out because I want to enjoy his suffering. When we reach the top, I give him a few moments to relax before I launch us off the top of the cliff. His screams fill my ears as we head towards a tree. I use my talons to grip the small tree and slide down, almost like a fireman's pole. Bark and tree-flesh litter the ground when we land. Dimitri quickly slides off my back and starts walking.

I don't bother shifting back to my human form, and he returns to his bear. It was going to be a very long night. My wolf is still tearing me apart mentally. She is going over the logistics of plotting out which possible towns Dimitri could have gone to. Every time he left, it was long after I had fallen asleep, which gives the woman an advantage at the moment. I know my wolf; she'll figure it out. I just hope I'm aware enough to stop her.

CHAPTER 4
Aurora's Wolf

I'm going to find that whore. I'm going to kill her and rip her head from her body and leave it on the bear's bed. How dare she touch what's mine? I silently stalk through the fifth town, scenting the air from my hidden position in the shadows. It's been effortless to overpower Aurora lately. With her body changing, preparing for the ascension, her mind has been distracted because of the surges in hormones and the increased drive to hunt.

Five hundred feet ahead of me I scent the whore, and yes, she's turning tricks in an alleyway—not a shocker. This will be an easy kill. The only question is, how long do I want to make her suffer? Hmm… minutes, possibly hours, or maybe even a few days of suffering would possibly please me. I will ponder this further while I wait for my opening. Once her john walks away, I strike. I stick to the shadows, moving silently towards her. My monstrous form looming over her from behind as I prepare to strike. With deft precision, I reach around her with my talons and sever her vocal cords, careful not to hit an artery. I just silenced the lamb and it was totally worth it. I throw her over my shoulder and run off into the night. Her blood is turning my white fur vermillion, its warmth running in rivulets down my back. The iron tang in the air is almost driving me to the point of frenzy. I must keep my wits about *me. I must do this the smart way so that the inhabitants are none the wiser to my mission.*

We make it to the woods about a thousand yards from the main house. I pause and close my eyes sensing where Dimitri and Andre are. Both are none the wiser to my escape and abduction. I drop the whore on the ground, watching her sad attempts at begging for her life. Sliced vocal cords make it so much easier to ignore her pleas. She's crying, and from the smell of it has pissed herself from fear. My night just keeps getting better and better. I wonder if my human counterpart will be proud of what I've accomplished for her. I mean, revenge is a great gift to give, right? I know what I'll do, I'll leave the head for Aurora. Hmm... leave it on her bed? Or maybe on her table? Either way, at least she'll appreciate the trouble I've gone through.

My taloned hand shoots out and sinks into the human's soft flesh. Blood slowly runs down, coating my talons as my grip slowly tightens on her. Holding her down, I strike quickly, wrapping my maw around her throat and slowly increase the pressure on her soft flesh. Warmth starts to flood my mouth, the coppery tang of her blood soothing my soul. Soft sniffles fill my ears. I'm not entirely heartless, so I twist my head violently, severing her head from her shoulders, ending her life quickly. I proceed to rip her body limb from limb before heading back home with her head in my hands. I can't wait until tomorrow morning; Aurora will be so proud of me.

~Aurora~

It's been several days since the fight with Dimitri. Several days where I keep losing chunks of the evening and most of the night. I woke up this morning covered in blood. And it's definitely not animal blood; it has a different texture and scent. That means only one thing; it has to be human. My eyes widen as I take in what's before me, screaming as loud as I can, I look around my room. My once beautiful room now looks like an active crime scene. Two sets of feet come thundering down the hall and my door blasts open, almost coming off its hinges. Andre shoots past Dimitri, then stops short and turns pale.

"Aurora, what have you done?? This looks worse than most of the horror flicks you and I watch." Andre studies me, then looks at Dimitri.

He's pale, really fucking pale. Then it dawns on me; my wolf must have made good on her promise. I feel horrible thinking about what my wolf may have done. "Aurora? Talk to me, baby girl. You and Dimitri are scaring me." Andre walks the spanse of my room looking at the chaos around us and positions himself by my open window. His fight or flight instinct is kicking in big time... damn bird.

I raise my hands, staring at the sticky, half-dried blood. "I've been losing hours the last few days... like I can't remember most of yesterday. After dinner too, now it is blank. I don't remember going to bed or anything." I start sniffing at my hand that's coated with sticky, half-dried blood; then I move my blankets. A severed head rolls off the bed and stops right in front of Andre. Andre screams like one of the old-school scream-queens and it honestly has that blood-chilling quality to it.

Dimitri has gone so pale he looks like he's going to throw up. I slowly slide out of bed and look around the room. Bloody paw prints cover the wood floor, from the doors leading to the balcony and straight to my bed. My wolf kept her promise to hunt the human. She's all smug in the back of my head, sitting there proud of herself. Dimitri is beside himself. His horrified eyes slowly drift to lock with mine.

Part of me is sorry we did it. The other part, the part that is all wolf, is sorry too; just not that the woman is dead. She's sorry it took so long to find the fucker.

"I'm sorry, D. I'm a monster... She's stronger... She's never been able to take over completely before. I need to go find the rest of the remains." I release a slow breath and take my pillow out of its pillowcase.

"Watch out, Andre. I need to take the head with me." Reaching down, I scoop up the head. Blood drips from the exposed arteries as well as what is left of the neck. Tendons and part of the spinal cord dangle beneath the ribbons of blood-covered flesh. After examining what was left of the neck, I determined my wolf had bitten her head off—what a way to go. I sniff at the scalp and recognize the scent. It's the same one that set me off the other day. My wolf had hunted down the woman that Dimitri slept with.

Andre loses it, shifting into his golden eagle, he shoots out the window. Honestly, I can't blame him. He's more of a pacifist than Dimitri and me. I don't expect the boys to help me clean up my mess. I'm just wondering what else I have done in the last forty-eight hours where I'm missing time.

"Aurora?" Dimitri snaps me out of my inner monologue. "I'll help you search. I... I know you didn't do this." Shaking his head, he seems to reconsider his statement. "I mean, I know you wouldn't have done it if you were aware of what was going on." His strong thick arms encircle me as he squeezes me to his chest, holding me. I wonder which one of us he is trying to comfort, him or me? I can't help but cry when Dimitri embraces me. I feel like a monster, yet here he is holding me. Slowly he releases me from the hug, and we both look at the double doors leading to the patio. We open the door and walk out onto the deck—more dried bloody paw prints. We follow my tracks into the woods, and about a thousand yards from the house, we find the woman's remains.

She was absolutely shredded. Bone fragments littered the ground, as well as chunks of muscle and sinew haphazardly thrown about. It was as if my wolf had a hunk of meat in her mouth, and thrashed her head violently around sending pieces flying. Slivers of flesh and blood clots hung like tinsel off the pine tree bark. The one small Douglas fir had her large and small intestines draped upon its boughs like a garland. What was left of the woman's clothing was ripped to shreds and hung like tinsel.

Further away on a small balsam fir tree, hands and feet hung off the boughs by their tendons. I'm guessing my wolf was feeling rather festive towards the end of her destruction. I stand there admiring her handy work, though maybe admiring is the wrong word for it. While I'm deep in thought, staring at the gut garland, Dimitri moves to stand next to me. I turn to look at him, and he's three shades of green and appears to be on the verge of wanting to puke. Gently I rub his shoulder, and he jumps back, startled by the contact. I let out a slow, sad sigh as I look around, taking in the full magnitude of what my wolf has done.

Scavengers were up in the trees, some with chunks in their talon's others just with bloody beaks. I shift and start digging a deep hole. My solution to the problem is to dig deep and bury everything. Dimitri realizes what I'm doing and shifts to help out. His bear is shoveling the dirt into a pile off to the side after I shoot it out of the hole I had made. Once the hole is deep enough, I shift back to my human form and begin throwing chunks into the hole. This is a forensic nightmare. It has become a fucked up scavenger hunt for all the missing pieces. I start singing "Dem Bones" to make sure I'm not missing any body parts.

"Really, Aurora? You think this is fucking funny?" Dimitri is pissed.

He honestly thought I was making a mockery of what we were doing. To be frank, I was so busy I didn't notice when he had shifted back to his human form.

"No, D, I don't think this is funny. It's the only fucking song I know to remember all the fucking body parts," I say softly as I pull the gut garland off the tree.

Dimitri was so angry he shifted back to his bear and returned to what he was doing. His reaction was rather upsetting to me. As much as he says it's not my fault, I know deep down he blames me. I remove the last of the hanging body ornaments then shift back to my wolf to continue cleaning. I claw up chunks of bloody moss and scraps of bark. If it has blood on it, it is going into the hole. After about two hours, and several searches in circles as far out as eighty yards from ground zero, we began to fill the hole in. Thankfully it was a ton easier to fill the hole in than it was to dig the fucking thing.

I suddenly feel a surge of energy run through my body, and it brings me to my knees. The surge was so powerful, it forced my shift back to my human form. What is happening to me? I feel like my blood is on fire. It feels like my wolf is ripping my body apart from the inside. I use a young ash tree to stand, only to fall back to the ground. Screaming out in agony, my voice a mix of my human and wolf.

Dimitri rushes over and shifts back to human. His large hands rest on my narrow ribcage, gently rubbing the muscle. The entire length of my body is going in and out of spasms each time the wave of power passes over me. My wolf's fur ripples across my skin as each power surge hits me. Skin-to-skin contact seems to take some of the pain away, but not all of it. I can tell he is in pain too but is trying to hide it.

"It's time, Aurora... You're ascending, which means your heat is about to start. We need to get you home." All I could really do is nod and close my eyes tightly. I feel like I'm going to die. As the pain increases, I notice it's starting to affect Dimitri; he can't stand either. He's in my hell with me. I scoot, so my back leans against his body, seeking any kind of comfort. My eyes snap open when I hear a branch break. It's Andre, he is back in human form, and he's notably concerned. Dimitri quickly explains to Andre what's happening to both of us.

He approaches me and scoops me up into his arms. "Come on, baby girl, let's get you some of that special tea and get you settled into bed for a very long nap." I snuggle against his bare chest and plant my forehead against his neck. His arms band tightly around me as we walk. As he carries me home he's able to feel just how strongly the spasms are. Every time one hits, he stops and tightens his grip on me. The poor man doesn't know what to do for a few reasons. Firstly, I know for a fact he's not used to holding a naked woman. Secondly, I'm not sure if he's ever witnessed an ascension before.

I need something, anything, and a nap sounded wonderful compared to the pain I'm currently in. I close my eyes and trust Andre to take care of me. We make it back to the house and through my double doors. In our absence, Andre had already cleaned up my room and changed my bedding. He gently lays me down on my soft bed, just in the nick of time, before the next spasm rips through my body. I scream and arch my back, lifting off the bed. My muscles tense and burn from the exertion. Sweat breaks out along my entire length and runs off me in streams; my bedding is soaked.

I hear a heavy thud, and Dimitri cries out at about the same time my pain spikes. There is nothing I can do to help him or myself at this point. He must have been on the phone because Andre quickly takes it from him.

"Elena, it's Andre... Aurora is ascending, and it's affecting the big guy too. Can you make it here? Yeah, I have the tea, I'm brewing her some now. She lost something, like at least twelve hours yesterday, and her wolf went all homicidal." I can hear him pacing my room, and then he goes down the hallway.

Eventually, I feel the side of the bed dip and open my eyes to see Dimitri; he looks like shit. I feel like I've been put through a food processor, I can't imagine what he's feeling because of our bond. "I'm so sorry, D... If I could sever the bond so you wouldn't suffer, I would." Guilt was suddenly all I was feeling at the moment, a soft lull in the sea of pain I was in.

Dimitri raises his large hand and rests it on my sweaty cheek. "Don't worry, little one, we bears are tough. We can survive anything. As for the bond," he takes a deep breath and lets it out slowly. "That will only be severed when you choose your first mate. That's something we don't want you to rush... that bond is forever. I don't want to see what happened to your mother happen to you." He looks down and away before getting up to sit in the recliner near the bed.

"What do you mean, D? Are you saying my mother was forced?" I quickly sit up straight and stare at him, my wolf flares to the front at that thought. She doesn't like the idea of being forced to do anything.

"Yes, that's exactly what I'm saying happened. Vlad, her Lycan mate, forced their bond, so he was the first mate. Her second mate, Mikhail, wasn't met with any resistance, and he was a bear like me. Nicodeamus, your mother's third mate, was a true mate. Their animals loved each other. He was an Ice Dragon. Your mom's fourth mate, Liam, was a Dire Wolf, and he met with no resistance either." He stares at his hands as he explains my mother's history, and then it dawns on me.

"Wait! Only a true mate can produce offspring." My eyes were focused on my hand as I shifted it.

"Nicodeamus is the reason my fur is white, isn't it?" I look away from my hand to Dimitri, and he nods slowly. Shit, my father is a dragon. Who knows how fucking long I'll live now?

Footsteps sound down the hallway. I look up to see Andre with the tea in his hands. Soft scents of lavender, honey, and hibiscus drift to me. There are a few underlying scents mingled in that I can't identify. "Baby girl," Andre says as he gently caresses my cheek.

"Elena said it's time to start drinking the tea she gave us. Without a mate, she says your temperament will be unpredictable." Andre looks down at the tea, his sadness tugging at my heartstrings.

"She said she needs to make several phone calls, and in three days' time, at the end of your cycle, she'll be here with the last, single Lycan males she can find." Slowly, he extends his hand out to me, offering the tea.

I carefully take it and drink deeply. It honestly doesn't taste too bad—honey always makes everything better, in my opinion. "If that's what she thinks is best, then I shall sleep. I don't want D suffering because of me." I offer him a sad smile before looking back to Andre. "Question for you… if, in theory, a suitable mate was presented to me, how will I know?" I mean seriously, I have two very good-looking males in front of me—granted one is gay, the other straight but my wolf is drawn to one and not the other. It's an honest curiosity.

Dimitri decides to answer me. "Your mother said it was like seeing a rainbow for the first time—like breathing." Dimitri gets a dreamy looks in his eyes. "Everything just clicked. That's how she described meeting your father." He watches me carefully, trying to gauge my reaction.

"I understand. Thank you, D." Without warning, I start to yawn. My eyes drift to my glass before I raise the remaining tea to my lips and finish it off. I yawn again before lying back down and snuggling myself deep into my blankets. "Wake me when Elena arrives." I yawn once more before falling into a deep sleep. Over the next three days, I only wake for short periods of time to eat and use the restroom before being given another glass of tea.

CHAPTER 5

Aurora

Waking up on what I'm guessing is the fourth day, the smell of bacon and lilacs assault my nose. Although the lilacs smell wonderful, I'm all about the bacon. Cracking one eye open, there sits Elena in the recliner in the corner of the room with a plate of bacon. Gods, I love this woman. It's been over a hundred years since I had last seen her, and she's barely aged. Being almost five hundred looks damn good on her. At most, she seems like she's in her mid-thirties, black hair, blue eyes, and a rather light build for a Lycan female.

"Morning Elena, is that bacon for me?" My voice is still scratchy and rough from lack of use. I stretch out my stiff body before accepting the plate of bacon from her.

"Princess, it's good to see you looking so well. You look so much like your mother." Gently Elena caresses my cheek. "She would be proud of the female you have become." She smiles softly as she watches me inhale the plate of food.

"I have brought you the last, single Lycan males that I could find." She quirks her lip and tilts her head to look at me before raising a brow. "I've also brought to you my son. He isn't mated and about a hundred years older than you." She smiles confidently. "I believe you two may be a good match. I do have to warn you though, he has a female he's been considering." Elena rolls her eyes. "Her father has been in talks with us about a betrothal. In the meantime, Dimitri and Andre are getting the boys ready for your inspection."

Okay, now she has my undivided attention. I have males. Willing males wanting to be inspected? What the fuck was I supposed to be inspecting? "Okay, I need a shower before I go inspect hotties. Oh, and coffee, plenty of coffee..."

I hear Elena giggle on my way into the bathroom and take the world's fastest shower. I mean seriously, I think I was in there like fifteen minutes max. I waltz out of the bathroom to find Andre and Elena holding a robe and coffee. "Why the robe?" I question as I slip it on before taking the coffee. Downing half the mug in a few gulps, coffee was definitely needed.

Elena stifles a laugh. "Because more than likely, if you scent your mate, your wolf will make herself known at that exact moment. It won't happen with the second one, but the first it's like *bam!* here she is!" She claps her hands together loudly to emphasize what will happen.

My eyebrows shoot up at the explanation, as Andre is laughing his ass off. "Okay, how does this work?"

She moves and opens the double doors so we can look into the yard. "Each male is standing in a different part of the yard, so their scents don't mix. All you must do is walk up and sniff. Your wolf will do the rest." She says it so matter of factly that, yeah, okay, not a problem.

"Andre, put "Sanitarium" by Metallica on for me. It's kind of fitting." I listen for the first few notes to echo through the yard before I step out onto the deck. Which way to start? Well, the question is answered for me quickly as Elena pushes me to start on the right side of the yard.

I guess counterclockwise is the order for the day. Slowly, I move towards the first male. His body language screams anxious, and his scent screams fear, which doesn't make my she-wolf happy. She assesses him as a weak male, not worthy, even before I get close to him. I lean in and sniff at his neck, just under his ear. The acrid scent of urine fills the air. Seriously? I can't believe he actually pissed himself. A growl escapes my lips, and he scurries backward. "Wuss."

That was the first and last word spoken to the coward. I snort a couple of times to clear the urine scent from my nostrils as I move towards the next male. He's standing stock still, his frame slightly muscular. Typical dark hair, dark eyes, and he's about an inch taller than me. So far, nothing exciting to write home about. I get closer and begin circling him. I want to see if I can throw him off his game.

Nothing yet. Leaning in from behind him, in a very dominant move, I sniff at his neck and smell perfume on him mixed with his male musk. Apparently, he took this meeting very seriously... not. I grab him under his arms, sinking my now extended talons into his ribcage, and throw him away from me. "Next time you visit a potential mate, don't smell like your last conquest."

The words are growled out, my full Alpha power behind it. He visibly pales, then runs off into the woods. Two down, two to go.

Hopefully, one of these two has balls and common sense. I swear what has happened to guys? They just don't make men anymore. My eyes seek out Elena, Dimitri, and Andre. The three amigos are up on the deck, laughing their asses off over this bullshit. I flip them the bird and stalk towards the next contestant, only the male is wrong. Poor thing, someone forgot to tell him he was male. He's built like a human male and shorter than me What the fuck!

I mean, really, has the gene pool gotten so shallow that I'm built more substantially than these so-called males? I am so disgusted by what I see, I bypass him completely and start towards unlucky number four. I stop in my tracks when he looks up at me. His eyes are sky blue, his hair is black as pitch. He's muscled, but not overdone. His skin is a golden brown, and scars litter his body, marking him as a fighter. Finally, an actual male! We lock eyes, and he doesn't back down. My wolf makes her presence known, and I feel my eyes turn to liquid mercury.

He smirks, and his wolf surges forward; his eyes are almost a white-blue. His wolf's eyes are beautiful. Only another Alpha can stare down an Alpha, and trust me; we are staring at each other. He begins to move towards me, and I freeze in my tracks. This is starting to get interesting. I hear Elena gasp, and the guys hush her. I'm studying this bold male, and in the back of my mind, I'm hoping he's the one. We stand about a foot apart, his nose in the wind catching my scent, his nostrils flare and his wolf rips into existence. He's beautiful, thick black fur, white-blue eyes, and long talon-like claws. If I had to venture a guess, he has to be about nine feet tall and is thickly muscled.

Ever so slowly, he lowers his muzzle to me. I tilt my head to the side, granting him access to my throat. I just submitted to this male without even realizing what I was doing.

Once his nose touches my neck, I get a good whiff of his scent... he's mine. My wolf doesn't want to wait to shift; she tears free and begins to sniff at him, rubbing her muzzle along his neck and chest. Damn, my bitch is the happiest I've ever seen her. Clapping erupts behind us, snapping us out of our little bubble. Elena has tears in her eyes as she runs down the stairs and hugs us both.

"My baby has found his mate!" She wraps her arms around the male wolf, jumping up and down while holding onto him. Her eyes move to me before she pounces and hugs me too. "Princess, you chose my baby boy. You bring so much honor to my home, thank you!"

Hold on, back that train up. I back away and shift again. Andre is ready with a pair of beach towels and hands me one. "What do you mean, Elena?" Puzzled, I look back and forth between her and this stud of an Alpha before me.

"Oh. Forgive me, Princess." Elena motions to the man with great pride, "this is my son, Sebastian Lupi. My first-born," Elena says as she introduces him. "He has trained for over two hundred years in the art of war and every known fighting style." She beams with pride telling me of her son's pedigree.

I nod as I move back towards him and wrap my arms around his taut, furred waistline. "Mind shifting back, big guy? I'd like to get to know your human side too." I smile, looking up into the wolf's eyes, he leans down and licks my cheek before I feel his body starting to break and shift back. Sebastian is easily six foot five and relatively easy on the eyes.

His arms tighten around me as he holds on. "I never thought you'd accept me." He speaks so softly, and with such reverence, tears threaten to break loose. "I've waited for what has felt like forever for you. I saw you as a baby in Dimitri's arms; you were so tiny and precious. Your scent called to my wolf and I wanted to protect you." He buries his face in my white hair, and I feel his warm breath upon my shoulder.

He's shaking slightly, overcome with emotion. I squeeze him tightly to me, holding on to him like I am afraid he will vanish. My protective instincts kick into overdrive because of his emotional state. "Did you know what I was to him?" I raise my eyes to look at Elena, watching her cry,

"If you did, how could you keep him from me?" My own tears run down my cheeks, sensing my mate's pain. Wait... I was feeling Sebastian's emotions, not Dimitri's? My head whips up, and I stare at Dimitri, and he holds up his left arm. The scar... its gone. I look down at my arm, my scar is gone as well. I run my fingers through Sebastian's hair in a soothing manner as I wait for Elena to answer me.

"Yes, child, I suspected, but you were far too young to have a male that was getting ready to ascend around you. His wolf would have demanded to complete the bond long before your body was ready." I nod slowly and nuzzle Sebastian as he scoops me up. Ever so carefully, he carries me up onto the porch and sits down, situating me on his lap. "I don't think he's going to let go for a while, child; you may have to get used to it."

I giggle and nuzzle his cheek. "That's okay; he can hold me for as long as he wants to." A muffled "forever" comes from Sebastian, and all I can do is smile like a lovesick puppy.

"We still have one matter to attend to, Princess, before you can complete the bond." There was a sadness in Elena's voice that made me raise my head to look at her.

Slowly, I nod and look at Sebastian, kissing his temple. "Let's get this over with. If I must battle, then I must battle." I stand and stretch, my bones pop and crack as I look back to Elena. "Set it up, have the witnesses ready, we do it the old way; wolf-on-wolf. Winner lives, and the loser dies." Everyone's jaws drop, shocked by how matter of fact I agree to battle. Apparently, I stunned the group into silence. Quickly, I turn and start heading towards my bedroom door, when a large hand grabs my wrist. I look down and notice it's Dimitri's. "Say what you must, bear. You have prepared me well. I am battle-ready." My tone is nothing short of full-blown Alpha and bleeds dominance. "No bitch will take what's mine without a fight."

"Aurora, I do not doubt your training. Though, with so few Lycan females left, you may wish to fight to submission." Dimitri is wringing his hands, looking at his feet.

I know he didn't want to question my desires, but I understand where he's coming from. "I will consider it, D, as long as she's not some insolent wench." I bare my canines at him and then look back at the group. "We leave in an hour." I watch as Sebastian battles his wolf to leave with his mother. I know he wishes to remain at my side, but until that other bitch dies or submits, honor states he's not entirely mine. I head in and pack only a day bag to take with me. The boys are quick to pack as well, thankfully. Honestly, the wait is killing me. I want to go. Within minutes we are heading to the battlegrounds.

CHAPTER 6

Sebastian

How could I be so dumb to accept the advances of Ravenna? I knew I had a mate, but a hundred years is a long time to wait. Now I've sentenced both females to battle to the death. My mother yells at Ravenna's father about protocol and traditions. He's insistent we sign the contract now before Aurora arrives so that it's binding.

But you can't ignore a mating call; it's impossible. I've scented my mate, currently in her adult ascended form, and damn, she is powerful. I almost feel sorry for Ravenna—almost. Here she is, strutting around the compound, in what she calls an outfit—that barely covers anything. From what I've been told, she's slept her way through the pack, trying to find a suitable mate.

I look at my watch for the millionth time when I hear the tell-tale sound of a diesel motor coming up the road in the distance. My wolf surges forth, bouncing with anxiousness; he knows his mate approaches. To be perfectly honest, I've never been happier in my life. Once this battle is over, we can complete our mating bond and move on to find the others she requires for her harem.

Dimitri and Andre hop out first as soon as they park and proceed to open the back passenger-side door. My mate looks stunning as she slips out of the truck. Her long, snow-white hair is braided down her back and on her muscular form, a blood-red Bodycon dress.

She turns to assess the crowd before starting to walk barefoot on our soil. Her eyes are swirling liquid pools of mercury. You can practically drown in the power that's coming off her in waves. Aurora lightly dips her head to me then locks eyes with Ravenna. Ravenna attempts to keep her eyes locked with Aurora but can't —she can't even look for more than a few seconds at a clip. You can tell Aurora is out for blood; the look on her face screams rage.

Aurora snorts before she looks to Elena. "I am ready to battle my elder." In a show of respect, Aurora drops to one knee and lowers her head to my mother.

Elena looks to Ravenna. "Are you also ready, child?" Mother is wearing her priestess robes for this occasion, a sign of her station within the pack.

A growl rips from Ravenna's lips. "There's no way she's Lycan! Look at her hair! She's an imposter! I demand my right to be mated to be honored!" She crosses her arms and smirks, thinking she has won.

Surprisingly, Aurora remains calm and stands slowly. "I am Aurora Marelup, daughter of Anca Marelup and Nicodeamus Tepish, dragon mate of my mother. I bare the royal brand."

She turns her right arm, baring it so it can be seen. As clear as day, the black, raised seal of the house of Marelup is there on her flesh. Most of the pack drops to one knee, including me. My true mate *is* the lost Princess. She continues to stare down at Ravenna and cants her head to the right. "Get in the ring, bitch. Let's see who the real Lycan is."

Aurora turns, giving Ravenna her back, which is the ultimate insult. Without warning, Ravenna charges at Aurora. Just before impact Aurora turns, grips Ravenna by the throat, and throws her into the ring. A slow shake of her head is all that is offered before Aurora shifts. Her wolf has gained mass that almost rivals my wolf's size, and she is easily seven, almost eight-feet tall, and heavily muscled. Her claws look more like talons, and on her muzzle she has snow-white scales. Ah, the ascension must have gifted her access to some of her father's gifts. This should be interesting, to say the least. She stalks forward, growling continuously at Ravenna, who still hasn't shifted yet.

"Shift and fight!" was shouted by someone in the crowd. Aurora stands there—statue-still—waiting for her quarry to shift. Ravenna knows she can't beat Aurora wolf-on-wolf.

"I wish to fight as humans!" Ravenna shouts. Boos echo around the ring before her father, the pack's Alpha, steps forward.

"Daughter, you will fight as a wolf. You disgrace our proud bloodline. To think, I whelped a coward!" Angus is beside himself, looking at his chicken-shit daughter.

First, she spoke ill of the princess, and now she is trying to change tradition. The pack starts to grow restless over her childish behavior. Aurora is clicking her talons together, waiting as patiently as an enraged she-wolf could be expected to wait. "You leave me no choice, Daughter." Angus forces Ravenna to lock eyes with him, and when she does, he forces her shift on her. She howls in pain, then lands on all fours. Her body contorted, breaking at odd angles because of the forced shift. She pants heavily, trying to regain some semblance of composure.

Her head whips up to see her father walking away, giving her his back. She's practically been disowned by her family for the disgrace she's brought upon them. You can tell when it clicked— when Ravenna felt she had nothing left to live for. Her wolf immediately takes over, having scented me on Aurora. Within moments, the smaller, black wolf is attacking the great, white wolf. It's kind of sad to say, but Aurora's wolf looks bored. She's playing with the smaller wolf, swatting at her and tossing her across the challenge circle.

Without warning, Aurora shifts back to her mostly human form. She only left her hands and feet changed to that of her wolf. Honestly, her shifted hands and fingers look more dragon than a wolf. Thick, rigid, white scales adorn her hands and fingers like armor. The talons at the ends of her armored hands look like velociraptor claws. Her tail still sways behind her, showing just how relaxed she truly is. There is a defiant smirk on her lips as she stares down the pissed off black she-wolf. With a flick of her hand, she signals for her to come at her.

As Ravenna charges, Aurora leaps up, right hand out and talons extended. She uses the momentum to send her over Ravenna's shoulder, sinking her claws into the she-wolf's throat. Aurora's left-hand shoots out and digs into the she-wolf's back. In one fluid move, she severs Ravenna's head and rips out her heart. Thick crimson fluid sprays the crowd as Aurora completes her finishing move. If I hadn't seen it with my own eyes, I never would have believed it.

Aurora lands gracefully, head in one hand, heart in the other, covered in her opponent's blood. She saunters towards me, shifting the rest of the way back to her human form. Her face is blank, nothing betraying her emotions at the moment. She dips her head in my direction, before heading towards my mother and her guardians.

Aurora drops to one knee and holds up Ravenna's wolven head and her heart to my mother. "I have defeated the challenger set forth before me. I offer you her head and heart to honor your home." My mother gently takes the offerings from her.

"I wish to petition for the right to claim my true mate, Sebastian Lupi." Her head is dropped in submission, eyes closed, waiting for the judgment of all the elders present. Aurora fought for me —for us. I am so proud of her I could burst.

"Come forth, Sebastian." Elder Grayson was the one to call my name. I move swiftly and drop to my knees beside Aurora. I lower my head in submission, as she did, and close my eyes as well. I hate waiting, but for her, I'd wait forever if I had to.

"It has come to our attention that some dark dealings have come to pass within the pack. This business of the Alpha using his position almost to force a mating when you had a mate already." Elder Grayson began to circle Aurora and me before speaking again. "How old were you, Sebastian, when you first discovered Aurora was your mate?"

I drew in a deep breath before answering. "Barely one hundred, Elder. Aurora and her guardians lived with us for a few months, before going into hiding."

Elder Grayson stops moving beside me. "How did you know she was yours, for one so young?"

I dare not raise my head or look at him like I want to. My wolf isn't happy he is questioning us. "My wolf knew by scent. I got to hold her as a baby. She was and is everything to me."

Elder Grayson snorts. "If you knew, how could you agree to start the process with Ravenna?" He puts his hand under my chin and raises my gaze. "You sentenced that girl to death today."

Aurora's growl could be felt by those close enough to her. Her eyes narrow on Elder Grayson, and his hand on my jaw. "Release my mate," she growls. Her voice takes on the pure force of her wolf, along with eyes, and canines lengthened. I watch as the fur starts to ripple across her flesh. Her wolf is fighting for control; she wants the elder dead. I just know it.

I rest a hand on Aurora's shoulder in an attempt to calm her. It didn't ultimately work, her anger is palpable. Immediately the elder releases me and joins the others. Aurora lets the full magnitude of her Alpha powers be felt as she slowly stands. Lesser wolves cower and whine, backing up slowly. Most of the elders begin to shrink back. Everyone except my mother; she just smiles proudly.

"Come, Aurora, let's feed you and clean you up. We have a mating ceremony to perform tonight for you two." My mother opens her arms, and Aurora, without hesitation, slips right in and hugs her tightly. She gently nuzzles my mother's neck, enjoying the affection being shown to her. It's kind of scary how quickly the switch flips. Aurora goes from hellhound to snuggle puppy in seconds. I can't help but smile, watching the two of them interact; it is a thing of beauty.

Aurora pulls out of my mother's arms and looks at me, smiling. She wiggles her index finger at me as if to say come here. I rise to my full height and slowly remove my button-down shirt, offering it to her. Typical Aurora, she cants her head to the side and slowly slips my shirt on, buttoning up the front. She lifts the fabric of my shirt to her nose and sniffs. A slow, gentle sigh escapes her lips as she raises her eyes to look at me.

"Thank you, my love." Those four simple words falling from her lips in almost a whisper rocks my world completely, tilting it on its axis. Aurora's steps are cautious as she approaches me—I can tell she is a little unsure of herself. Her hand rests over my heart, and her eyes lock on where her hand rests.

"I do not enjoy killing lesser beings. But I will burn the world to the ground to protect what is mine." She leans forward and kisses my chest over my heart before looking up into my eyes. Her own eyes are human, a pale steel-grey, and I know the woman had said what was in her heart, not the wolf.

"Aurora, my love, I feel like I've waited a lifetime for you. I will continue to wait until you are ready. I am yours, you are mine; we are one." I rest my hand over hers as I speak, a slight swirl of mercury surfaces in her eyes then vanishes. Both woman and wolf agree. We turn, hand in hand, heading to the main hut to catch up with my mother. I bet she's already counting how many grand pups she wants to have. I shake my head and laugh to myself as several females rush up and try to steal Aurora away. She's instantly a big, growling mess.

"Ladies, my mate isn't used to being handled. Just ask her to follow, I'm sure she would like to get cleaned up before the ceremony." Aurora nods slowly, and hesitantly follows the females, stopping to look where I am. I almost want to laugh. This badass bitch just ripped her opponent's head off and ripped out her heart, but is concerned about following a bunch of females to a bath.

A large hand lands on my shoulder, turning my head slightly to find Dimitri. He has that psycho Joker smile going, and it looks kind of disturbing. "What can I do for you, big guy?"

Dimitri's eyes bleed gold, then back to hazel. "Not much, future Prince. Our girl did good today, *Da?*" He crosses his arms over his chest—he's fucking huge, six feet tall and easily almost four hundred pounds of man-bear.

"Aurora was phenomenal. That finishing move, holy shit, it gave me chills. But seriously, I hate that part of the tradition. Usually, it's two males fighting, not females—there's so few fertile females left. To lose one is a hit to our species as a whole." I look out across the great hall watching everyone preparing for tonight's ceremony.

"There are even fewer Great Bears, if there's any left, besides me." He looks down at his beer stein and then takes a long pull of the amber fluid.

"I knew that day, way back then, that Aurora was yours." He draws in a deep breath, getting lost in the memory. "Not many hundred-year-old males would want to fawn over a pup all day." I smile thinking about it. Those were the best three months of that year.

"You were the only one that could get her to stop crying. I believe in my heart she knew you were hers back then too." Dimitri's eyes lift to meet mine. You can tell he is holding back laughter as he begins to speak. "I kept the shirt you gave to her to soothe her until your scent was gone. Man, did that little hellion have a fit to end all fits that day." He starts laughing hard. "She clawed the hell out of Andre and bit his nose when he leaned over to take the shirt away."

"That wasn't funny, Dimitri! That was so many shades of wrong!" Andre bellows from the other side of the hall. Damn eagle has excellent hearing and eyesight.

I start laughing just as hard as Dimitri. Man, if only I could have seen baby Aurora go postal because my shirt was taken from her. I was so distracted I didn't notice my mother emerging from the alcove. In my mother's hands, she is carrying a blood-red, crushed velvet tunic. A smirk crosses her lips as she hands it to me. Don't get me wrong, I love Aurora with everything that I am... but holy shit! I'm finally taking a mate, and she kind of scares me. I don't care that she's a princess, but fuck me, she's the last Lycan Princess and fucking lethal. Honestly, I'm more nervous that I will fuck this up and not make this perfect for her. Quickly I run over to my good buddy Pete, and give him instructions for what I need him to do for me. I'm hoping that Aurora likes camping and that my favorite spot pleases her. Otherwise, this is going to be a very long and miserable night, potentially.

CHAPTER 7
Elena Lupi

I knew when my sister had sent that tiny, snow-white haired baby to me she held great power. Dimitri had bestowed upon me the gift of knowing Aurora's true birth parents. To think the dragon was the true mate of Anca amazes me. I knew that Anca wasn't fond of the Lycan Alpha. It was a political mating more than one out of love. Now, to see the woman that Aurora has become makes my whole heart swell with joy.

My son was instantly taken by her when he met her. He held her every day and halfway into the night every night. I knew what she was to him. To watch him miss her and pine for her all this time has been torture. There's only so long a male can hold out on urges, and he impressed me, waiting fifty years before touching another female. I knew nothing would ever come of it.

Then there's that psycho, Ravenna, who thought using her father would get her the prize she wanted. Sadly enough, it had almost worked—*almost*. Even if it had, if his true mate showed up, Ravenna would have been tossed aside like the trash she was. My eyes drift towards the head and heart I had placed on the ceremonial table. At least the wicked bitch is dead and no longer an issue. Watching Sebastian interact with Aurora's guardians makes me so happy. The first leg of her journey is now complete, and the next is very difficult.

My hands glide over my scrolls. I'm searching for the one on the dire bloodlines here in the states. Looks to be only one Alpha left here, and he's somewhere in the Grand Canyon. He's been blessed with four sons; one set of twins, and two single births. Sadly, the jackass sends the females to battle the prisoners he's collected over the years. No female has survived the Wendigo or the Ice Dragon he's got. I suspect the Ice Dragon is Aurora's father. If I'm right, and she can survive long enough to battle him, he will know his bloodline by scent and not harm her.

Herbs are gathered by my acolytes and placed in their proper places upon the table. I arrange the dagger and the bowl, even though I know neither of them wants a hand binding; they will use their canines to mark their mate. Both are warriors and strong, stronger than most that live in these current times. Aurora will gain the strength of my son after they complete the mating tonight. Each mate will gift her a particular attribute unique to their species. The Dires, there are so many possible gifts… wow, there are so many possibilities. She could gain shadowmancy, their toxic bite, a traditional wolf form, and the list goes on. A throat clearing makes me look up to see my beloved son waiting for permission to approach.

"Come in, please. After all, this is where you need to be." I smile at him and come out from behind the table to embrace my boy. It doesn't matter how old he gets, he'll always be my little boy.

"Mother, must we have Ravenna's head and heart present? It's kind of weird for a mating ceremony." He scrunches his nose like he always does when something is distasteful to him.

"Baby boy, I was honored by your mate with these gifts. They deserve to be in a place of honor. That, and to remind the others to not fuck with the two of you." Yup, I can be the evil priestess when I need to be. With all the bullshit concerning the Alpha, he needs to be reminded where the real power lies. That power is in a pure-white Lycan hybrid named Aurora, my future daughter-in-law. My son starts to laugh; he's learned to read when I have a wicked thought.

"Mother? You're trying to scare the Alpha, aren't you?" He tilts his head and looks at me, smirking.

Damn, I'm busted. He freaking knows me too well. I raise one hand to my chest in the *who me* motion, and he laughs harder—yup, totally busted. Moments pass and the pack starts filtering into the hall, taking their seats.

The Alpha approaches me and glares. "So, how much damage did my daughter do before her demise?" He just smirks—almost laughing. What an asshole!

Before I can answer, Aurora makes her entrance. The doors bang against the wall making everyone jump, including the Alpha. "No damage. She wasn't strong enough, fast enough, or skilled enough to lay a single claw on me," Aurora practically growls out her sentence.

"If you want Alpha... you can meet me in the ring in the morning, and you can see for yourself if it was just a fluke." Her eyes swirl between mercury and steel-grey—it's quite apparent she is fighting for control at the moment.

Thankfully, my son moves and touches her arm, drawing her attention to him. I let out a relieved breath and nod slowly, signaling for the lights to be lowered and the candles to be lit. I raise my hands slowly, drawing the pack's attention to the front of the room. Once everyone's eyes fall on me, I begin.

"We have gathered here tonight to bear witness to the mating ceremony of my son, Sebastian Lupi, and Princess Aurora Mare-lup. We bore witness to her strength and power today; we felt she was the true heir to the Lycan throne." I move and start to pour red wine into the chalice.

In my right hand, I grab hold of Ravenna's heart and hold it up high. "As in ancient traditions, I was offered the heart of her enemy. I, in turn, offer the heart to the wolf Goddess Morrighan! May she smile upon this union." I take the heart and place it on the copper platter, then set it aflame. As it burns, the flames change colors several times until they turn white before the heart turns to ash. A smile crosses my lips, having witnessed the white flames; the Goddess has accepted our offering. I raise my hands again.

"Our Goddess has accepted our offering!" The crowd erupts in cheers; it truly is a blessed day. I turn my gaze back to the smiling couple before me. "As per tradition, I must ask if any in this hall objects to this union before we proceed." Silence greets us for several moments before the Alpha steps forward.

He has a wicked grin on his lips, I know he's up to no good. "I claim my right as Alpha to take the princess as my own!" A bold statement, but also a fact. He doesn't realize a true mating trumps his claim. Sebastian and Aurora begin to growl at him. Over half the villagers are growling at him as well. It's about to get really interesting.

Aurora's laughter rings out and fills the hall. She moves to stand before the Alpha. The full weight of her dominance ripples throughout the room. Her eyes are pools of liquid mercury as she stares at him. He's trying like hell to keep his eyes locked with hers. He squirms where he stands, and shortly after the staring contest begins, he turns his head and lowers it. Aurora shifts her right hand and places a talon under his jaw to raise his eyes to meet hers. "You are not worthy. You are a weak, pathetic excuse of a male."

She scrunches her nose, giving him a look of disgust. "Look at yourself; you pissed your pants all because I stared at you, you pussy." Aurora turns and faces Sebastian, locking eyes with him. Wave upon wave of power come off both of them, but he doesn't submit. Aurora smiles and approaches him.

Her eyes close, and she touches her nose under his jaw in submission. She holds her position until he releases her. Steel-grey eyes meet Sebastian's white-blue, the eyes of his wolf. Ever so slowly, she bares her neck to him. Sebastian leans in with an open mouth and lightly bites her throat, holding her there. It's more for show, but it's a massive symbol of the trust between these two titans.

Once he releases her, he stares at the Alpha. "With all due respect, Alpha. She'll kill you in a heartbeat without question. That is if my wolf doesn't beat her to it." Sebastian's voice holds the growl and power of his wolf.

The Alpha lowers his head and backs away. He mumbles that he withdraws his claim as he runs out of the building. "Okay, so now that, *that*," I wave my hand in the direction of the departing Alpha, "bullshit is over, let's get back to the important part—the sharing of blood to start the bond. By scent and sight, your wolves have accepted each other. Now by blood, they become one. You have two choices: cut your palms, bleed into the wine, and drink; or, you can go traditional and bite each other. The choice is truly yours."

As one, they turn to look at each other. No words pass between them as they shift to their wolven forms. The unexpected shift makes many of the pack nervous, others sit there in wonder. A traditional bonding hasn't been done in public since my day.

Aurora chooses to submit first and bares her shoulder and throat to Sebastian's black wolf. He closes the distance between them and licks the area he intends to bite. A slight nod from Aurora and Sebastian opens his muzzle and clamps down on the muscle between her neck and shoulder. He holds her like that for what seems like forever, her white fur stained red from her blood.

Carefully, he releases her and licks the wounds clean, healing them instantly. Aurora raises her head and nods slightly again, and he crouches down a bit for her. That almost two-foot difference in height makes all the difference. When Sebastian is ready, he rests his taloned hands on her wolven hips to stabilize himself before baring his throat to her. Aurora slowly lowers her muzzle to his shoulder and begins to clean the chosen area. Her eyes turn to watch Sebastian for a moment; he nods, letting her know he is ready.

Aurora draws in a deep breath and opens her muzzle to bite at the muscle between his neck and shoulder. Her taloned hands rest on his shoulders, careful not to slice him to ribbons. Sebastian's blood could be scented in the air but not seen. When she feels she held him long enough, she releases her grip on his shoulder. Gently, she cleans his wounds, sealing them instantly. Both wolves turn to face me.

"I bless this union. May their lives be filled with love and longevity... and many pups!" I had to throw that in. The look on both of their faces is priceless.

In the corner, Aurora's guardians stand there like sentinels. Poor Andre is having a hard time with his little girl growing up. He's an emotional mess but still standing tall and proud, even with his puffy eyes. Aurora and Sebastian bow to me before they leave the hall out the back door. Now is the time for their hunt and the true mating to occur. At least some things are still kept private, thank the Gods. I move towards her guardians and shake both of their hands. "Gentlemen, we have succeeded in our missions. Aurora has ascended and found her first mate. I call that a win."

I watch Dimitri rubbing the spot where the binding mark once was. His eyes eventually find mine. "*Da*, we did. Now it's just a matter of time before time catches up to Andre and me. Don't get me wrong, we are grateful for the extra time, but now we know the end is near. We just hope we live long enough to help her ascend the throne and take her rightful place." Dimitri hugs Andre to him and holds the overly emotional bird to his great chest.

I study them closely, and the sands of time have begun the run. Delicate wrinkles now grace the creases of their eyes. A sprinkle of grey hair can be seen on their temples. A soft sigh escapes my lips as I watch them. I feel horrible about what's to come. My sister's magic gave them the extra time, and perhaps I can extend it again. I leave them to have their moment and walk back to my hut to start studying my sister's notes. Maybe I'll find a solution for them. I can only hope.

CHAPTER 8
Sebastian

Both wolves run through the woods far away from the village of my birth. The sun is starting to set as we come upon the place called Mirrored Lake. The water is so calm and still it's like looking at a mirror laid flat on the ground. The surrounding area has heavy timber as well as an apple tree grove that has fruit available. I come to a stop at the edge of the water before shifting back to my human form. Aurora cautiously approaches the water's edge then shifts back to her human form. She slowly tilts her head to the right and studies the area... it's absolutely breathtaking. You can tell she's watching the sun setting over the mountain tops. The sky is streaked with reds, blues, purples, several shades of oranges and yellows. I move and lightly place a hand on her lower back before gently kissing her cheek.

"I hope this is acceptable to you?" I was nervous about my choice of where to take her. This particular place held so much meaning for me; it's where I made my first kill and learned to shift and fight. Aurora smiles at me and moves in closer, resting her head on my chest.

"It's beautiful, Sebastian! Can we stay here for a while? I can't wait to see the moon upon the lake's surface." Her smile made the long run worth it. Gently I guide her to a small grove of apple trees. Under the oldest tree, I have camping gear and a cooler set up for us. Aurora begins to bounce up and down. Apparently, I have chosen wisely. "Awesome, I've never been camping before; this will be an adventure!" She bounds away from me to look around at all I have prepared for our first night together.

Suddenly she freezes and begins to growl. Her wolf bursts forth from her body and takes on a defensive stance as she begins to back up towards me. Seeing my mate shift so quickly, I decide to shift as well. My sizeable black wolf moves to stand at her right flank, staring in the direction she is. A pale being reeking of death, decay, and sulfur begins to amble through the woods towards us. Its face looks like the being from the old black and white movie Nosferatu.

Aurora's eyes narrow; she knows what it is. It's a Strigoi—the same creature that had a hand in the destruction of her bloodline. Silent communication passes between us. I shift back to my human form and look for the phone I packed. Quickly I call Dimitri and tell him what is standing before us. It was Dimitri's worst fear. The Strigoi sensed when Aurora came into power and began to hunt her. I keep my eyes on Aurora as she circles the Strigoi, sizing it up. Dimitri gives me detailed instructions as to how to destroy it.

"Aurora, we must take its head! And don't let it bite you; it's poison!" I yell as loudly as I can. Quickly I shift back to my wolf as I spot a second creature approaching. I know this is going to be a fight to the death. Aurora's guardians are on their way to help us, just in case. Backup isn't far behind, now we need to dispatch these two before it gets too dangerous.

Aurora charges at the Strigoi, making sure to stay out of range of its swiping distance. Her talons sever its left arm from its body—blackened blood pulses out of the artery poking out of the remnant of the creature's arm. The second Strigoi starts going nuts, smelling the blood from its companion. It's dark eyes, burning red like blood, have taken on an unearthly glow before it lunges at me. I dodge, barely getting out of the way of the crazed creature.

My taloned hand reaches out and catches the back of the Strigoi as it passes me, ripping its flesh to ribbons. Blood pours down its back, and its movements are slowed from the strike I delivered. Both Strigoi are moving slower from blood loss. The one Aurora is fighting now has a massive chunk of his thigh missing and can barely remain standing.

Dimitri's bear is seen breaking over the top of the ridge. Damn, that male is freaking huge; he makes a Kodiak look small. He charges forward and into battle, knocking Aurora's Strigoi to the ground and ripping its head off. While Dimitri is busy with the first one, Aurora joins me with the second one. Both of us now circle the lone Strigoi, it screams—calling for help—but no one answers.

The last Strigoi doesn't stand a chance being trapped between Aurora and me. Her eyes flair to life, and the liquid mercury of her eyes seems to glow brighter for a mere moment. Suddenly she lunges forward, her taloned hand extended with her fingers splayed wide as she aims for the Strigoi's throat. With a flick of her wrist, the Strigoi's head is severed from its body. Blackened blood sprays in an arc, painting the once green grass onyx. The body falls with a thud at her feet, blackened blood oozes from the severed arteries, coating the ground. The thump of the severed head landing near draws our attention away for a moment, before our eyes refocus upon the remains in front of us. The threat is now over, and the Strigoi bodies turn to ash and blow away with the wind.

Dimitri shifts back first and walks over to us. "You both did well. Congratulations on your first Strigoi kills." He claps his hands briefly.

"It's been over two hundred and twenty-five years since I've seen these fuckers. It's only going to get worse from here." His eyes move skyward, watching Andre's Golden Eagle circle overhead. He is doing lazy circles in the air, keeping watch for any more surprise visitors.

Aurora, still in wolf form, walks away from the group heading towards the water. Her normally snow-white fur is now spotted like a dalmatian from the Strigoi's blood. Once in the water, she shifts back to her human form and begins to wash away the blood from the battle. I watch her, hypnotized, my eyes transfixed on everywhere her hands touch.

"Sebastian?" Dimitri says, trying to draw my attention back to him. "Shift back, we need to talk." Dimitri is all business all the time, and the look on his face at the moment proved that this is about to get serious.

Quickly I resume my human form and move my hands over my erection, trying to cover it—I'm failing miserably. "Thanks for getting here so quickly. How the fuck did those things find us so fast? I thought we had time." My voice held concern as I look between Aurora in the water and Dimitri before me. I'm not panicking, just shocked that the Strigoi arrived so quickly.

"Andre and I will stay within howling distance tonight. You must complete the bond. She will gain power from you and you from her." Dimitri's eyes drift to Aurora and linger there longer than I think would be decent. My own heated gaze caresses every single visible inch of my mate's curvy form.

"Each mate she adds, she will gain a gift from them, and thus it spreads to the others as well. Your mother told us where the local Dire Wolf pack is." Dimitri tilts his head, making a very stern face at me. "So, when you two get your act together, that's where we're heading next. They are somewhere in the Grand Canyon in some old Indian dwelling." Shortly after Dimitri finishes speaking, Andre lands.

All you can see is Andre shaking his head and throwing his arms about. "Wait! We have to play hide and go fucking seek to find her mates? Do I look like the dude from *Pickers*?" Andre has a *what the fuck* face on as he looks between Dimitri and me. We both crack up over the frazzled look that Andre gives us.

The laughter carries to the water, and Aurora's head snaps up as she stares at us. Slowly she walks out of the water. Rivulets of water caress her curves in a hypnotizing manner. Each droplet catches my attention, my eyes follow their path hungrily. Aurora smirks, looking at my state of being—my poor penis is rock solid, the head is turning purple and leaking. Aurora raises an eyebrow looking at it, then up to me. "That looks painful. What'd you do? Slam it in the cooler lid, or did one of those things hit it?" And there you have it—her innocence on display. Dimitri's and Andre's jaws drop. I honestly don't know what to say. Aurora just smiles at me then moves to grab a towel.

"As for the others. We'll find them, and I'll take what's mine." She raises her hand and taps a finger on her plump lips.

"Speaking of which, Dimitri and Andre, you need to leave." She waves her hands, making a shooing motion.

"I have a mate to claim, and I refuse to do it in your presence." She crosses her arms over her chest, staring at them. Dimitri and Andre almost fall over each other trying to leave. Andre takes to the skies, and Dimitri shifts back to his bear and lumbers into the woods.

"So, Sebastian, how do we do this?" The look on my face must be priceless. Aurora flat out asked me what we needed to do to complete the bond. Dimitri and Andre are long gone, so there was no one to use as a distraction.

"Well, Aurora, I was hoping to ease into this to make it special for your first time." My eyes drop to the ground at my feet. I've had sex so many times I've lost count, but this time means something. My eyes meet hers for a brief moment before looking down and away again. This is my mate, the one I'd be spending the rest of my life with. Aurora's hand gently caresses my jaw, raising my gaze to meet hers.

"I won't lie to you, Bash; I'm nervous. Instinctually I know what I need to do. But instincts and practical application are two different things." I watch her shift her weight nervously.

"But I trust you. You're my mate, my forever, and I know it's insanely soon... but I feel like I love you already." She leans in and gently kisses my lips.

"Don't tell the guys I'm a big softie; they'll never let me live it down." She smiles and winks at me before moving to sit on the picnic blanket. A gentle pat was given to the spot next to her for me to join her. I laugh and move quickly to be at her side. Aurora opens the basket and starts spreading out the food I brought for us. There are several types of meats and cheeses, two kinds of wine, and water. For dessert, there is a homemade apple pie. The amount of thought I put into this moment pleases Aurora and her wolf.

Ever so carefully, Aurora dishes out food onto plates for the two of us. With a deep cleansing breath, she lifts the plate for me and offers me my food first. Her eyes remain locked on me until I begin to eat. Once the first morsel is swallowed, Aurora begins to eat.

"Why did you serve me and wait? We are equals." I am puzzled by Aurora's actions, so why not ask?

"Well, Dimitri and Andre both said tradition dictates I should serve my first mate before myself." She shrugs her shoulders. "It's the way things were done back when my mother ruled and her mother before her." Her eyes drop to her lap, where her hands are tightly clasped.

"I'm sorry if I didn't do it correctly. The guys did their best trying to teach me, but I'm stubborn and willful, and honestly, don't give a shit half the time." She raises an eyebrow and looks up at me to find me smiling and trying not to laugh. My smile must be contagious because soon, Aurora begins to laugh. "What's so funny?" She cants her head to the side.

I reach out and pull Aurora onto my lap. "Fuck tradition! We'll make our own as we go along!" I nibble on her throat and make her giggle. I reach out and grab a piece of meat, then offer it to her. Ever so gently, Aurora takes the offered meat and eats it. Her own hand reaches out and grabs a piece of meat to offer it to me, and I take it in my mouth and eat it. An hour passes as we take turns feeding each other. We are so relaxed with each other, it is just what we need to settle our nerves.

I pick Aurora up, making her squeal. I have her now straddling my lap, facing me. Her eyes move over my body, then back up to my face. I lean forward and capture her lips, kissing her slowly, savoring the moment. Breaths between us begin to deepen as the kiss grows in intensity. Aurora starts to paw at my shoulders, leaving fingernail tracks from my spine to my biceps. She doesn't understand what she wants, but instinctively she knows what she needs. A deep approving rumble reverberates deep in my chest. Aurora's scent thickens with her arousal as she starts to become more aggressive.

I can't hold back anymore, and my wolf demands I take our mate now. My erection is throbbing, thick and hard as steel, pulsing in time with my heartbeat. I grab hold of Aurora and flip her onto her back and come to lay down over her. I'm not about to give in completely to my wolf. I refuse to be rough and set a punishing pace her first time. No, the man was in control, no matter how much my wolf howls in the background. My lips come to rest against Aurora's.

"Baby, this may hurt, I'm not a small man." I kiss her again, looking into her eyes for some sort of acknowledgment. Slowly she nods and nips my jaw. "I'm going to go slow. Stop me if you need to." I'm worried about her comfort; I love her too much even to cause the slightest bit of pain. My hand slides between her thighs to position myself at her entrance. Aurora is soaked, absolutely beyond wet. I slide myself through her moist lips, coating my length before starting to enter her.

Aurora inhales quickly as she adjusts to my girth. Her eyes lock with mine, and she nods again, showing she is okay. I stop when I meet with resistance. Hesitating, I know this is the part that is going to hurt her. My mouth drops to her shoulder over my mating mark, I sink my teeth in hard as I slam forward, breaking the barrier. Aurora grips me tightly, wiggling from the pleasure my bite is bringing her. Slowly I begin to move, setting the pace for our mating. The slapping of skin, pants, and moans can be heard in the distance. Aurora is whining, sounding more wolf than woman as she approaches her climax. When she finally cums, her screams morph to a long haunting howl. My own howl soon joins hers as I, too, reach my peak.

We lay there cuddled up, tangled within each other's arms for what seems like hours. We consummate our mating many times throughout the night, deepening our connection and strengthening our bond. In the morning, it will be time to begin the hunt for the Dires and whatever may come after that.

CHAPTER 9

Aurora

I close my eyes as I sit at the lake's edge. I can feel precisely where Sebastian is, and if I concentrate hard enough, I can almost see what he's seeing. A gentle breeze blows and shifts, and in the winds I smell Dimitri and Andre approaching. Thankfully the Strigoi that attacked had only been scouts. Although by tonight, they will know that their scouts were killed and that I was now a threat.

Heh, they don't know the half of it. I'm sitting here, with my head thrown back, enjoying the breeze with my eyes close. I'm still trying to figure out what gift I received from Sebastian when Dimitri decides to interrupt my thoughts.

"Princess, we should get moving. The Strigoi won't attack during the day so we can move quickly, and the village won't get attacked." He spoke with truth and logic—he's learned not to fluff things with me. After all, they raised me to be a no-nonsense kind of girl. Give it to me straight, and I'll respect you more for it.

"Fine, D." I roll my eyes. "Have Andre fly ahead and tell Elena what happened with the Strigoi. Also, tell her I'm going to need that map she said she had." Standing up, I stretch and crack my back.

Faint pink lines cross my ribs like tiger stripes from Sebastian's grip on me last night, and I can feel D studying them. "Don't stare, D, it's creepy." I smirk, looking at him as I head towards Sebastian to help him finish packing up the site.

The sneaky male has a golf cart hidden nearby, so we load up everything in it. My eyes drift back to Dimitri. "D, please drive the cart back. I wish to stretch my legs before getting trapped in the truck with three stinky boys." I playfully pinch my nose before turning back to look at Sebastian.

"Race ya!" I shout as I run and shift in motion. My great, white Lycan glides swiftly and soundlessly through the woods heading back to the village.

To my surprise, Sebastian is on my heels. Guess I gifted him with my speed. That may come in handy in the future. We weave in and out of the trees, almost playing tag as we approach the edge of the forest. Suddenly stopping, I look about... hmm, something isn't right. The scent, it's wrong. Raising my muzzle in the air, there's a scent of blood carried in the breeze.

In the distance, I stop and prick up my ears to listen closely and discern what I hear around me when suddenly I hear Andre screaming for help. We run towards him without a thought. The village center looks like a scene from a horror flick. Several wolves lay dead, and there are just as many ash piles. Sebastian takes off looking for his mother as I prowl the village. I catch the scent of a single surviving Strigoi hiding out in the meeting hall. Without a second thought, I leap onto the roof and let loose a warning howl, so no others will approach. Sadly, it has the opposite effect, and the surviving wolves begin to gather. We listen to the screeches of the trapped Strigoi.

The sun will destroy it if it comes out, so I think the smartest thing to do is let the sun in. My talons begin to rip at the metal roof, opening it up like a can of tuna. Light begins to flood the hall. I stick my head down into the hole I created and see where it's hiding. It's blocked in a corner, trapped by the beams of light I let in. Now was the time to fry it. Quickly, I leap to the other side and rip off the roof directly over its head and watch its body burst into flames. The Strigoi's screams fill the air until its body is frozen in mid-scream with no more sound coming out.

Satisfied that I ended the threat, I leap down and the villagers drop to one knee before me. All except the Alpha, that dumb ass decides to walk up to me. "How dare you bring this threat to my people! Many have died because of you!" he snarls at me, pointing a finger.

"I hope they rend the flesh from your bones and drink your blood like wine." He stands there all cocky, thinking his title will protect him. Over his shoulder, I see Sebastian, Dimitri, and Elena. I didn't want to do this, but I cannot let him poison my people anymore.

I shift back and stand before him, my eyes that of my wolf. "It's amazing how you have short periods of time that you have balls —no brains, but balls. I'd almost respect that if I didn't scent the terror oozing off of you." I narrow my eyes at him.

"Not one of the Strigoi fell by your claws. No, you hid in your cellar waiting for the sun to come up so you could claim the glory to the survivors." I shake my head and circle him.

"You forget your place in the hierarchy. You forget that Alphas have no power while a Royal still lives." I smirk at him then point a finger in his direction.

"You are a leader with a handed down title from a weak bloodline." Jabbing a finger in Sebastian's direction, I continue. "My mate's bloodline is older than yours, from the old country where our kind orginally comes from."

I circle him with my eyes narrowed. "You, you're a thin-blooded, American Lycan no history, no lineage. I'm ending your rule today," I say, baring my canines at him. "Step down and submit... or die. Your choice." I give him my back and close my eyes. Sebastian feels what I am doing, and he locks onto the Alpha, watching his movements closely. I see every move through Sebastian's eyes without having to turn.

"Like my daughter said, she's not pure Lycan She's part dragon and unfit to rule!" He charges at me, and just before impact, I regain my Lycan's form and sink my talons into his chest straight to his spine. I hold him there, feeling his heart beating against my forearm. Blood pulses out and around the hole in his chest and down to my elbow. He's in such a state of shock that he just stares into my pure mercury orbs. With one quick flick of my wrist, I end him, ripping out his spine in one fluid move.

I shift back, his spine still in my hand. My arm bloody to my elbow as I turn to face the gathered crowd. "You are my pack, my people. I will fight for you and protect you. All I ask is that you train hard in the old ways." I raise my clean hand and wave at Elena to come forward.

"Elena and her family have faithfully served my family for countless generations. I ask her to serve me now. Watch over our people; guide them in the old ways. Her word is my law. Those that stand against her will die by my talons." I address the survivors who all nod and bow their heads, showing I've gained their respect and loyalty.

I turn to Elena, "Train them well in the battle skills. War is coming, and I'll need every strong Lycan at my side for the final battle." I pace back and forth. "Gather the rogues and the ones the old Alpha exiled, bring them back into the pack and give them purpose." I kiss the top of Elena's head before moving towards my shocked mate.

I hold out my hand and offer him the spine of the old Alpha. "For you, my love. Do with it what you will." I walk off towards his hut, listening to his mother comfort the survivors. I've chosen well, she knows these people, and she'll do right by them. In the meantime, I need to clean up and pack. We have a road trip ahead of us.

I drag out the guitar and amp I found in Sebastian's room and sit on the front porch to tune it. Usually I like playing Ax7, but today is a little different. Instead, I start playing Megadeth's "She-wolf," letting the notes carry through the compound. My head is down, my eyes closed, and I'm lost to the music. In my head, I'm singing the song. But somewhere around the first chorus, I hear several voices join in singing the lyrics.

I smile as I look up to see it's Sebastian and several other young males. One joins in with his guitar, playing the backup rhythms for the song. We jam out, and I bask in the glory of how my mate and his wolf are staring at me while he sings. I stand up and start walking around playing the song, and eventually, it turns into a full-out performance for the pack.

The young male playing back up approaches as we bounce back and forth toward the end of the song, taking turns playing the lead rhythm. It's a thing of beauty when you can be in sync with another. I see Elena approaching, and she smirks at me. I look to my new buddy and change it up. I hit the opening riff of "Of Wolf and Man" from Metallica. Peter—I find out his name—is grinning from ear to ear as the pack sings the lyrics as we play.

Elena stands there enjoying the pack's flow; they are alive and acting as one, as a pack should. I breathe new life into them. Slowly I move toward Elena, still playing along with Peter. "Can I help you, pack master?" I smile at her as I thrash through the cords, and everyone begins to howl along with this part of the song.

"Princess, you have performed many miracles for your people." She smiles. "You freed them and gave them a purpose. We are blessed to have you." She pats my shoulder as I hand the guitar off to my mate, who starts up an early 90's tune.

"I stuck a new author's book in your bag. The female main character reminds me of you." Okay, that got my attention.

"Oh, is she a wolven badass like me?" My smile spreads wide like the Cheshire cat—or is it the cat that swallowed the canary? Either way, it isn't an innocent look.

"Definitely not. It's a mob book. She shoots this girl..." She waves her hand in front of her, then adds, "just wait 'til you read it. With the way you handled the last two threats, she's right up your alley." Elena has that innocent as fuck look going on, so I know she's up to something. Now I really need to read that book.

I shelve that thought at the moment and turn to look at my people. *My people...* I never thought I'd be saying that. I was kept separate, raised off-grid for over two hundred years, all because of my bloodline. Now I have a pack, a mate, and other mates I must still find. I feel like I'm playing an advanced game of manhunt, well, a literal manhunt.

I stand here watching everything unfold and ponder what my parents would think of me at this moment. Am I too brutal? I mean, my death toll is rising, and I haven't traveled more than four hundred miles in the last week. I'm mildly concerned as to how high it will reach before the final battle. I've killed a woman, an Alpha's daughter, and the Alpha. So only three in the last week... not horrible, maybe. Dimitri once told me I was going to need an army to take back the castle. A pack's loyalty is to its Alpha. So, unless I'm sure of the Alpha's fealty, he cannot live. I must ascend to take over the pack. Many cogs in the machine, so many pieces to the puzzle, but I clearly understand how they fit together.

Then it dawns on me. Sebastian's gift is battle strategy. I never had the ability to plan things out to this level previously. This is freaking amazing. Speaking of that hunk of a Lycan, he walks straight towards me. "You look deep in thought, love. Everything okay?" He smiles and sits next to me, taking my hand in his.

"Just a lot to process. I've done so much, yet it's just the tip of the iceberg." I rest my head on his broad shoulder and take comfort in his presence.

"Oh, and I figured out that I gained your gift of battle strategy. That is a most excellent gift to receive." I smile, and he starts laughing.

"Great, I made the perfect weapon even more dangerous!" he says, still laughing and smiling, so I know he's just teasing me.

"But on a serious note, good decision on killing the Alpha. He would have promised backup for the war then left us to drown.

He's always been a self-serving asshole." Fan-fucking-tastic. I didn't read him wrong. I'm not sure if I'm more happy or relieved at this point.

"That's exactly what I was pondering. You know I'm going to have to challenge and kill the Dire Alpha to secure his pack for the war." My face is dead-serious, not even a slight sign of joking in my tone. Sebastian's face drops, the joking smile falling from his lips.

"I know, love. If I could bear the weight of all this death for you, I would." He kisses my cheek and hugs me. Giving me the love and support I need. It's not his fault he hasn't yet realized I'm not some Disney Princess that needs saving. I'm like Selene from *Underworld*... but a wolf instead of a leach. I'm a trained killer; it's all I've learned since I could walk.

"Killing doesn't bother me, love. I know in a sense it should, but it doesn't," I say, shrugging my shoulders. "It's a means to an end. I don't know how many of the Strigoi still enslave any of our people." Slowly I stand and start pacing back and forth.

"I fully intend to do everything within my power to free our people and take back my mother's castle. If I have to slaughter every Alpha between here and there to get the army I need... then so be it." I stop right in front of him and look him in the eyes.

"They are either on my side or in my way." The last line is accented by my Lycan, making her presence known.

Dimitri and Elena walk up halfway through my little tirade. Elena wears a look of concern, while Dimitri just looks smug. "Now there's that fire I've been waiting for! You are ready, Princess. You are ready to become a mother fucking Queen." Dimitri picks me up, hugging me tightly.

"That fire will spread in the hearts of your pack-mates; our strength will become theirs. It's both a blessing and a curse, how a pack works." He releases me and backs away. "One strong Alpha can influence the whole pack either to greatness or to ruin. I know, little one, you will inspire greatness, just like your mother did with the entire nation." Dimitri cups my cheek gently and smiles.

"If any of the old-timers live, they will see your mother in you and follow you without question." He bows slightly and backs away.

"Say your goodbyes, it's time to go. We have a long trip to our next destination. Only twelve hundred miles to go." He smirks and walks off, heading to the truck where Andre is throwing what looks like mine and Sebastian's bags under the cover in the bed of the truck.

I look back at Sebastian, and he seems like he's in a bit of a shock. "Are you okay, love?"

He double-blinks and then locks eyes with me. "Most of your plan is solid. But are you sure killing off Alphas and dominating packs is the way to win the war?" he asks, puzzled. Then adds, "I mean, the Dire pack alone is like four to five hundred strong. If they revolt, we have one hell of a battle ahead of us." He makes a valid point.

"I look at it this way: the Dire Alpha has four sons, odds are at least one will be *the* one. Worst case, I take two of them as mine. They will stand with their mate. Thus, it's in their father's best interest to play nice, or he dies. It's really pretty black and white..." I start cracking up because of the unintentional fur color reference. Thankfully Sebastian gets it and starts laughing.

"Please try not to kill everyone off, hmm?" Sebastian's request is filed in the maybe pile.

I'll divert him with boobies later since they seem to distract him. My plans are solid, well, for the most part. Then again, I like flying by the seat of my pants. I like to change it up on the fly, so my enemies have no clue what the fuck hit them. I wink at Sebastian and take off running towards the truck. "Shotgun!"

I am so excited about the gifts that Elena has given me. There are several books in the bag, all of them some form of reverse harem romance. She chose mostly new authors because she liked giving people a chance. She had strongly suggested that I read the purple book first. Elena said her main character was like me, a badass bitch that took no shit. I've got to respect that.

She also said the books would give me a good idea of how to handle multiple mates and what may happen once I find them all. It's kind of starting to feel like a horrible episode of Poké-mon... Gotta catch 'em all. Gotta hunt them all down? I mean, really. What happened to the days of the males pursuing the females? Wait, I know what happened. I'm supposed to be fucking dead or not even exist. But those mother fucking Strigoi found me. Do I have some fucked up magical lo-jack on my ass or something? I open up and start reading the first few pages of the book and damn, this will get good; I can just tell.

CHAPTER 10

Sebastian

I can't believe she just yelled shotgun and took off like that. She's taking this hunting for her mates thing better than the rest of us. Mostly I'm concerned about her safety, especially after the first attack of the Strigoi. Mother has trained me well for the last two hundred years to be ready for what was ahead of us. Underneath it all, I believe that mother has an ulterior motive behind all this.

I know Aurora's guardians have trained her well because she's fucking lethal. Like scary brutal, like *I'm concerned for the rest of the world* deadly. So far, I've witnessed her kill my suitor and the Alpha without breaking a sweat. Not to mention the one-night stand Dimitri had that she killed. Yup... better make sure I keep my mate super happy, so she doesn't go all homicidal on us.

My mother stops me halfway to the truck. "My boy, here's all the information I have on the pack you're looking for." She hands me a thick envelope. Inside it has a map, a family tree, and a breakdown of all the key players in the pack. The Alpha has four sons, three mates, and a love of barbaric gladiator games. Mother grabs my jaw to make me face her.

"Don't let the bear and bird enter the den. They don't trust anyone other than other wolves," she says, concerned with trying to educate me.

"There's a rumor the Alpha may have Aurora's father and a Wendigo. The Wendigo will lose its magic if its antlers are broken off. Remember what I tell you." She grips my jaw tighter to make sure her point was heard.

I nod slowly. "I hear you, Mother. I will tell Aurora about the Wendigo, but I'm not sure saying anything about her dad possibly being there will help keep the peace."

Mother releases me and kisses my cheek. "I will see you soon, my boy. By the time Aurora summons us, the pack will be whole again and the exiled returned." Mother smiles at me and walks back towards the village.

She's up to something; I can feel it. The question is, what did she do? Changing my focus, I make my way to the truck. Aurora apparently is playing DJ for this road trip because I can hear the music from here. What does she have in her hand? Hmm... it looks like books. Oh, shit, what did mother give her? Looking closer, I can make out a skull, and she seems the most excited about that one. Just the cover art has me concerned. Just what Aurora needs: more inspiration to rip people's heads off. I climb into the back seat, sliding mother's care package out of the way and get comfortable. "What are you reading, Aurora?" My interest is piqued. She is so engrossed in the book, it takes her several moments before she answers.

"I'm reading a new reverse harem mafia book. According to the back, it's full of sex, blood, hot guys, and a mob war." She smirks and then winks at me.

"It sounds right up my alley. I'm at war, I have a hot mate, and about to collect others." She shrugs her shoulders.

"So far, there's been plenty of bloodshed with more to come. I wonder if she rips someone's heart out like I did." Aurora smiles sweetly at me and grips my hand. "I love you, Bash. And I'll kill anyone who stands against you." As comforting as her declaration is, it's just as scary. She looks at me so innocently. Deep down, I know she's dead fucking serious when she said she would kill for me. She's already done it twice. I can feel through the mate bond she's calm and at peace, so her words are from the heart.

I squeeze her hand back and smile at her. Ever so slowly, I raise her hand to my lips and kiss her knuckles gently. "I would burn the world to ash for you. I love you so fucking much." My words please her, I can tell. Deep down, something does and doesn't sit well with me making that declaration. Brushing that confusing feeling aside, I refocus on my beautiful mate before me.

Slowly she nods her head and lays her head against the headrest to watch me. At the moment, I have her full and undivided attention; her book temporarily forgotten. "Mother gave me directions to the Dire's lair and instructions on how to gain passage." Both guardians have entered the truck and made themselves comfortable. Dimitri gives me a nod, so I proceed.

"Andre, the ascent is vertical, so Aurora and I need you to scout it out before we start our climb. Once you determine it's safe, we'll shift and use our talons to make the climb." Shifting my gaze left, I look at Dimitri,

"Dimitri, you need to make sure we have our packs secure and keep the getaway vehicle ready to go." This is the exact moment his bear makes itself known, and a soft rumble escapes his lips.

"I'm going with you. I'm Aurora's guardian! No pup will keep me from my duty." He is deadly serious, but Aurora's growl—because he raised his voice—silences the entire truck. Her liquid mercury eyes are locked on him; he is now the target of her budding rage.

"Aurora, you must understand, it's dangerous. You are the only family that Andre and I have left in this world. It would kill me if anything happened to you on our watch." I look between Dimitri and Andre; the poor bird has tears in his eyes. Dimitri's words struck a chord with him.

Aurora takes a deep breath and her beast retreats. Her eyes move between Dimitri and Andre, trying to gauge their emotional state. "I love you both. You are the only family I ever got to have, the only ones I've ever known." She reaches out and gently touches them both.

"We are preparing to enter a den of wolves that with one bite can be lethal. There's a very good chance that Bash and I are immune because of our bloodlines," Aurora says, tilting her head.

"There is little to no chance that you and Andre are immune, Dimitri. I couldn't live with myself if you two died because I couldn't protect you. My heart would break into a thousand pieces if I lost the two of you." She sighs softly, trying to keep it together.

"I'm treating this like we're walking into an ambush. I'd rather be over-prepared than not prepared at all." Aurora speaks with a wisdom far beyond her years. None of us can argue with her logic; it is solid.

To break away from the heavy emotional topic, I start again with my mother's information. "I have intel on the den and the ruling family. Apparently there are four heirs involved, two single births and a set of twins." Aurora's eyebrows shoot up at the mention of the twins.

Oh, dear Gods, what did my mother tell my mate? If she were shifted, her freaking tail would be wagging right now. I know that look—mental note, give her plenty of dick before we storm the castle. "Okay, so back to the important stuff. The Alpha holds gladiator type fights between prisoners. It wouldn't shock me that one of us will have to battle to prove our intentions to him." That thought makes the boys feel uneasy. Aurora looks bored; I know she loves to battle, so the idea of a fight is like second nature to her.

"Okay, let's get this show on the road. There's blood to spill and naughty books to read!" Aurora ends the meeting quickly.

"Come on, D, fire up that diesel, and let's get rolling. Twelve hundred miles isn't getting any shorter just sitting here." She nudges the grumpy bear, and he turns the key—bringing Aurora's beast she had named Black Betty—to life.

I never thought I'd see the day a female would give her truck a female's name. Aurora fiddles with the radio until she finds a station she likes, and it's a bit odd when she puts on a pop radio station. Dimitri visibly cringes when some female pop singer begins to sing about a dark horse. The smirk that plays on my mate's lips makes me want to kiss it off her face. She's so damn adorable it almost makes you forget the beast within. I continue to flip through the papers my mother gave me, learning all that I can on the long drive to Nowhere, Colorado.

Twelve hundred miles is going to take forever with as slow as Dimitri drives. I know bears are slow, but damn, at least go five miles over the limit. We're going to die because he's over-cautious. "Hey, Dimitri, I know this diesel is quick; I can see the tuner head from here. Can we bump the speed up a bit?"

Dimitri's eyes dart to mine, then down at the dash. "What's a tuner head, and where is it?"

Aurora's head whips around to give me a death glare. I just fucked up big time. "Sebastian is seeing things, D, just use the gas pedal more; it's the long vertical one on the right side. It makes the truck go Vroom Vroom." Aurora is in a wise-ass mood, as well as pissed off—longest road trip ever.

Her eyes lock on me again. Yup, I'm in trouble. "So, Sebastian. As the first Lycan to need glasses, how the hell are you?" She's used my full first name twice now. Definitely in the doghouse. Dimitri and Andre both laugh at me.

"Well, love, since your beauty is so blinding, it's not shocking that I need glasses. To look at you for a long period of time is like staring at the sun. All I can see is you, and nothing else matters." Aurora narrows her eyes again at me; I just can't win. Then she shakes her head and turns back around to read her book. I may be safe.

"Andre, take the file from Sebastian and tell me about the four sons. I'm curious," Aurora says with a playful tone to her voice.

I fold the sheets up and stick them between my thighs, thinking they were safe. Nope! Andre reaches down, brushing the back of his hand against my cock and balls, and grabs the papers. The look on my face has to be priceless. I mean, I am more in shock that he had the stones to go near my balls. Aurora snorts as she watches Andre's antics. My mate just let another male touch my balls! What the fuck! I look from my crotch to Andre.

The bird just smirks. "I can see why baby girl is smiling. You, my boy, are stacked!" He smiles sweetly at me, then looks back to Aurora.

"Hmm, looks like the firstborn is named Johan. He's four hundred and thirty-five years old, six foot six, and about two-hundred and thirty pounds. He's a politician in the pack serving as beta to his father. Johan is unmated but does have an arranged mating coming up this winter." Andre twirls his finger in the air as if to say *whoop de doo*. I can tell he's not impressed by the pack's beta.

"The second eldest son is Alexander. Hmm, he's on my team, so that's a no go for you, sweetie." Andre pauses to read the next part and grins at Aurora before reading the next line.

"Now, the twins are interesting. Jayceon and Dominik are two hundred and eighty-seven years old. Dominik is the pack enforcer, standing at six feet three and two hundred and fifty pounds." Andre waggles an eyebrow at Aurora before continuing.

"He has served this country as a ghost, whatever that means. Jayceon, or Jayce, as he prefers to be called, is a historian and organizer. He's currently dating a packmate, Sinclair, and was previously involved with a Chrystina. I'm guessing he doesn't care what gender he dates." Dramatically, Andre pauses and raises both eyebrows looking at Aurora, watching for her reaction.

Aurora purses her ruby red lips listening to Andre, carefully waiting for him to continue. "Jayce is six foot one and two hundred and ten pounds, more brains than brawn from what it says here. Elena has footnotes that she believes the twins will be the best match for Aurora." Andre passes the papers forward to

Aurora, and she starts looking at the pictures and bios, weighing the pros and cons of all the males listed.

Aurora turns around and looks right at me. Her eyes flicker between her's and her Lycan's; they appear to be formulating a question. "What's your opinion of the males listed, love? You are my first mate and I value your opinion. Because if none of them is a true mate like you are, who do you think would be the best fit for the political alliance?" Slowly she turns to be able to look at me, studying my facial expressions.

I'm glad to see that my gift of strategy is serving her well already. She isn't just looking at the pretty faces and all the muscles... she is being tactical. That line of thought will serve her well with all we have to do before us. "The beta wouldn't be bad, but I'm not sure having another potential Alpha in the pack would be a great idea. There would be fights for dominance and possession constantly. The second born being gay wouldn't help at all there; the bond at best would be weak." I draw in a deep breath.

As much as I hate admitting it, the twins look to be her best option. She's smiling, looking at me; she knows her assessment is solid and is just looking for confirmation. "The twins look to be the front runners for this pack. Sadly, there are very few Dire Wolf packs left, so the selection is meager." Aurora nods slowly before turning back around.

"Fucking Strigoi," she mutters before picking her book back up.

I look over the remaining sheets in the file my mother had given us. Surprisingly she had a geographical survey of the Nankoweap Ruins. There must be hidden tunnels leading into the den from the ruins that humans haven't found yet. Andre has scooted closer, looking over my shoulder at the diagrams.

"If I fly up here," he points to the eastern edge of the ruins, "I can catch and ride the thermals across the face of the site to get a look inside. With it carved into the cliff face, I won't be able to glide silently in and out. I'd have to fly around, which means they'll hear my wings." Andre is thinking like a military man. It makes me start to question what they had done before I came to know them.

"I have a question for you, two guardians. I remember the night you arrived. It was dark and storming. Both of you were wearing armor with crests on them. What was your position before becoming bound to Aurora?" I needed to know who was with us and what they can do to help in the final battle.

Dimitri's eyes find mine in the rearview mirror. "I was the queen's sword, her personal guard, and her enforcer. I had my room right off her chambers when she became pregnant with Aurora." He looks down briefly.

"We lived in a time that King Vlad had caused a lot of civil unrest because of his treatment of the Strigoi. Lycans were originally their daytime guardians. Pets, if you will." He shakes his head slowly.

"The Lycan's began to rise in power as they discovered the females took on their mates' powers. It's why Aurora now thinks strategically... it's because of you." He motions to me. "That was one of the gifts you've given her. Nothing else new has manifested yet, but who knows what other gifts she'll gain from you as the bond grows." He shrugs slightly.

"Andre, back there was the spymaster of the castle. Since Golden Eagle shifters are so rare, he could sit in his shifted form anywhere in the castle and no one gave him a second thought, thinking he was just a trained pet." Andre smirks at Dimitri's comment.

"Shortly after Anca started taking mates, she had Andre and me bonded. It's similar to a mate bond, but its purpose is more strategic than anything else." He waves his hand slightly.

"It's why when I was bound to Aurora, Andre's life was also extended. I've been teaching Aurora different fighting styles since she was able to run." He smiles fondly. "As new forms became available, I'd join the classes, learn new skills, then come back and train Aurora. It's not that I didn't think she could handle the outside world; I didn't think the outside world could handle her." Dimitri's eyes remain on the road.

I watch his face morph throughout the conversation. He's taken his job very seriously over the last two hundred years. Something deep down tells me at some point, it stopped being a job for him and it became a passion. Through all of his hard work and effort, Aurora is as efficient and lethal as they come.

Out of nowhere, Aurora starts laughing hysterically. Like out of control, belly laughing, to the point the noise stops, but the open mouth laughter continues. "What's so funny, love?" The look she gives me makes me think I'm going to regret the answer.

"Well, the main character... she has a thing for her associate." Aurora does the air quotes when she says associate. "She goes to visit him and he's banging this chick from one of the businesses." Her eyes drop to the page, then looks back up again.

"So, he's going at it like a champ, and from the sound of it, he was getting close. So, she pulls out her gun and aims it at the female's head." Aurora makes a gun with her fingers.

"Soon as the girl sees her, she shoots her in the head. Blood everywhere, the guy is freaking out. Totally something I would do." She nods.

"Then again, I prefer my talons. I'm more of an up-close and personal kind of girl." She just fucking smiles! Smiles and laughs about a chick getting her brains blown all over the place.

I'm concerned. Dimitri clears his throat. "Aurora, your Lycan bit the head off of my one-night stand just because I forgot to shower before seeing you." He glances at her, and she is still smiling and nodding before he looks at me in the rearview.

"Good luck!" He fucking smirks at me. What in the nine hells have I gotten myself into? Poor Andre is fucking pale, and Aurora is still laughing when she holds her hand up.

"Remember how we had to play manhunt for the missing body parts after we found the severed head in my bed? My Lycan must've been really pissed at you, Dimitri!" She's still laughing. I would almost think my mate has become unhinged, but unmated she-wolves can be quite unpredictable at times.

"How is finding a severed head in your bed funny, Aurora?" I had to ask, though I think I should have kept that question to myself.

"Okay, so Andre and I have a movie night at least once to twice a week. I think it was the week before that we had a Godfather movie marathon." Aurora turns to sit sideways with her back against the door so she could look at me.

"In one movie, the boss wakes up with a horse head in his bed. I guess my Lycan decided to bring her prize to bed with us." Aurora exaggeratedly shrugs her shoulders after explaining, then goes back to reading her book like nothing fucking happened.

We continue to drive through the night, switching off every six hours so we can sleep in shifts of two. I honestly don't think anyone slept when Aurora was driving. She has a lead foot and a love of that tuner mod that makes that diesel of hers fly like a bat out of hell. At this rate, we should reach our destination in two days tops. Perhaps not sane, maybe not in one piece... but we'll get there sooner rather than later.

Dire Wolf Compound

I received an email today from Elena of the Lycan pack to the north. The old Alpha has finally fallen. To my surprise, the lost princess had done it and taken over the pack. Per protocol, Elena informed me that Aurora was on her way to meet my sons. Now I can finally have my revenge on her parents for the slaughter of my old pack at the hands of the Strigoi.

Slowly I move to my desk and look over the prisoner list. Nicodeamus is still alive. *How fucking long do damn dragons live?* I'll set him as the last opponent, as usual. I still have the Wendigo and several Dire's will save me time from killing them if they die. I am almost salivating, thinking about the bloodshed to come.

Maybe I'll let the Princess live and take her as my mate and increase my power. I'll use her to take back her mother's throne then murder her in her sleep. That would give me the Lycan pack and keep my pack under my control. *Now to plan the battle... who should I have her fight first?* Hmm... I'm going to start it off easy for her and let her warm up with several Dire prisoners. A knock sounds at my office door while I'm deep in thought.

"Enter!" I shout and don't bother looking up. By scent I know it's one of the twins. "I need you to prepare some prisoners for battle." I raise my eyes up, briefly looking at Dominik, then back down to the prisoner list.

"Pick three of our best Dire fighters, The Wendigo and the dragon. Make sure they are fed and in top shape for Friday. Drawing up to my full height, I cross my arms over my chest to look directly at my son to gauge his reaction.

"We have a visitor coming. She's supposedly the missing Marelup princess. As far as I know, that child died with the queen. Regardless, if she's anything less than the heir to the throne, she'll die swiftly in the early battles." Waving my hand dismissively because, in the end, her life won't matter for long, no matter what her bloodline.

Dominik steps forward to look at the prisoner list. "Alpha Lucian, are you sure this is necessary for one female? I mean, they are in such short supply as it is. To lose one is the loss of several potential pups."

Dominik regards his father's cold, calculating assessment of the list. It's clear he's already signed this female's death warrant. "If I may be so bold to ask, why is she coming here?" Dominik furrows his brows, looking at me quite curiously, studying me like I had taught him to do to assess a possible threat.

I draw in a deep, irritated breath. "The old order of things requires the she-wolf princess to take mates from all four clans as a political alliance." I hold up my right hand with four fingers up.

"Do the math boy... that's four mates—three other dicks to try to race to knock her up first." I huff irritatedly.

"The Shaman from the Lycan pack didn't state if she has a mate yet. Part of me blames the old Alpha for the deaths of thousands of our pack mates." I narrow my eyes as I look up to my son.

"I want his seed to die. Then again, if she's not his spawn, perhaps letting her seek a mate here would be to my benefit." I go deep into thought again and turn away from my son. Before leaving, Dominik takes the list and the printed letter with him out the door to do my bidding.

🐺 🐺 🐺

~Dominik~

Once out of my father's sight, I race to the suite I share with my brother, Jayce. The door almost comes off its hinges with as hard as I hit it. Jayce just about falls off his stool from the shock of my arrival. "Shit, Dom, what the fuck's going on? Where's the fire?" Jayce stands up and moves towards me, resting his hands on my shoulders, his eyes search mine for answers. I smile briefly before starting to explain.

"Remember the Dragon, Nicodeamus? How he used to beg to be set free to find his hatchling?" I raise both thick, black eyebrows hoping my brother will remember.

"Yeah, he was babbling about the hatchling again about two weeks ago. Something about an ascension and full access to power." Jayce throws his hands up in the air. "You still haven't told me what the actual fuck is going on." Jayce is a little pissed off and puzzled by my actions.

"Jayce, if she's who I think she is, we are going to have one pissed off dragon on our hands. The Princess isn't lost anymore." I pace back and forth anxiously. "She's coming here to look for a mate." I motion out the balcony doors, to the desert beyond them.

"Father wants her to battle the prisoners before getting to meet any of us." Gripping my hair, I'm stressing the fuck out; no female should have to battle for a mate.

"Okay, so if you're right and she's the princess and the dragon's daughter, Father is going to be in deep shit." Jayce taps his chin in thought.

"Especially since dragons and dragon kin share power when they are close to each other. If she can wield her father's ice, we are going to be ice skating in the middle of the desert." Jayce is pacing now, his nerves getting the better of him too.

"Calm down, brother. I'll protect you as I've always done, don't worry about a thing." I step in front of Jayce, attempting to get him to relax.

"I kind of hope she's related to the dragon. Father has gone further down the rabbit hole and is losing what's left of his mind." I raise my hands several times in frustration, then point down in the dungeon's general direction.

"We have a Wendigo here! Those things are the most fucked up abominations I've ever seen." Roughly I run my fingers through my hair again.

"If she's the dragon's daughter, she'll win." I half-smile. "Her father will sense she's his kin, and then they will turn on our father. Then his reign of terror will be over." I say it and partially regret it—kind of. Lucian has been nothing but cruel to our brother, who's gay, and Jayce for being bi.

I do my best as a brother to protect them. Now I have a chance to free all of us from the hell we're in. "Get some rest, Jayce, and lay low... Father is in a mood."

I leave our suite and head down towards the dungeon. I pass the guards on duty, and they leave the area thinking I'm just as cruel as my father. A misconception that I have had to foster in order to survive. My eyes survey the Dires and the Wendigo that the princess must fight. They are quite sturdy but shouldn't be too much of a challenge. As I approach the Ice Dragon's cell, there's an immediate drop in temperature. Icicles hang from the ceiling. "Nicodeamus? I have news for you." I see his glowing, silver eyes regard me.

"What is it?" Slowly the massive male moves towards the bars, his left arm missing from the Strigoi war. His good hand grips the bar. There's a tinge of hope in his eyes. A healthy dose of fear throttles through my system as the much larger predator regards me. There's a tiny part of me that hopes he accepts the information I bring him in a positive way and does not go into a rage ahead of time.

"It's not all good news, Nicodeamus. There is to be a battle here tomorrow night. You are the last fighter, like always." His eyes drop for a moment, the years of being a slave in the gladiator pit weighing heavily upon his weary soul.

"I believe your daughter is on her way here. She is coming to claim her Dire mate, but my father wants her to battle for the right," I say and back up, slightly prepared for anything.

His head whips up quickly, and the slits of his dragon bleeds through his silver orbs. "I was right. I've been feeling her all these years." His gaze drops just before he begins to pace.

His bare feet slap upon the stone as he moves back and forth. "She has ascended; I felt her touch my power." He opens and closes his hand several times.

There's a subtle shift in his mood as the ramifications of the news I've delivered him hits home. "Your prisoners do not stand a chance against her. You are a good, strong male with a good heart; I hope she chooses you."

Nicodeamus winks at me then smiles. "As for my battle with her, we will not fight. Our animals will not permit it. She is dragon kin. Just by entering your den and being close to me," he smirks, "she will be able to use my powers." An evil grin crosses his lips as his hand moves to rub where his arm once was.

"I will finally get my revenge against the traitor." Nicodeamus slowly turns and paces around the cell.

"I need to eat and regain my strength. My daughter will need me." His eyes, now back to human, lock on mine.

"I feel her; she's already taken her first mate and has gained gifts from him." Lightly he strokes his beard before he looks back at me.

"Prepare yourself as well as your brothers that they may do right by her. I will speak to her once she's within the den and will share my knowledge with her." Nicodeamus goes and sits down on the edge of his bed, watching me.

"I'll send more food to you, and drink. I swear on my life I will do all that I can to protect the princess and reunite you two." My eyes turn golden as my wolf surges to the surface; he agrees that it's time to stage the coup. I bow slightly to the dragon king, my fist to my chest over my heart. He returns the gesture before I head back upstairs. I walk back towards my suite and move towards the balcony. Pushing the doors open, my eyes search the vast desert before me. Night has fallen, and the temperatures are steadily dropping.

Slowly I raise my binoculars from the table to scan the desert. I see a flickering light far out in the desert. Quickly I switch to the telescope and try to focus on that flickering light. It's definitely a campfire and a large black truck. Figures are moving about the fire, and they appear to be large bodies. So far, I'm not seeing anything that would make me think the princess is with them. Just as I am about to walk away, a large white Lycan comes into view. In its maw, a pronghorn hangs limply, obviously dead. "Holy fuck!" I accidentally say out loud.

Quickly I look around to make sure no one has heard me. When I am sure the coast is clear, I find myself watching the campsite, hoping to see the princess again. At about one in the morning, all the motion around the fire ceases—bedtime for them and me. Tomorrow is going to be rather interesting indeed.

Morning comes too quickly for me today. My nerves are on edge as I know what is going to happen. I don't want to fight my brothers, but I will if I have to. Our father has poisoned my eldest brother for years, and he's the only one I have to worry about standing against me. I promised the dragon king that I'd protect the princess. Last night I got to see her beast with my own eyes; she's definitely dragon kin. Today's battles will be a walk in the park for her. I dress quickly and make my way into Jayce's room.

"Wake up, Jayce! There's a lot we must do today!" He's curled up with his current boyfriend—limbs all tangled together.

"Go away, Dom!" Jayce waves his hand in the air, trying to shoo me away. I use his pool cue and poke him several times until he growls at me.

"Damn it to hell, Dom, go the fuck away! Don't you see I'm not alone!" He buries his face against the male's back, between his shoulder blades.

"Jayce, we have a very important visitor today, and we need to talk before they arrive." That gets his attention. His head pops up, and his eyes focus on me finally. I hold out his robe to him.

"Go shower. I'll explain as you get cleaned up." Jayce's face becomes solemn as he leans over and whispers into his boyfriend's ear; it is time for him to leave. The man rises and doesn't bother to dress when he walks out of the suite and into the main den.

I turn to look at Jayce. "Having fun pissing Father off with your latest conquest?" I say this half-joking, half-serious as well. He knows how Father treats our gay brother. Why he wants to bring torture on himself is beyond me.

"You know I love making him uncomfortable. Especially with how shitty he treats our mother most of the time." I can't disagree with him on that count; Father treats our mother like shit. Dire's don't need a true mate to breed, just a female in heat. It's sad, really, and it's the only reason our numbers are so high. Jayce finally gets in the shower and starts to bathe.

"What if I told you the dragon is right? His child lives. I have it on good authority that she's on her way here to find her mate." Jayce's head pops out of the shower to look at me, shocked.

"Are you fucking kidding me? Like, are you serious? She lives? Father said the queen died before the baby could be brought into this world." Obviously, Father didn't know the whole truth... Nicodeamus did, and up until two weeks ago, he hadn't mentioned the child in years.

"Jayce, we must be ready. If Nicodeamus is right, the winds of change are blowing. Our only decision is: do we help the princess or let Father kill a female Lycan?" I hate the idea of Father killing a female... any female. There are so few females left and even fewer that are fertile. To lose even one more life is a crime.

Jayce's answer is simple. "We save the princess. It's the right thing to do." There is a finality to his words, and all I can do is nod. He may not be the strongest of us, but his heart is always in the right place. For an omega to take such a strong stance is a rarity.

"Father said to be in the viewing room behind the tinted glass by ten in the morning. I'm going to make sure our brothers are all ready." With that, I search for the others, anxious to see what kind of female the dragon's daughter is.

CHAPTER 12
Aurora

Camping in the desert isn't as fun as I thought it would be. We can see the ruins from where we have set up camp. At one point, there is a single spot of light that flickers for a moment on the cliff face. I watch the area for a while before I finish my hunt and return to camp with the pronghorn I killed for dinner.

My Lycan is getting restless. There's a strange energy I'm feeling; it's making my blood hum. I can't explain it, but I feel like a part of me that has been missing is so close that I can almost grab it. I walk the outskirts of the camp for most of the night before Sebastian makes me follow him back and go to bed.

We're on the move again early this morning, the adrenaline pumping through my veins in anticipation of what's to come. We could be walking into a trap. Then again, a trap could be fun at this point. It's been five days since I killed the last Alpha, I'm about due for some carnage. The boys go over the hypothetical plan while I stand over here like, let's do this.

After a short drive, we arrive at the ground below the ruins. There are plaques and various other tourist crap for those that will never see the ruins up close. While the boys chat, I move to the rear of the truck and grab my go-bag for the ascent. I double check the contents while Andre flies around, assessing the ruins. Sebastian moves up alongside me and rests a hand on my lower back.

"Ready, love?" He's got one of those megawatt smiles that usually melts my insides, but today his smile seems forced. Those eyes of his are as blue as the bluest sky; I can get lost just staring up at him. I can tell he's worried about this being a setup. And I'm ninety percent sure that this whole thing *is* a setup. Something is off. I mean, there's no security, no sentries; at this point, I'm not feeling super safe.

I just smile and nod, looking at him. "Let's go. The cliff won't climb itself." I shrug out of the summer dress and shove it in my pack. The shift comes easier than usual; my blood is singing to me. I swear I feel like my strength has been amplified. Half of me wants to ask Sebastian if he feels it also, but I don't think he does. He's not acting any differently than usual; it's just me. I feel like I chugged a half dozen energy drinks and some espresso.

Once Sebastian's Lycan is beside mine, Dimitri helps us strap on our go bags for the climb. My usually growly bear looks nervous about us going without him. I lightly nuzzle his cheek, and he smiles at me.

"Be safe, princess. Not all wolves favor the ruling family." He sighs before looking up. "If I'm correct, this alpha was the son of the current alpha before the attack. Their pack was almost wiped out because of the Strigoi." He raises an eyebrow at me.

"So, don't expect a warm welcome." Sebastian and I nod our heads then look up at the vertical climb before us.

Andre approaches from behind. "I didn't notice anything out of the ordinary. Though one building looks like it's got fancy double doors recessed out of the line of sight." Slowly, Sebastian and I nod, then leap for the wall. Our sharp talons sink into the stone as we make our climb. Thankfully it doesn't take us long to make it to the ledge of the ruins.

Sebastian is the first to scout the area as I shift back and get dressed. He returns to me and shifts back too. "There seems to be an entrance in the far-back, right corner. I think we should start there." My eyes follow the path that he points out and we start walking in that direction. As I approach the door, the humming in my blood seems to increase. I carefully reach out to grip the handle on the wooden door, and frost begins to spread across the wood.

Sebastian and I both stare at the frost and the door. We are both puzzled as all fucking hell as to what's going on now. "Maybe it's because of who my father is? I mean, you did say my Lycan has gained white scales on my muzzle." I shrug my shoulders, confused.

"I also noticed I have dragon scale gauntlets that go all the way to my talons. I wonder if I can blow ice fire. I mean, is it frost flames?" I raise an eyebrow curiously. "Okay, whatever it is, an Ice Dragon freezes things with."

Ugh, it's so frustrating not knowing what the hell I am becoming and not knowing what kind of gifts—besides scales and frost touch—I've gotten from my father. Sebastian's shoulder delivers a light hit to the door, and it splinters and falls to the ground in a wintry mess. We glance at each other and enter the hallway.

Sebastian takes the lead, and I follow behind him, just in case. Besides, he would never let me go first. He is dead set on protecting me. We make it to a foyer, and several males are standing about, looking right at us.

Sebastian speaks first. "The alpha is expecting us. Elena sent word a week ago to him." Two of the guys disappear down the hallway before returning with a man in a suit. He isn't muscular in the least, and he looks to be in his decline.

"Ah, welcome, esteemed guests! Come this way so we can speak." He turns and heads back down the hallway. The question is, do we follow? Yeah, why the hell not? I move forward, and Sebastian is close on my heels. We enter a room with a one-way mirror and a balcony overlooking the gladiator pit. I move towards the mirror and stare at it.

My Lycan surges forth, her liquid mercury eyes studying the glass. I can see outlines behind the mirror. Two appear to be the same height; one is built heavier than the other, one tall and thin, and the last tall and muscular. The two males of the same height move closer to the glass; I can almost feel them. I cant my head to the side then straight again.

"What do you want, Lucian? You have your sons behind the mirror watching us. To what end? I'm not exactly sure. My gut tells me you're going to add conditions to meet your sons. So? What are they?" I cross my arms over my chest as I watch the myriad of emotions flicker over the alpha's face. Apparently, I've read him too well, and he's not used to it.

"You're very wise, princess. I do want something, and I do have conditions." He moves to lean his back against the mirror.

"I'll give you two options. The first is that you forget my sons and accept me. Your other option is to fight in the pit, and if you live, you get to meet my sons." He smiles in a way that would make the Cheshire cat jealous. He is definitely off his rocker if he thinks he would ever get his grubby paws on me.

I walk over and lean my back against Sebastian's chest. Immediately his arm wraps around my shoulder. "I'll take option B. I'll fight in your pit." I start to laugh.

"I have to battle before I meet your sons... the dick better be worth it!" Sebastian laughs behind me as he tightens his grip.

"Say the word, my love, and we leave." His head lowers as he moves my sundress to the side to show his mating mark upon my shoulder. His mouth comes to grip the same place, making me squirm slightly.

"I came to fight, my love. Apparently, Lucian wants to see if I'm worthy of his sons." I look up into Sebastian's eyes before kissing him chastely.

I turn back to look at the alpha. "At least let me see who I'm fighting for. After all, if by some fluke I die in the ring, I want to see the four males that had the chance to see me." I move forward, slowly placing my palms flat on the table, staring at the glass. What I didn't expect was for the frost to spread from my hands across the table.

"As you wish, princess. Though I do have to warn you, I have one dud of a son. One who can't make up his mind what team he's on, one that's betrothed, and the last one that is in love only with his armory. So, good luck." He flicks the switch, and the reflection disappears from the mirror. I can see the twins and the other two males clearly.

It is the twins who catch my attention through the glass. I watch as the males regard me. The two older ones don't even appear to be interested at all. The twins, though, their wolves are making themselves known. Dire's know their mate on sight, Lycan's need to see and scent their mate. I would definitely have something else to fight for. I *need* to win. I need to kill all my opponents and then the alpha to free my mates from under his rule. But my question is, will the other sons side with daddy dearest or their brothers?

"Gentlemen, let the games begin, shall we? Give me my first opponent, and I'll give you their head." The twins begin to hit the glass trying to break through; their drive to protect is admirable. I return to Sebastian.

"Protect the twins." My eyes lock with his, and he gives me a quick nod. That's all I need to be able to enter the ring.

As I'm led out of the room, I get close to the glass. The twins are still pounding on it, trying to break free. I press a kiss to the glass, leaving blood-red lipstick behind. The lighter built twin is beside himself, and the stocky twin looks pissed. Good, one has a temper —they'll be just fine. I follow the alpha down a series of hallways that lead down deeper into the den. I scent so many bodies and species down here that my senses are on overload. Then there's that hum that's getting stronger.

Daughter?

I hear the words in my head. Cautiously, I look around to see if anyone else heard the voice. I listen to it several more times before I think of a response.

Dad?

I mean, I never met the man, and as far as I knew, he was over two hundred years dead. I feel a wave of relief wash over me. Wait, dragons can communicate telepathically?

Nicodeamus? My mother's dragon mate?

Part of me wants to cry. I still have family left. I not entirely without my bloodline. Tears threaten to break free. I have to make myself mad to not alert the alpha to what was going on.

Yes, little one. We don't have much time. Lucian plans to kill you in the ring. Use my gifts, my strength. When we come face to face, we will burn this place to the ground.

His voice holds such confidence and authority, I can't help but smile. Now I know where I get my *don't fuck with me* attitude from. I walk with more confidence and bounce in my step.

In my mind's eye, my father shares years of information: our history, our family, and the night of the attack. The alpha is the one that helped the Strigoi breach the castle's defenses. For that, he will pay dearly.

"Are you ready, princess?" The sarcasm is strong with this one. I give him two thumbs up and turn my back to him.

"Yup, let's get it done." I crack my knuckles and my neck, getting my limbs loose. I'm as ready as I'm going to be. The great doors open, and I hear the roar of the crowd. Closing my eyes, I start hearing the Megadeth song "Crush 'em" in my head. The opening line fits so well, and I start singing the first lines out loud.

Poor Sebastian must think I've lost my mind, entering the ring singing. I need to focus, and one of my favorite training songs makes me feel like my mentor is right beside me. Opening my eyes, scanning the arena, they fall on Sebastian and the twins. This is the first time they will see me shift. It should be worth seeing the look on their faces. Especially now that my father taught me how to use the frost in the shift; it should add a whole new element to my theatrics.

I breathe in deeply and let out the deepest, most haunting howl I can muster as the shift takes me. Frost seeps from my every pore as my body takes on its new shape. I embrace my father's magic and let it bond with my Lycan. By the time I am done, the arena is dead silent. Not a single sound besides my breathing can be heard.

"Hell yeah, babe!" I hear Sebastian shout. He knew through the bond about the influx of power I have gained. My mercury eyes seek out the twins. Their eyes glow golden like their wolves'. Yes, we are one. Bring on my opponent!

The door across from me slams open, and a rather large Dire Wolf comes charging out and skids to a stop. I don't think this poor bastard was expecting me. I roar at him, my voice a mix of wolf and dragon. His scent screams he's frightened; that's good. Two more Dire's come out behind him; this is about to get interesting. I raise my right arm before twitching my finger at them, signaling for them to attack. All at once, they charge. Now the fun really begins.

CHAPTER 13

Dominik

Holy fuck, what a day. Aurora is the princess, our mate, *and* part dragon. Can today get any more fucked up? My brother Jayce and I race to the balcony with Sebastian close on our heels. He's trying to reassure us that she'll be fine. But damn, every female we know can barely hunt for herself. We just found our mate and we aren't ready for her to die yet.

Halfway into the suite, Sebastian's knees buckle, sending him to the floor. He's panting heavily through whatever is happening to him. He appears to be in immense pain the way his face is contorted and his jaw clenched tight.

"Shit, that hurt. I hope Aurora knows what she's doing." He looks up to me.

"She's tapping into her father's power. They are close enough for her to do it now. Fuck did that pack a punch." His eyes are swirling between an almost white-blue to his regular sky blue.

If the mating bond can do this, I'm almost afraid of the power she's wielding at the moment. I go and help Sebastian to his feet and we make it to the balcony to see her enter the ring. I can't believe my ears; she's singing while entering the ring. Sebastian laughs, saying how the pack is in trouble now.

Her gaze finds us, and she smiles just before tilting her head back, allowing her long white tresses to flow down her back. Her crimson lips twist up in a mischievous smile before letting out the most bone-chilling howl I've ever heard in my life. Fur ripples over my arms as my wolf fights me for control. My bones and tendons tighten as her howl echoes through the pit, calling forth my wolf. He wants nothing more than to be at his mate's side when she battles. I agree with him, but it's not our place at the moment. Looking to my right, I can see Sebastian and Jayce having the same problem.

We look at each other briefly before watching Aurora shift. Her body bends and breaks, reforming to that of her great, white Lycan beast. Every inch of her body is covered in frost as the change takes hold of her. Her beast grows larger by the second, far larger than any female Lycan in recent history.

Unlike your average Lycan, her's has white dragon scales along the length of her muzzle as well as armored gauntlets with talons. Holy shit, she has dragon talons instead of the normal Lycan claws. Aurora flexes her hands several times, looking over her weaponry before looking around the arena briefly. She appears to be bored with the way her long, white tail sways slowly behind her. A couple of quick stretches later, and the double doors in front of her are thrown open.

One Dire Wolf comes running into the arena. Aurora looks bored with only a single wolf arriving. The roar that comes out of her mouth is the thing that nightmares are made of. A chill runs down my spine hearing the tone that comes out of her mouth. The male in the ring is terrified, his body shaking; that is until two more join him.

Aurora raises her right arm and bears the royal seal. Fuck, she *is* the lost princess. To attack royalty is an immediate death sentence. The Dires move as one towards her, and her fingers spread, exposing her talons. They aren't even claws; they are fucking talons—long, curved, and lethal.

In one fluid motion, she flicks her hands out, catching the two leaping in the air at her, and rakes her talons across their throats, severing their heads from their bodies. Blood sprays everywhere as the decapitated corpses hit the ground. Her snow-white fur stains vermillion as she stares down the last remaining wolf.

Her rage is palpable in the air. Energy crackles around the arena as if a thunderstorm is approaching. As the final wolf charges and leaps, Aurora catches it in midair. Her talons sinking deeply into the ribcage of the Dire. Blood oozes freely from the wounds she has dealt him as his feet dangle off the floor. The poor wolf whines, whimpers, and squirms, trying to free itself from her vice-like grip. Her eyes lock onto my father as she rips the Dire in half; bloody entrails dangle from the two halves in her talons.

She throws the upper half of what is left of the Dire at my father's balcony. Blood splattering all over the white marble and some of it manages to land on my father's face. The hind end in her talons falls to the ground as I swear her beast smirks at my father's reaction. He isn't happy that she threw the body at him, his lip still curled up in a snarl. Personally, I find it funny.

The carnage in the ring is unlike anything I've ever seen in all my years of watching these battles. Aurora turns and looks back up at us, trying to gauge our reaction to her brutality. I bow my head and raise my fist to my heart. I witness my brother and Sebastian repeat what I have done out of the corner of my eye. Aurora lightly dips her head to us and raises her taloned fist over her heart in return.

My only question is, how far is my father going to take this farce? He's up to something; I'm just not sure what. The door to the right opens, and the energy in the air changes. The air becomes thick and humid. Fog begins to roll into the arena, making Aurora adjust her stance to face her new foe.

I know what it is: the Wendigo. It stands almost equal in height to Aurora's Lycan. But where Aurora has bulk, the Wendigo is gaunt with bones protruding out of its half-rotted flesh. Its face looks like the skull of a bear with terrifying teeth and a blue tongue that can be seen tasting the air. Upon its head are great horns like that of a stag. Its eyes are deep-set, glowing red orbs like that of the demon that it is. Its arms are long and at the tips of the boney digits, sit razor-sharp claws.

The two titans begin to circle each other. One more terrifying than the other. Height wise, they appear to be equally matched. Both have white fur matted with blood. Aurora takes a quick swipe at the Wendigo's chest, ripping a layer of flesh off it. The creature doesn't even seem phased by it. But the look on Aurora's face tells me she noticed something we can't see from where we are sitting.

I turn to Sebastian. "Is she okay? I mean, I know you can feel her." His eyes never leave her in the ring.

"She's fine. My mother told her about the Wendigo and how to kill it. She's just making sure what my mother knew is accurate before she goes on the attack." His tone doesn't sound concerned; instead, it almost sounds detached and bored. In my opinion, his reaction isn't appropriate for what happening currently. I'll file this tidbit of information away to process later. My eyes return to watch Aurora move about the ring, testing the creature.

"It's better to test than to be sorry. Aurora's very wise." I walk over to Jayce, who's still beside himself, and I wrap an arm around his shoulders.

"She'll be fine, you'll see!" I have to have faith in our future mate. I refuse to have any negative thoughts about the female my wolf has chosen. The Wendigo suddenly roars and charges at Aurora. She jumps to the side, barely getting out of the way in time.

Unfortunately, the Wendigo's claws catch Aurora's ribs, slicing thin lines along her right side. The scent of Aurora's blood has put the creature into a frenzy. It's not thinking straight, and Aurora takes full advantage of it and charges.

Quickly she drops down and sweeps the legs out from under the creature, causing it to land flat on its back. Her talons come down swiftly, severing the horns from the Wendigo's head. The creature's high-pitched scream fills the arena, blackened blood oozes from where the horns once were. Aurora grabs the horns and drives them down into the Wendigo's arms, pinning them to the earth below it.

Aurora's taloned hands take on an unearthly glow as frost begins to gather in her hands. She drives her talons into the creature's chest and rips up quickly. Within the now hollowed rib cage lay a human curled up in a fetal position. It is the man the Wendigo possessed to enter this world. Aurora's Lycan studies him before ripping him free of the creature's remains.

Once the human is free, the Wendigo's corpse ignites, burning blue in the center of the ring. The man is covered in a black, viscous material, almost like a cocoon. Aurora cants her head left and right several times, studying the man before ripping his head free of his shoulders and throwing the severed head onto my father's balcony.

She roars again, looking around the arena, calling for her next challenger. The massive doors on the far side of the stadium opens—a deep bellow echoes throughout the arena, followed by a blast of blue flames. The temperature in the arena drops quickly as frost and ice begin to coat the available surfaces. An Ice Dragon lumbers into the arena; his head mere feet from the roof. His white scales are thick and armor-like—with each scale having a thick raised ridge with a sharp spiked tip. Not only would the scales protect him, but they would also slice his attacker to ribbons.

It is quite scary to see such a battle-hardened warrior lumber in on three legs and missing a wing. His scales tell the tale of his years of battle, not only here but in his past. His silver serpentine eyes search the arena then lock on Aurora. He raises his head high and blows his flames down upon her. Wave upon wave of blue-white flame encapsulates Aurora. The fire itself seems to roar and crackle as they fall from the dragon's great maw. Aurora doesn't even try to evade the dragon fire. We can't see her as the flames begin to coat the arena floor.

My eyes shoot to Sebastian, and he is calm as all hell. How the fuck can he be calm when our mate is getting burnt to a crisp? The fucker just smiles. Sebastian exudes an unearthly air of confidence that is a bit unnerving. Slowly, his eyes turn to me. "They are showing how powerful Aurora is. She's immune to his dragon fire because she's his daughter."

Well, now that makes more sense. The crowd is quiet as the flames recede. Aurora stands there, her fur cleaned of blood and her wounds healed. She begins to walk towards the dragon and shifts back to her human form.

The dragon lowers its great horned head to her, and Aurora places a hand to his cheek and kisses his muzzle. She turns to face the crowd, choosing this time to shift partially. Her hands look like white armored gauntlets all the way down to her white talons. Her legs break backward and are that of her Lycan—a light dusting of fur-covers her most intimate of parts. Aurora walks to the middle of the arena and locks eyes with our father. Her rage is evident by the trail of frost she left in her wake.

"How dare you imprison my father! Your lost dragon king! You have betrayed the royal family! You have betrayed your people, Lucian!" Aurora calls out our father, the alpha.

He claps his hands and starts laughing. "What does a little bitch like you think you can do to me? I have five hundred Dire Wolves at my command." He raises his arms as if to gather his forces, but none move. Not one single being except my eldest brother—his beta—moves to his side. All the others begin to move to the far side of the arena, behind Aurora and her father.

Aurora looks over at her father's dragon. He's missing his front, left leg and wing on that side. She begins to growl low in the back of her throat. "You want to see what I can do? So be it." She rips her eyes away from her father to gaze upon the gathered wolves within the arena.

"My people, I'm going to apologize now for what I'm about to do." She shifts the rest of the way rapidly and howls... ripping the wolves from all of us. None of us have control when her Lycan calls to ours. My body breaks and reshapes to that of my Dire Wolf far faster than I've ever shifted before. I look to my right to see Sebastian and Jayce both have shifted just as quickly.

She summons all of our animals, and only a true alpha could force the shift of an entire pack at once. We leap down from our balcony to flank Aurora, moving in sync to stand at her side. Her father stands like a great sentinel behind us. The rest of the pack fills the arena, slowly closing in on my father. Do I feel bad for Father? Not one bit. The way he treated my brothers because of whom they love... he deserves everything he is about to receive.

Aurora breaks free of the pack and bolts towards my father's balcony. Her father's wing shoots out about midway between her and the balcony. Aurora leaps up and grabs onto her father's wingtip and uses it to launch herself up and into my father's suite. Next thing you know, my father is flying through the air with a tremendous, white Lycan hot on his heels; they land within seconds of each other. Aurora monopolizes on her momentum and pins him to the ground. Her head lifts to lock eyes with her father.

He shifts back to human and approaches Aurora and my father. "You killed my family. You allowed the Strigoi passage into the castle. You took my arm, and in my grief, you made me a slave in your games."

He nods to Aurora, only to have her grip my father by the back of his neck to lift him off the ground. "My daughter was swept far away to be raised without me because of you." He extends a single finger and touches my father's stomach. The flesh turns to ice spreading slowly over his body.

"The time for me to show mercy is long over, Lucian. Now you will know my pain. But know this, the Strigoi will die, and my daughter will be queen in her castle. You," Nicodeamus smiles sadistically, "on the other hand, will just be a memory. A blip in time to be easily forgotten in years to come." Ice covers my father's body completely. He is frozen solid—kind of like Han Solo in carbonite.

Nicodeamus takes my father's frozen body from Aurora and throws him to the ground, smashing him to bits. Johan comes out of nowhere, sailing through the air with Father's rapier in his hands. He heads towards Nicodeamus and closes the gap quickly.

Before he can get close enough, Sebastian's Lycan slams Johan to the ground. The force of Sebastian's impact knocks the rapier from Johan's hand and the air from his lungs. Aurora is way too calm for what is going on. Her eyes locked with her father's, and they stare at each other for a moment. I'm guessing they have an in-depth conversation in the middle of a foiled assassination attempt.

Nicodeamus makes a graceful sweeping motion towards Johan, and Aurora walks over to where Sebastian has him pinned. With every step, Aurora returns slowly to her human form until she stands beside her Lycan mate.

She threads her fingers through the fur on the back of Sebastian's head. A single hand raises up, caressing his ear as she leans down to stare at Johan. She speaks to him in the most condescending tone she can muster. "Poor, little beta thinks he's wolf enough to attack my father." She keeps tilting her head from side to side, assessing him. "You have been weighed and measured. You simply aren't wolf enough to breathe the same air as me."

Her gaze falls on Jayce, and me next. "Please forgive me for what I must do next. We will not be safe if he's allowed to live. Your father's will has poisoned his heart and mind." Her eyes remain bouncing between mine and my brother's as her fingers glide through Sebastian's thick, black fur.

This dominant-as-fuck female before us is asking for our forgiveness. My brother and I choose this moment to shift back to our human forms. We glance at each other quickly and nod our heads at her. Jayce makes a heart with his hands—being the softy that he is. That little gesture earns him a smile from Aurora before she moves before Johan again.

"I sentence you to death for the attempted assassination of my father, the dragon king." She raises her hand and shifts it, allowing her talons to catch the light in the arena. The talon on her index finger touches the artery on the right side of Johan's neck. And ever so slowly, she applies pressure. We watch the skin flex and bend before finally granting passage of the sharp tip of her talon.

Every beat of his heart, a little more blood pumps out and runs down his chest. Aurora almost seems fascinated watching the blood flow. Carefully she removes the talon from the artery and moves to the other side to repeat the process. Now two streams of blood flow slowly down my brother's chest. With surgical precision, Aurora pierces the brachial artery in his right arm, causing yet another stream of blood.

She's bleeding him out slowly. For some reason, she skips the other arm and goes straight to his femoral artery, and slices it open just above his left knee. Now that one really pumps the blood out. His face grows pale, and yet he doesn't utter a word. Johan doesn't beg for his life or even to be spared.

Not that I think Aurora would have spared him at this point. She finally got her father back, and Johan has tried to kill him. I understand she needs to make him suffer, but to what end? Her head tilts one last time and moves forward.

"It's nothing personal, but you tried to kill my father after your father tried to kill me. It's only fair." Just before he loses consciousness, she uses her talons to rip his heart out. Her eyes lock on the final twitching of Johan's heart before she offers it to her father. Nicodeamus takes it with a smile before she walks off toward my father's remains. Her talons gain purchase on his frozen skull as she lifts it off the ground.

Carefully measured steps carry her back to where her father stands. She drops to one knee and holds up my father's head to him. He takes the offering then pulls Aurora up into a hug. It is probably the most surreal thing I have ever seen.

He holds his daughter with his only arm while my father's hair is wrapped around his fingers, and my brother's heart dangles off of his pinky. "My baby... My beautiful, powerful baby. I never gave up hope I would see you again!" Nicodeamus nuzzles the top of her head softly, crying into her blood-soaked mane.

Aurora starts crying as well, holding her father tightly, afraid she will lose him again. Nico shakes his hand, freeing him of his presents to grip her better. Aurora looks like she has a Kung Fu Ninja death grip on him. Lord, help the being that tries to end this hug-fest. I think there would be another body hitting the floor quickly.

CHAPTER 14

Dominik

Sebastian moves up slowly and cautiously. "Aurora, love? We should appoint someone to watch over the pack until we need them. And don't forget we have Dimitri and Andre waiting outside for us. You know how Andre gets; he's like an old mother hen." Aurora's head lifts, and she nods slowly. Her eyes find her smiling father looking down at her.

"Daughter? Do Dimitri and Andre still live? How can this be?" Nicodeamus looks puzzled because, by all rights, those two should have been long dead by time alone. Both types of shifters are not very long-lived by shifter standards.

"Yes, Father, they live. The elder dame bound them to me until I found my first mate, Sebastian. I fear now they may not have much time left." She turns to face Jayce and me. "Can we trust Alexander? Will he lead in our stead while we are gone?"

My brother and I think long and hard about it. "Yes, we believe he would. Father always mistreated him because he's gay. Trust me, he will be thankful and most faithful to you for freeing him from our father." I say with great finality, truth rings with every syllable that passes my lips.

Out of the corner of my eye I notice Sinclair, my brother's lover. Jayce stands stock still watching him approach, afraid of what Aurora may do to the competition. Jayce's fear is palpable in the air as he watches his lover approach. Without a second thought, Sinclair closes the distance and hugs onto Jayce for dear life. I am prepared to intervene if needed, but what could I do? It is my mate and my twin—possibly having to choose between them is breaking my heart.

Aurora shocks me as she moves slowly and touches Jayce's shoulder. "If this is where your heart truly lies, I can and will release you from this fragile bond." Her eyes are the pure mercury of her Lycan. She is anxious, and you can scent her sadness in the air. Aurora is trying to do what is right for my brother. My older brother Alex hears the whole exchange and waits to see what Jayce chooses.

Jayce takes in a deep breath and kisses Sinclair hard on the lips. "I'm sorry. My wolf and I want her as our mate. I never thought I'd find my mate; I thought we had forever." He glances back to Aurora, who has tears streaming down her face. She's ready to release him if that's what he wants, even if it causes her pain.

Aurora shifts quickly and runs across the arena. She leaps high into the air and lands a good twenty feet off the ground. Her talons sink into the wood and mortar as she climbs higher and higher until she reaches the alcove just below the roof. It was the first time Sebastian witnessed his mate run from anything. He just stands there in a state of shock. His eyes swirl between his normal sky blue and that of his wolf. It appears that they are battling each other for control.

"Sebastian!" I yell at him to knock him from the trance he appears to be in. Slowly he looks at me, then back in the direction Aurora had fled. Everyone, now watching the alcove. "Why did she run?"

Sebastian draws in a deep breath, grabbing everyone's attention. "She's not good with handling anything outside of rage, desire, or apathy. The possibility of losing a mate before really having him fucked her world all up."

His eyes find Jayce's. "Choose whatever will make you the happiest. She wouldn't have offered you an out if she didn't mean it. Besides, I think you've figured out that she doesn't hold back when something pisses her off or gets in her way."

Jayce nods and looks towards the alcove then back to me. "Dom, please go talk to her. I need to talk with Sinclair a bit, and I'll bring Alex up to speed while you try to make Aurora happy."

I smile at my brother and bring him in for a quick hug before heading to the side of the arena. A hand grips my shoulder, turning my head slightly; it's Nicodeamus, and he is smiling. It's kind of terrifying that he's smiling at me right now. "Son, she's hurting and volatile. Tread softly and talk with your heart. Her beast isn't going to listen to reason right now." He spoke from a place of years of wisdom, his connection to his daughter giving us insight into her emotional state...

"Is it safe to approach her? I mean, we're not bonded yet, and she's wedged in a small area." I wasn't afraid of being attacked. I was more fearful of setting her off on a rampage.

"Soon as she can scent you, you'll be safe. Be patient with her. Perhaps the company of your wolf will help her once you get up there." He smirks at me because there is no visible way for me to get up there.

I stare at where she is hiding, then look back at Nicodeamus. "Mind giving me a lift? My wolf isn't like hers, and I can't climb walls like she can."

Nicodeamus starts laughing and walks away from everyone before he shifts back to his dragon. He looks from me to the alcove and back again before opening his huge taloned hand, waiting for me to walk into his grip. Well, here goes nothing. I walk towards him—poor Jayce is in panic mode, and Sebastian has to hug him to keep him from chasing after me. Once I am in the dragon's grip, he rears up on his hind legs and stretches out his arm, and places me on the ledge of the alcove.

Glowing mercury orbs find me swiftly. She is curled up against the back wall, hugging her knees to her chest. I slowly shift into my wolf and belly crawl over to her, whimpering the entire distance. The great white Lycan in question lies down and curls up around my wolf. Never in my existence have I felt like a small wolf until now. Slowly she starts licking the back of my head, grooming me as if I am the one that needs comfort. When she moves to get a better angle, I can start grooming her.

After a while, she stops and shifts back to her human form. "Your wolf is beautiful, Dom." Her fingers thread through my thick, obsidian fur as she examines the path her fingers blaze.

"Father must like you to lift you up here. I'm sorry I took off as I did." Her voice quivers with emotion.

"I was afraid of Jayce's rejection. I was afraid that my Lycan would kill his lover in retaliation." She lowers herself to lay her head on my ribcage, curling into me for comfort. "I'm glad you're here, Dom. I don't think I could take Sebastian coddling me."

Her fingers continue their exploration of my wolf's body. Her fingertips are getting dangerously close to my sheath. I can feel my body responding to her proximity. Her own scent is starting to change as she scents the change in mine.

I turn my head and nip at her exposed shoulder. I didn't expect that she would move her head to the side to expose her neck to me. My wolf is ready to claim her right here, right now. He isn't giving me control anytime soon. We nudge her with our muzzle, and she moves onto all fours.

Apparently, our princess is a bit of a freak behind closed doors. My wolf is in the driver's seat as he moves behind her—his long broad tongue laps from her clit through her soaking wet folds to her engorged entrance. Her moan makes our fur stand on end. We lick her like an ice cream cone, enjoying her sticky sweet taste on our tongue.

"Please, Dom," is all she says as she looks back over her shoulder at us. Who am I to deny my mate what she is begging for?

I hesitate, knowing my wolf won't be gentle, nor will he go slow. She shakes her ass at us one last time, and he surges forward, mounting her quickly. Quickly we thrust forward, burying ourselves to the hilt. Aurora moans at her sudden fullness and draws in a deep breath as she wiggles again. Her movement spurs my wolf to bite her shoulder hard to hold her in place as he decides to fuck her as hard as he can. Our dew claws dig into the tender skin near her hips so we don't lose our grip of her as we pound her relentlessly.

The sloppy wet sound of our cock sliding in and out of her is music to our ears. Her voice changes as her orgasm grips her. Her muscles grip us tightly, rhythmically pulsating while milking our cock. We won't last much longer; our balls draw uptight as our mating knot forms just before filling her with our seed. Soon after we orgasm, my wolf releases his hold on our body and allows me to shift back to being just a man. The mating knot is still in place as I kiss at the bite my wolf gave her.

Aurora turns her head to look over her shoulder at me and just smiles. "Totally worth it."

She starts giggling to herself, and then I feel it. I feel another presence beside myself. It's a somewhat confusing feeling, half elated and at peace, the other part angry. The mixed emotions have me baffled. Aurora looks to be quite happy and content at the moment. The second emotion is definitely puzzling me. As we lay here together, my mating knot finally releases so I can pull free from Aurora's welcoming depths.

"What am I feeling? Better yet, who am I feeling?" I pull her onto my lap, waiting for her answer. I know I feel her, but is that also Sebastian I am feeling? She snuggles into my lap, and without warning, she bites my shoulder near my neck. Everything I was feeling becomes clearer. I'm feeling Sebastian, and well, he is none too pleased my wolf took part in the claiming.

"He'll get over it," Aurora says rather matter of factly after she cleans my mating mark that she just made. "Let's go. I'll have to shift and carry you back down."

Slowly she stands and stretches by the entrance. I watch my seed drip freely from her pussy before she shifts back into her Lycan. She gives me a short bark as if to say *get over here*. I climb onto her back, lock my arms around her neck, and use my thighs to hold onto her rib cage. This most certainly is a strange turn of events. I'm holding onto my mate for dear life as she takes a running leap off the ledge towards the wall that seems miles away.

Sadly, I must admit I think I saw part of my life flash before my eyes as we sail through the air. The landing leaves a lot to be desired; it is jarring and sudden. Through the bond, I feel her joy at my dismay, and I can feel Sebastian's state of panic over what she had just done. Aurora is definitely enjoying this way too much because about halfway down, she launches us backward. All I can think is, *this is it; I'm going to die because my mate is insane.*

A large, taloned hand shoots up out of nowhere and snatches us out of the air. Nicodeamus has decided to join in on her fun and my panic. Thank the gods I have such great control over my bowels; otherwise, there'd be a mess I'd have to clean up later. Nicodeamus places us on the ground, where I promptly slide off her back and move away slowly. I thought I was in the clear until Sebastian's fist meets my jaw, stunning me for a moment.

"What the fuck! You took advantage of her emotional state, you fucking heartless bastard." Just as he gets ready to strike again, a large, white maw comes between us and starts growling at Sebastian. Aurora makes him back away and rethink his course of action.

Her shift comes quickly as she moves to get in Sebastian's face. "I love you, Bash, and I appreciate what you're trying to do. But if you ever hit another mate for doing what I wanted, you and I will be brawling," she growls out.

"I touched his wolf's sheath." She jabs her hand in the direction of my cock.

"I waved my ass and soaked pussy in his face. I taunted them 'til they gave me what I wanted!" Her hands clenched into fists.

"I needed to feel something other than death and sadness. I needed to feel like something other than the monster I become when I'm forced to kill." She begins to pace between the two of us. Her hands coming up to run through her hair, almost violently, over and over again.

I can see what he meant when he said she doesn't deal with emotions well. I choose, at this point, to back away slowly. This part of the fight is between them, not me. My gaze finds my two brothers and Sinclair huddled over by the exit.

I move slowly over towards the group. "Hey, guys, what's going on?" They all appear to be happy to see me, so that's a good start.

"I'm going to accept the title of pack master until Aurora calls for us." Alex is his usual get-to-the-point self. His eyes fall to his nails before he speaks again.

"It will be nice to get the pack back to the way it was before Father lost his marbles." I nod slowly and look around. The pack is moving slowly, interacting like I haven't seen them do in the last fifty years.

"That's great to hear, Alex. I'm sure you'll bring about much-needed changes here that have been long overdue. You're one of the most compassionate and understanding people I know. You'll make a great leader." I embrace Alex then look at Jayce and Sinclair.

Sinclair seems to be in disbelief over what's happening, and Jayce is getting frustrated. "How are you two doing?" I figured I'd ask in case my twin needs backup. Sinclair was always a very needy bitch when it came to their relationship. Jayce's wolf is showing, and Sinclair looks like he is on the verge of tears.

"What could she possibly do that I can't do, Jayce?! I've been with you for almost fifty years!" Sinclair huffs, completely in touch with his inner bitch.

Jayce shakes his head and draws in a slow, measured breath. "For one, she can give me pups. Two, she's not a needy bitch like you are. Three, she's my fucking mate! That won't change, no matter how much you beg!" Jayce flails his arms.

Jayce's screaming gets Aurora's attention, and she sprints over to stand behind Jayce. She is still human for now, but who knows how long that will last. Her face comes alongside his, and she speaks softly next to his ear. "Are you alright, sweetheart?" Her arms wrap around his shoulders as she stands on her tippy toes to rest her head on his shoulder.

"I'm fine, your royal hotness, just trying to get Sinclair to understand that it's over and that I choose you." He made probably his smartest move of the night, leaning his head against hers and placing his hands on her arms. Not only do his words please her, but he also immobilizes her in case she wishes to attack. Because after all, if she moves wrong, she'd end up hurting him too, and she wouldn't ever do that.

Sinclair starts to move towards them, and he appears angry. Aurora isn't having any of it. Her eyes burn molten mercury, and scales ripple over her forearms as she growls at Sinclair. "Choose wisely, male. Jayce has chosen; his word is final. He is my mate, which places him on my level. To move against him or me is to move against the throne." She releases Jayce and moves him behind her. Sinclair slowly lowers his head looking down.

Aurora isn't budging at all, and she has made her stand. Once Sinclair moves off, Aurora turns and kisses Jayce. "I'm sorry you had to go through that." Her eyes return to human grey as she moves to embrace Jayce. They hug for a very long time before they break apart.

Aurora steps away and moves close to Alex. "I heard you accepted the position." She holds her hand out to him, her royal brand facing Alex.

"I do, my queen." He bows his head to her, already proclaiming her queen.

"I will be fair and just and treat everyone better than my father had treated me." He grasps her hand tightly and shakes it. He lifts his head, and they smile at each other.

"Thank you, Alexander. Please prep your people for war. Free the prisoners that were unjustly imprisoned. If any wants to fight alongside us, they are welcome. The guilty prisoners execute them. There is no sense in being imprisoned for life." Alex nods along, taking notes on his phone. He is the organizer of the sons, so he is perfect for this role.

"Oh, and Alex, I need the Dire's with the toxic bite to be trained for assault." That gets his attention.

"For assault, my queen... like assassins?" Alex is quite curious about where her thought process is going. I nod along, sensing where Aurora wants the team to be.

"Yes, Alex. We send them in, almost like scouts, to weaken the forces already in place." Aurora starts drawing in the sand. Nicodeamus moves up alongside her and starts adding to the drawing. She draws a place that she's never been to. Somehow she knows the layout of the castle grounds.

Nicodeamus takes over drawing at this point. "If the Strigoi didn't completely destroy the castle, they will hole up in the bottom chambers in the center during the day." He points to the structure in question. "A daytime assault will be the best bet. If we can gather other Ice Dragons, we can freeze them in their tracks and behead them."

It's kind of scary to think that Aurora was raised without her father, and their thought processes are perfectly in line. She looks at her father's drawing, pointing at parts of it, and you can see the gears turning. "Father, what if we use the tunnels to the south and send the Dire's in through there?" She has a puzzled look on her face, mostly because she's unsure how she knows these things.

Nicodeamus starts to laugh, which draws Sebastian to the group. "I'm so glad to see that you remember all that I've shown you in your dreams over the years. I wasn't sure what you learned in your sleep." He hugs Aurora tightly as he gazes upon us. "Come, all is settled here. Let's head back to your guardians, Aurora."

My brother and I return to our suite to pack. It's time to go and plan our next moves as a pack. Jayce still seems off, but his spirits are much higher than they were earlier. I think Aurora verbally claiming him made the difference in his mood. I guess we shall see. After all, we are about to meet the two men who raised her for the last two hundred plus years.

CHAPTER 15
Nicodeamus

After all these years, I finally have my little girl. She is everything I have dreamt of and more. Though I must admit, she took after me so much. She has my white hair and silvery eyes, but her face and build are all her mother's. And her Lycan has some distinct dragon qualities to it—for example, her talons and the white scales. Her Lycan's muzzle is far longer and broader than your run of the mill Lycan. It killed me to have to sit back and feel her battle without me. Even though I knew she would defeat the challengers without an issue.

The draw on my power had been intense, and she's far more potent than I could have ever imagined possible. When I walked out and saw her Lycan standing there without fear, it made me beam with pride. She trusted me completely even though she didn't know me, per se. We stood against the alpha together, and it warmed my heart that she was there with me.

Now we move slowly through the tunnels to come out somewhere near where Aurora's truck and guardians are waiting for us. Aurora is ahead of me between Sebastian and Dominik, with

Dom in the lead. The other twin, Jayce, is still with the brother we left in charge of making sure the transfer of power went smoothly. I think I'm more anxious about being free after all this time. I haven't seen the skies in over two hundred years.

We approach the sealed passageway, and Aurora looks back at me, sensing my unease. She breaks loose of her mates and comes to my left side to wrap her arms around my waist. "I've got you, Daddy... no worries, I'll protect you." Her smile is infectious and warms my soul. I'm *Daddy* to this grown woman. It brings tears to my eyes, hearing her call me that.

"Thank you, little one. I love you, baby girl. I always have and always will." I kiss the top of her head and nod to Dom to open the passageway. I squint my eyes as the first rays of light flickers through the opening. It feels like forever since I've seen the sun or smelled the fresh air. I move slowly with Aurora, looking outside, amazed by how little this area has changed since my imprisonment.

Dimitri and Andre come rushing over, seeing Sebastian exit first. They immediately start asking about Aurora. She steps out next while I remain in the shadows for a few moments, just taking it all in. She is smiling and laughing as Dimitri hugs her and spins her around in a circle. The next moment he's shaking a finger at her as she tells him about the new body count. His head whips to the opening, then back to her quickly as he processes what she's told him. I still live. Andre and Dimitri come running over to the passageway and drop to their knees before me.

"M'lord," they say in unison, still looking at the ground waiting for me to speak.

"Rise, my friends. You've done a glorious job with raising Aurora. I am forever in your debt." They both look up at me, astonished.

It's now that they finally notice I'm missing my left arm. Andre looks like he's ready to cry, and Dimitri isn't sure what expression is appropriate at the moment. "I lost my arm the night of the invasion. The now-dead alpha was the one that took it. With the help of my daughter, I got to take his life tonight. It's been a very good day." I smile at them, and they look between Aurora and me several times. I guess my daughter is more like me than I realized.

Aurora moves to my side and snuggles in close. She was choosing me over her three mates; it truly soothes my soul. In all the years I dreamt of my child, I never pictured the strong female before me. When I would dream walk to teach her in her sleep, her animal never revealed their gender or even their fur color. It was very protective of her even in her slumber. Perhaps her Lycan is more dragon than I first suspected.

Dimitri is the first to approach and kneels before me. His bear surfaces as he looks up to my daughter and I. "M'lord, if I had known you were captured, we would have come for you sooner." His head lowers, and he looks to the ground. I guess, in a way, he blames himself for not knowing.

"Dimitri, do not blame yourself. You carried precious cargo; my daughter, last of her name. You performed a great service to our people and me. I am forever in your debt." I gently place my hand on his shoulder. "Rise, old friend." Aurora moves off to the side and into Sebastian's waiting arms. Dimitri slowly stands, and I can see clearly now that he is starting to age.

Whatever magic that has extended his life is fading slowly. I move forward and hug Dimitri, bringing the big old bear in close. I missed having my trusted guardian at my side. Few from the past still live, yet those that should not be here are still alive. My eyes find Andre; he is another that has outlived his species lifespan.

"If there is anything I can do for you and Dimitri, name it and it shall be yours."

Dimitri backs up and hugs onto Andre. His eyes dart to where Aurora is standing with her three mates. Slowly his eyes return to me, and I can see a sadness deep within their depths. "I fear we will not be able to serve in the final battle as we are now." Andre begins to sniffle and hides his face against Dimitri's chest; he fears death. Dimitri looks down at his faithful companion and sighs. Perhaps there is something this old dragon could do.

"We can try something; it's old magic and might not even work for long." I look down, staring at my hand as I shift it, looking at my snow-white scales and long, white talons. Even after all these years, it is odd to only have one arm. My dragon's eyes lock onto Dimitri before I look up and over to Aurora.

"Daughter, I need your assistance." Aurora and her mates look plenty puzzled by my request before they come running over without question.

"Yes, Father?" She cants her head to the right looking up at me. Her Lycan surges to the surface, sensing my dragon's urgency. Her eyes fall to my shifted hand and arm, then back up to my eyes.

Our animals are in deep conversation that even I'm not privy to. Aurora's hands shift quickly, and then plucks two scales off my wrist. She turns and promptly plunges her talon into Dimitri's chest and sinks the bleeding side of my scale into his skin. She repeats the process even faster, with Andre knowing how sensitive the bird is. Once her task is complete, her hands begin to glow with frost. Her eyes lock onto the scales, and she presses both frozen palms over the scale transplants, cementing them to their new hosts. She draws in a deep panting breath then collapses from the exertion. Dominik is the one to catch her before she hits the floor. He cradles his greatest treasure against his chest, rocking her gently.

"I'm not sure how much more time my scales and Aurora's frost will grant you. But for now, it will slow the process that has already begun." I speak truly; I'm honestly not sure how long it will give them. For Aurora's sake, something is better than nothing; she will need their guidance and wisdom to train the troops. They both look down at their chests then over to Aurora, who is still sleeping.

"We need to get moving. Dominik, do you or your brother have transportation? As we are not all going to fit in that." Motioning to the black truck that isn't far from where we are standing.

"Yeah, we have a couple of vehicles we can take. Where are we headed?" Jayce is the one who answers and now looks to Sebastian—apparently, he is being recognized as alpha while Aurora is incapacitated.

Sebastian moves forward and sniffs the crown of Aurora's head, then kisses it before turning to me. "We'll head to my birth pack. My mother will be most pleased to see that you live, my king." He bows slightly to me. Too alpha to fully submit, yet smart enough to show ample respect where it's due.

"Sounds like a solid plan. Let's depart as soon as possible. It will be nice to have a bath and sleep in a real bed again." I turn to Dimitri and smile.

"I'll ride with you, old friend. We have a lot of catching up to do." Dimitri nods and starts heading towards the giant black monstrosity that they call Aurora's baby. Baby? An odd thing to call a structure of metal—it doesn't live or breathe. Nor does it resemble my daughter in stature or scent. Andre notices my puzzlement and moves closer.

"Aurora calls the truck her baby because she loves it. It's her most prized possession, besides her guitar." Ah, she has placed a term of endearment and possession on a lifeless object. So much has changed since my capture. Like I'm supposed to ride in this metal beast. Dimitri hops behind what looks like a wheel and does something that makes it roar to life.

Black smoke billows from the beast, and in that moment, I feel at home. Perhaps it is part dragon? I decided to pace around the loud metal beast. I touch it, and its scales are more rigid than my own. I sense no life from it, yet it makes noise. What other wonders will I find now in my newfound freedom? After my second lap around the smoking beast, Andre opens it up. I peer around what he is calling its *door* and see two rows of what appear to be soft seating. It's like a carriage, but there is music playing in it, and the wind blows out of holes in the front.

"Have you captured tiny musicians and frost sprites to have music and cold air?" I stare into the slotted holes, looking for the beating of the sprite's wings.

I hear muffled laughter from Dimitri, and Andre is holding his breath, trying not to laugh. "I demand to know what's so funny!" I turn and stare at them both in turn.

"Has my daughter wrongly imprisoned sprites and tiny musicians?" I attempt to cross my arm over my chest and wait for a sound explanation. "Oh, and the dragon whose smoke comes from this metal beast, how dare you let her capture and imprison her kin!"

Dimitri is the first to compose himself and turn to face me. "M'lord, a lot has changed since the last time you walked free.

We are sitting in what is called a truck. It does not live; other than us, there is nothing alive in it." He motions to each object as he names it.

"The air blows cold because of an invention called an air conditioner. This right here is a radio, and it allows us to find all different types of music. No one is needed to be awake or present to hear the music." I nod along slowly as he explains the wonders I am witnessing.

Never in my wildest dreams did I imagine any of these things before me. I still stare, puzzled at the knobs and buttons that are before me. Each one does something... what will they think of next? Dimitri pushes buttons on the thing he calls a radio, and soon, the sound of an orchestra fills the vehicle.

I smile; it reminds me of the last time I was happy and free. "Thank you, old friend, this is a gift." I reach over and pat Dimitri on the shoulder before leaning back to listen to the music. A rumbling that you can feel in your chest destroys my peace. A sleek-black, metal beast comes straight for us super-fast. I was getting worried, but Dimitri starts laughing when the car suddenly turns and covers us with dust.

Aurora jumps out of the left side of the vehicle and walks over to Dimitri's door. "Hmm, I cut it a tad bit too close. I got my baby dirty. We're gonna head back to Sebastian's pack, so try and keep up!" Before I can get a word out, she hops in through Dimitri's window and flips down a panel, hits a few buttons, and the sound of the vehicle changes.

"There, just woke up a few extra ponies so the beast can keep up with the harlot. Hi, Daddy!" She smiles at me before popping back out the window and running back over to the car.

"Is she always like this?" I watch my daughter jump back into what Dimitri called a *HellCat* and take off, leaving a cloud of dust in her wake.

The harlot is far away, and we can still hear it clearly. It makes me remember the days when dragons flew free and were the lords of the skies. My eyes lock on a metal bird overhead—what I wouldn't give to go back to when it was simpler.

"Yes, she's always like that. Free as a bird and reckless, with an obsession with speed and power." Dimitri's eyes lock on the switch box Aurora had fiddled with, then shakes his head, dismissing it.

When his foot hits the pedal, he quickly figures out what she had meant. The truck launches itself forward much faster than any of us had anticipated. "Holy shit!" he screams as his knuckles turn white, holding onto the steering wheel. I watch the numbers in the middle of the dash get higher and higher, and we gain ground on Aurora at breakneck speed.

I lower the window and stick my hand out, feeling the wind rush over and around my fingers. It feels like I am flying again. Without a second thought, I stick my head out the window to feel the wind in my face. I was robbed of flight, so this would have to do for now. I hear Andre yelling at me to get my head back in as he panics over my safety. At least some things didn't change; he's still a worrywart. I resume sitting in my seat when Andre leans forward and ties me to the chair with a strap.

"What is the meaning of this, Andre? You dare to restrain your king?" My dragon makes his presence known as his slits burn through my silver eyes.

"It's called a seat belt, M'lord. It's to keep you safe in case of an accident." He looks quite sheepish, having to explain it to me. I look down at the offensive belt, then back to Andre.

"Fine, it can remain for now. Next time, warn me before you decide to restrain me for my own good." I breathe out sharply, and a frosty mist escapes my nostrils. I wasn't thrilled, but he did have my best interest in mind, so I couldn't stay completely mad at him.

I drum my fingers on the windowsill as I watch the miles fly by me. We've been on the road for several hours already, and they said we still have a few hours to go. Being terrestrial is the worst fate ever. I could have already been at our destination if I still had both of my wings. I could have carried everyone. It was a lifetime ago when I last had the wind in my face.

There's an odd ringing noise in the truck, and the music stops playing, and I see my daughter's image on the screen in the dash. "How is my daughter in the truck?" I point at her picture and inadvertently, unbeknownst to me, answer the phone call.

Her image is now gone, but I can hear her. "Hey, guys, time to stop for food. We're at the diner about five clicks north of your position." I tilt my head to the side and stare at the screen.

"Aurora, baby how are you in the truck and the diner? What witchcraft is this?" I look frantically between the screen and Dimitri; who, by the way, is laughing at me again.

"Daddy, it's called a telephone. Dimitri's phone was answered when someone touched my picture on the truck's screen. It's safer than taking your eyes off the road to fiddle with the phone. I'm sitting on the hood of Dom's car talking to you at the diner." She was so helpful. I look around the truck and see her picture on the rectangle object in the cupholder.

"I think I found that thing you call a phone. It has your picture on it. Did a witch make this?" Aurora and Dimitri start laughing at me now.

I'm starting to get mad about being laughed at. "Why must you laugh at me? I swear I'm ready to set things on fire if this continues." Soon as the words leave my mouth, everyone goes silent. I look around and see the diner in the distance.

"Well, we know where I get my lovely temperament from!" Aurora giggles before the line clicks and the music returns.

I look at Dimitri. "What did she mean by that?" I was honestly puzzled by my daughter's statement.

I feel I was relatively calm. I used to burn things and then question the survivors. I fully believe that my temperament has improved quite a bit. I guess I came off a bit smug, evidenced by Dimitri's eye roll. We pull up next to the Hellcat, and the truck stops and becomes quiet. Hmm, that little black thing makes it move and makes it stop. I'll have to question my daughter later about what it is.

Andre comes and opens my door; I go to exit and am suddenly stopped. The evil belt he put on me is still in place. How do the others tolerate this horrid thing? It most certainly gets in the way, but I see its possible uses. My daughter is surrounded on three sides by her mates. Sebastian is being incredibly dominant and possessive of Aurora. Out of the three, only two have been fully claimed by her, but Sebastian seems to have problems sharing.

"Everything okay?" I look at each one of them in the eyes. Sebastian and Dominik can maintain eye contact for a decent amount of time, whereas Jayce can barely raise his eyes. Hmm, two potential alphas and one omega. This is definitely going to lead to problems down the road.

"I believe so, M'lord," Sebastian answers me first.

"Dominik just needs to learn what being chosen as the first mate means in our family." Sebastian's wolf flairs to the surface and emphasizes his point. Ah, now I understand what's going on. A soft growl escapes Dominik's lips at the end of Sebastian's statement.

"I see..." I state plainly.

My eyes find Aurora's; she's mildly distressed by all of this posturing these young pups are doing. "The first mate's role is to help their queen make levelheaded decisions. It's not to rule or dictate the direction of the pack. The last king that did that ended up losing his kingdom and his mate and pair bonds." My eyes churn liquid mercury to accentuate my point.

"I've already seen a first mate destroy a pack. I will not let it happen with my daughter." I motion for Aurora to join me.

Swiftly she untangles herself from the guys and snuggles into my side. When she looks up at me, I see her mother's eyes so clear and pure. It makes my heart ache to see those eyes again. I have to remind myself this is our daughter and all I have left of my beloved Anca.

"Thank you, Daddy." She squeezes me tightly again as she begins to move us towards the diner's entrance.

At the door, a woman stands dressed like one of the serving girls we had in the castle. She asks how many in our party, which thankfully, Aurora answers her with seven. "Why was she asking about a party when we are just passing through?" I furrow my brows because to be quite honest, I am puzzled. Aurora just shakes her head and guides me to the table, pushing me to the side closest to the wall. Ah, I see what she did; she's protecting my left side. Something here has her on edge, and I can feel her animal bristling near the surface.

Jayce slides in next to Aurora and begins to rub the back of her neck. Slowly she begins to settle down. I wonder what set her off. "Let's get some food in you, sweetie. You'll feel better with a full tummy." Jayce speaks to her so lovingly, and she instantly responds to it and rests her head on his shoulder. Her beast settles as well, once the other males join us finally. Jayce continues to pamper Aurora throughout the meal, distracting her from the petty, childish bullshit that Dominik and Sebastian are portraying.

At this point, I am quite thankful that at least one of her mates has his priorities straight. Aurora's eyes find Dimitri, and he kindly orders for the table. I have a feeling this is going to be one very long and exhausting journey.

CHAPTER 16

Jayce

What in the world have I gotten myself into? Not only has my ex gone totally mental, blowing my phone up to the point of lunacy, but Sinclair is never going to understand the pull of the mating bond because he only likes men. He'll never feel the way your blood sings the minute you see your mate for the first time. He'll never experience that first kiss that sets your whole world on its axis.

I get to sit behind Aurora as she drives after the diner debacle. I can't believe that Dom and Sebastian can be so petty. Aurora chose to sit next to her father, and I decided to shield her from their shit. I mean, come on, get over it! Then it became a pissing contest as to who was going to pay the bill. Dear lord, guys, just whip them out and measure them already. My brother is across from me, checking in on the pack while it's Sebastian's turn to sit up front with Aurora.

I can tell she's aggravated as she's dead silent, not a single peep out of her. My eyes glance towards Sebastian, and his thumbs are flying over his keyboard, texting someone. "Mother has the alpha's house ready for us when we arrive," he states flatly.

"I've already texted Andre to let them know what's going on," Sebastian says, his tone flat and authoritative.

Aurora just nods then tells her phone to pair to the car. The familiar ping that the connection was made is heard. She grabs her phone for a moment and scrolls through songs on her phone. She searches out the song "Devil" from Shinedown and looks into the rearview. Her eyes are that of her beast's as she looks at everyone in turn.

Oh yeah, the silent ultimatum was read loud and clear. Well, at least by me, it was. Dom's eyes shift for a moment, and he nods briefly. He goes back to texting our other brother, whom we left in charge of the pack. Everything on that front, at least, is calm and quiet.

Her eyes fall on Sebastian, who doesn't even look up at her at all. Oh, you can see she is getting angry; the corner of her right eye starts to twitch. She has so many subtle facial cues, like how she's gritting her teeth and the tenseness in her jaw. Her eyes keep shifting back and forth between human and liquid mercury.

The temperature in the car starts dropping quickly. It is only when Sebastian begins to see his breath does he bother to look over at her. Her canines are visible, and her knuckles are white with how tightly she is gripping the steering wheel. The muscles of her right bicep twitch and flex as she white knuckles the wheel.

"I hope you accomplished something great while you ignored me." Her tone is all beast; it is growled out and accented with a frost after bite. He sighs and turns to face her. I don't know if that was his smartest or dumbest move to date, but I'm thankful I'm back here.

"A half dozen rogues have returned to the pack. Some are semi-feral, most are okay. Mom has the feral wolves sedated until your return. She figures either they will live or die by your talons depending on their actions." He draws in a deep breath and lets it out slowly.

"I just hate that the weight of the world is on your shoulders. I can handle some of this responsibility for you, and Dom can help as well." He shrugs his shoulders and rolls his eyes.

"I don't think killing everyone who doesn't agree with you is the best course of action," he says just before crossing his arms over his chest, trying to drive his point home.

Aurora cuts the wheel hard and puts us into a spin. She doesn't care, she is at her breaking point, and Sebastian has finally pushed her last button. Once she stops us from spinning, she slams the car into park, gets out, and starts pacing.

"Who the actual fuck do you think you are?" Her eyes flair and begin to glow the liquid mercury orbs pulse with untold power.

"Telling me what I should and shouldn't do!" She is partially shifted and quite terrifying. Dom and I stand back as she faces off with Sebastian.

Dimitri and the guys finally catch up and stop dead in their tracks. Aurora is so worked up, she is between forms and freezing the ground around her. "Can you do anything?" I look to Nicodeamus, and he shrugs his shoulders then shakes his head no. Fantastic, we have an Lycan-dragon hybrid, pissed off beyond all recognition, and not even the dragon can stop her. My eyes fall on Dom next. "Brother, can you do anything?"

Dom just starts laughing. "And have her get mad at me too? No way, brother; he buried himself. I'd like to see him claw his way out of this one." Some help my brother is. I begin to pace and watch the fight. Sebastian isn't fighting back, and Aurora is mostly yelling at him, so it isn't Defcon one; we are maybe a three or a two-ish. Not total nuclear war, but definitely not at peace.

Then I have my most brilliant thought. I strip out of my clothing and shift to my wolf. I begin to belly crawl to her, whimpering. That gets her attention. Her head snaps up as she turns to look at me fully, checking me for wounds. She immediately shifts back to human and kneels beside me, her fingers thread through my thick, obsidian fur as she checks my body over for injuries. I roll over, giving her my belly.

Aurora smiles when she figures out that I'm in one piece and begins to rub my stomach. Success! I got her out of rage mode, and now it's cute snuggly Aurora. She starts to laugh as I lick her face and paw at her several times. I get up quickly and shake out my fur and play-pounce her, knocking her onto her ass. Now she's hysterically laughing, and officially, we are back to Defcon five. I move closer and let her use my shoulders to pull herself back up to standing. Am I feeling a bit smug? Yes, yes, I am. I freaking prance past Sebastian and my brother to get to my clothes.

Nicodeamus pats me on my shoulder and tells me I did well. Now that's worth every slightly degrading moment, and her father appreciated what I just did. Quickly I return to my human form and dress, not wanting to hold the group up if they're going to get rolling again.

Dimitri is the first to approach me once I am fully dressed. "You did good, son. You read her correctly, and you were exactly what she needed at the moment. You bring balance to your brother's brashness." The Great Bear pats me on the shoulder then starts walking back to the truck. He's truly a man of few words.

Carefully, I move between Aurora and Sebastian and look between them. "Are we okay now?" Being the omega at times has its advantages. Like now, I'm not even remotely considered a threat. I'm not even a contender for the crown. To be honest, I don't want it.

Aurora and Sebastian nod and move towards the car. Aurora suddenly stops and turns to me. "Care to drive, Jayce? Or would you rather Dom drive? Either way, I'm climbing in the back and taking a nap." She smiles softly at me and tilts her head towards the car.

I look to Dom, and he makes the key in the ignition motion to me, signaling he'll drive. "Dom can drive; after all, it is his baby. I'll climb in back with you, and you can use me as a pillow." There's the smile I was looking for.

Aurora's smile can light up the darkest night. She walks past Sebastian and kisses his cheek before moving to me and taking my hand. There's that tingle that only she can give me; goose-bumps move up my arm, and the flutters start in my belly. The humans call it butterflies, which is the giddy feeling you get from the person you love. I draw in a slow, deep breath and smile. We stop in front of Dom, and she kisses his cheek as well and whispers a quiet, heartfelt *thank you* to him. My normally stoic brother cracks a smile and caresses the back of Aurora's neck before drawing her close to kiss her temple before releasing her.

We walk in silence to the car; it is nice just to be able to be in this moment with her. When we reach the car's passenger side, I open the door and let her slide in first. Carefully I slide myself in place behind the passenger seat, press my back against the window ledge and prop a leg up on the seat. Aurora watches me with rapt attention until I signal for her to lie down on me. The back seat isn't huge, nor is it all that comfortable, but at least if I can keep her comfortable and safe, then I've succeeded. Aurora moves slowly, like the calculating apex predator she is, her eyes roaming over my body and the way I have positioned myself.

"Jayce, are you sure you're going to be comfortable? I mean, the hard plastic against your back can't be comfortable." Aurora's concern for me warms my heart and eases some of the pain I feel after breaking up with my long-term boyfriend.

"I'll be fine, sweetheart. I'm more concerned about you. You've had a rough couple of weeks, and I'd like to be able to take care of you for a while." My choice of words must have set her mind at ease. She leans forward and kisses me lightly on my lips, lingering there for a moment, looking into my eyes. Slowly her eyes swirl mercury, then back to grey. She and her beast are in agreeance; they completely accept my wolf and me.

My wolf stirs for a moment, just long enough to see Aurora smile at having seen him. A soft yawn escapes her lips before she snuggles against me—her hip against my groin and the bridge of her nose against my adam's apple. Gently her forehead comes to rest against my neck. I wrap my arms around her, holding her firmly to my chest. I must admit that this is one of the best moments of my life.

My brother and Sebastian get in the car and break me out of the bubble I was in when they both turn to look at us. I'm not good at reading alpha-types well. I mean, they both continuously look pissed. Seriously, if men could have a resting bitch face, these two have perfected it. I smile, what could they possibly do that wouldn't send Aurora into a rage for disturbing her?

For once, I feel I possess the ultimate power by having the nuclear bomb we call our mate, sleeping on me. The rumble of the Hellcat comes to life, causing Aurora to stir slightly. I simply tighten my grip and inch us down in the seat a tad to make both of us a bit more comfortable. She's out cold in my arms, and I'm the luckiest wolf alive. It doesn't take long for the engine's rumble and Aurora's soft breathing to lull me to sleep as well.

Who knows how long we slept for, but before we know it, we are at our destination, and some woman is asking for Aurora. My eyes crack open first, and slowly, I look around to get my bearings. I notice Sebastian opening the driver's side door up and sliding the seat forward. He leans in slowly and smiles, seeing our precious cargo still sleeping so soundly. His head tilts to the side, studying her and her positioning on me. The fingers of her left hand have a death grip on my shirt, and her right-hand grips my forearm.

Sebastian starts laughing. "I guess Dom's driving scared her in her sleep. At least she didn't see what I had to see on the way here." He widens his eyes in mock horror and smiles before he starts rubbing her hip.

"Wake up, beautiful. Mom is getting impatient about seeing you, you know how she gets. She has to make sure you're in one piece after your journey," Sebastian says, his voice and facial expression don't match yet again. His tone versus the look on his face is saying two different things.

Aurora shifts slightly, causing my cock to stiffen instantly. It's been years since a woman has had such an effect on me. Quite honestly, I am fucking amazed and impressed at the same time. I watch her eyes blink rapidly then finally open. She stretches and yawns, opening her mouth wide. Sebastian and I are both shocked to see her canines have dropped. Was it a moment of aggression, or was she scenting my arousal?

Her beast is present when she turns those pure mercury orbs on me. Her smile is completely predatory, her pearly white teeth on full display. I do believe she would take what she wanted to whether I was ready for that step or not. Well, my cock is a traitor, and fuck, he'd sell our soul to the devil to get lost in her for a few hours, days, years... In moments like this, being omega sucks. I lower my eyes and submit to her. My mate is a dominant alpha, and there is no way I'd be able to hold my own against her.

Lithe hands swiftly cup my cheeks and pull my head up so that my eyes meet hers. They are human again and look quite concerned. Tears threaten to break free from her eyes as she looks me over quickly. "I'm so sorry, Jayce. She got away from me a bit. I'm not that type of alpha. All my mates are equals in my heart. I hold none over the others." Gently she kisses my lips when I nod, acknowledging her statement. I know deep down she said it more to remind Sebastian of his place and help me accept mine.

I am equal to three alphas; that thought is very foreign to me. Sebastian mentions the others are waiting, trying to tear her away from me. Aurora's eyes drift back to Sebastian, and she lets out a soft growl, baring her canines at him. Our girl doesn't like being told what to do. That was a very simple lesson to learn, but the muscle-bound male hasn't figured that out yet—easy points for me. Eventually, she extends her hand to Sebastian, and he helps her slide out of the car.

This little wisp of a woman wraps Aurora up in a hug and snuggles into her so tightly. Aurora looks almost panicked as the woman continues to hold on. To me, it is absolutely the most adorable thing I've ever seen. I take this moment to extract myself from the car and join the others. My eyes flitter between Sebastian and this little woman, then it dawns on me, she's his mother.

Dom moves over to bump into me and starts to snicker. "I don't think our girl is overly comfortable with physical contact." It was true, Aurora didn't look overly thrilled, but she also didn't look like she was going to harm the little woman. Her eyes find mine, and she extracts herself from the woman's grip and starts to drag her to us.

"Elena, I must introduce you to the twins!" Aurora has that mischievous look to her, and I just knew she was up to something. Elena looks between Dom and me and just smiles, then pulls Aurora down to her height and whispers in her ear. Aurora's cheeks turn bright pink. Quickly she pulls back up to her full height, looking back and forth between my brother and me, then back to Elena and blushes more. Oh, dear Gods, what did that sprite tell her?

Aurora clears her throat, then places her hand on Dom's shoulder. "Elena, this is Dominik. He was his pack's enforcer, and now he's mine." A gentle kiss is placed on Dom's cheek, and he nods lightly to Elena.

Aurora then comes over to me and straightens out the collar on my button-down. "This sharply dressed hunk is Jayce. He was an advisor and historian to the alpha and beta in his pack. Now he shall be my voice of reason." She snuggles into my side for a moment then kisses my cheek. Sometimes there's an advantage to being an omega.

"Elena, you won't believe who we found!" Aurora is squealing and bouncing up and down like an excited child. Apparently, none of us have ever seen Aurora like this because we're all fucking puzzled.

"Daddy!" She screams at the top of her lungs then sprints over to her truck to try to drag him out into the open.

Elena looks at Sebastian. "Daddy?" Her brows are furrowed, and her confusion is quite evident. All the screaming and squealing has started to draw a crowd. It appears the entire pack is now in the central courtyard.

Sebastian simply nods his head as Dimitri and Andre approach. "Apparently, the Dire Alpha took the Dragon King hostage during the Strigoi attack. He also cut off the King's arm." Elena and Sebastian both look towards the truck where Aurora is in a heated discussion with her father. Heated is a relatively poor choice of words since the ground and the truck are now covered by a thick layer of frost.

I start shaking my head as I move towards the truck—my brother and the others yelling at me not to go, that it would be my funeral, and so on. My hand slowly grips Aurora's shoulder and rubs her neck gently. "M'lord, what seems to be the problem?" Addressing the dragon directly was scary as fuck. Then again, so was the nuclear winter they were plunging us into.

His dragon eyes lift and regard me. "I am not the king I once was. The focus should be on you and her other mates with her, not me." He gently rubs the socket where his arm used to be. His sadness is palatable, and yet there is a hint of fear with it as well.

"M'lord, your presence and wisdom will be a great asset to your daughter and her mates for the upcoming war. You know these creatures, their habits, and what their weaknesses are. Your involvement can be the deciding factor for our victory." I appeal to his honor and sense of duty. Most importantly, I am appealing to his desire to protect his daughter. I can feel the shift in his mood almost immediately, and a smile graces his lips.

"Daughter, you have chosen well. You have a wise and reasonable mate." Nicodeamus slides out of the truck at this point and wraps me up in a one-armed hug. "Let's go see the pack, shall we?" I remain tucked into Nicodeamus's side as we head back to the others.

Everyone—including the other mates—all kneel before the dragon king. He smiles gently at everyone and keeps me tight to his side as we move to the alpha house. Aurora opens the door for us, and once everyone is in, she turns to the pack. "Prepare a feast! We shall welcome my new mates and father properly." The pack erupts in cheers and begins to scramble to prepare for tonight. Aurora presses her back against the door and slides down it laughing. "Well, that went better than I expected!"

Sebastian moves and crouches down in front of her and shakes his head at her. "For being the alpha of this ragtag bunch, you can be so silly at times." He leans forward and kisses her lips, and caresses her cheek. "Good thing you're cute even when you're homicidal."

Aurora smirks and looks around the living room. A Lycan skull and vertebral column are hanging on the wall. A huge smile graces her lips as she jumps up to look at the bones on the wall. Moving swiftly towards her trophies, she almost knocks Sebastian flat on his ass in passing. "Aw, Elena, you shouldn't have! I love it, and the little plaques are absolutely precious!" Aurora's fingertips trace the edges of the plaques as she reads each one.

Out of the corner of my eye, I catch Sebastian facepalm and shake his head. "Really, mom?" His eyes are an ice blue, almost white, as he stares at his mom. Elena is laughing so hard at him.

"Oh, come on, you know she loves it! Why wouldn't you want her prizes on the wall of your home?" Elena comes up beside Aurora with a Swiffer and begins to dust the bones.

"It's disconcerting, Mother." Sebastian states flatly.

Dimitri looks like the cat that swallowed the canary. In his hand is a cooler that I overlooked before. My eyes find my brother, and he rolls his eyes. He quickly points at Aurora, cutting the head off move, signals seven, and then points to the cooler. Holy shit, she has my father's and brother's heads and the others in the cooler. I'm feeling a little ill at the moment when Aurora looks at me. Shit, she knows I figured it out.

"Elena, Mother... I have seven more for you to prepare to go onto the wall. Maybe over there." She points to the wall space to the right of the head and spine. She's actually fucking serious about wanting to put their skulls up. What the actual fuck am I witnessing? I start to back up and run into a hard, warm body.

Large hands grip my hips. "Where are you going, little omega?" Sebastian whispers in my ear.

Lightly he nips my earlobe as he watches Aurora interact with his mother. "Disapprove of our mate's collection? Honestly, it disturbed me in the beginning as well. The Lycan's head is the female I was betrothed to, and the spine belonged to the alpha." Sebastian cants his head with that sexy smirk on his lips. He's just as out there as Aurora is; apparently, keeping parts of your enemies is a Lycan thing. His deep breathy, baritone voice makes my cock stir. I feel it heat and swell to life, pulsing in time with my heartbeat.

Why does he have to be so fucking sexy? He kind of looks like that vampire Damon. Sebastian is the full package: dark, brooding, and oozes sex appeal. I could easily lick him for hours. I wonder how Aurora would feel about her mates having sex with each other?

Speaking of that crazy female, she's dancing around with the heads in her hands, spinning in circles. Sebastian turns me around in his arms, so my hands land flat on his taunt muscular chest. His eyes shift to that of his wolf, and our hard cocks are side by side, pressed against each other. Time has officially stopped; the rest of the room falls away, and all I see is Sebastian leaning down to kiss me. His lips are smooth as silk when they first touch mine. His kiss intensifies and becomes hard and demanding; our teeth hit just before he bites my bottom lip and draws blood. I can't help but moan into his mouth as I feel my cock pulse. It was one of those intense kisses that makes your cock leak with anticipation. My fingertips grip his shoulders tightly as we grind against each other. Out of nowhere, there's a flash of light and then another.

Aurora is standing on a chair not far from us, taking pictures with her cellphone. Her eyes are pure mercury, and I can smell her arousal. So apparently, our girl likes to watch. "Okay, guys, that was hot!" She jumps down off the chair, walks over, and sticks her hand between us, gripping our cocks and wet pants.

"Ooh, someone was having a good time." The way she's biting her bottom lip ramps up my desire.

I really want Sebastian to make me his bitch, and yet I really wish to have Aurora dominate me as well. She slowly brings her wet hand to her lips and licks our essence off her skin. That thick, wet muscle of hers coils around her fingertip as she laves up every single drop. I'm so close to cuming it's not even funny anymore. Sebastian looks like he's in the same personal hell I'm in. As quickly as she fucked my world up, she moves away towards Dom. That motherfucker has the nerve to smile at me right now. I have the absolute worst case of blue balls in the history of blue balls, and he's smiling. He leans slowly to nip at Aurora's neck; without warning, she sweeps his legs and puts him to the ground.

"It's not nice to taunt your brother!" She stands over him, her eyes churning liquid mercury as she stares down at him.

"He's still fragile over his breakup, and if he can find comfort with Sebastian, then so fucking be it! If I catch you giving him a difficult time, I'll beat your ass myself." Holy fucking hell, that was even hotter than the kiss that Sebastian just gave me. She stood up for me. I look to the others, and they are slowly clearing the room to get ready for later.

My eyes land on Sebastian, who can't stop smiling at me. "She loves you, Jayce. She's protective of what's hers. She'll wait until you're ready to be with her, with no pressure. In the meantime, you know where to find me." He smacks my ass so hard it's still stinging. My cock starts to twitch to life again; apparently, I have a new kink. Time to go shower and rub one out before dinner. My life just got very interesting.

CHAPTER 17

Andre

I never thought I'd live to see the day my little girl would find her mates—and two being bi-sexual. When I was young, if you even showed interest in someone of the same gender you were put to death. So being a gay Golden Eagle was a touch depressing. I just got to witness the most open display of attraction I've ever seen in my life. To be quite honest, it was hot as all hell. I felt my nether regions twitch to life for a few moments.

Over my shoulder, I hear a young lad clear his throat. Slowly I turn to look at him, and he smiles at me. Hmm, today may be getting interesting, after all. My eyes fall back on Aurora; it warms my heart with her level of acceptance of her mate's and my choices. I draw in a deep breath as tears threaten to break loose, I feel the love in the room, and it's the most beautiful thing ever.

Dimitri chooses that moment to come over and give me a side hug. "You okay, old friend?" He looks down at me with that smile he gets on a rare occasion when he's feeling sappy.

"Aye, just remembering our baby girl when I used to get the chance to mother the hell out of her. I know I'm not a mom. Hell, my bollocks prove I'm not a mom. But out of the two of us, I've always been the gentle one." I look at my soft hands and my wrist where Aurora's bracelet she made me so very long ago still rests.

"I wonder how long we have left." My eyes well up further, and the tears break free rolling down my cheeks in streams. I blubber like a bloody idiot, but I can't help it. I can't see myself or Dimitri without Aurora in our lives. My hand absently moves to touch the scale the dragon king gave us. Who knows how much magic is in it or how long it will sustain us? My heart hurts thinking about leaving her when she needs us the most. She's only gathered mates from two of the clans, and there are two left. I turn and embrace Dimitri, burying my face in his strong shoulder.

A small, warm hand lightly touches my shoulder. Turning my head to find Aurora with Nicodeamus at her side. Her eyes hold unshed tears as she looks between Dimitri and me. "Father told me what's happening; I don't know what to say or do. I don't want to lose you two." Tears pour down her cheeks at her confession. She quickly snuggles herself between Dimitri and me, and the three of us start balling our eyes out. Aurora's lithe body shakes as she sobs uncontrollably; Dimitri and I try to hold her and comfort her. Deep down, I'm afraid of what will come when Dimitri and I pass to the great beyond. Aurora's inability to process emotions is a concern as she cries in our arms.

The double doors to the alpha's house fly open and slam against the wall. Sebastian and Dominik are both completely shifted, looking for danger. Jayce comes walking from the other side of the hall to stand before them. "Nothing to worry about guys; they're having an emotional family moment." Both males shift back to their human forms and move closer to us; both males lay a single hand on Aurora. She seems to calm almost immediately. Her head slowly raises to look at each mate in turn. Wordlessly she shimmies out of her guardian sandwich and moves to her mates. All three surround her and hold on until she stops crying.

"We're going to take her to our room and comfort our mate," Sebastian states calmly and with the authority of an alpha.

Dominik bends and scoops Aurora up into his arms, cradling his precious cargo tightly to his chest. Jayce, who is the most in touch with his emotions, kisses the crown of her head. "I'll draw a hot bath for you, Aurora, and I'll give you a massage while you tell us what you need from us." He gives the other mates a look—probably the most dominant look I've ever seen from him. The other guys just nod and smile as they croon softly to Aurora.

Watching them move as a unit makes me smile; I know in my heart of hearts that she will be taken care of no matter what. My eyes find Nicodeamus and he's smiling. "You two have made wonderful parents for my Aurora. I am forever in your debt." He sighs softly as his eyes move between Dimitri and me.

"I can see she's become more than an assignment to you. She's the child you two never got to have. For that, I am sorry that your lives were put on hold for her. I am grateful, however, that she's known love her whole life. For that, she is blessed." He bows at his waist to us. A king is bowing to us; it's going to take some time for that sink in.

"We are the ones that are blessed with the gift of time we have had as your daughter's family. We have been blessed with the countless extra years her life has given us. We only wish to live to see her ascend the throne—like her mother hoped she would. God's willing, we will be granted long enough to do just that." I sigh deeply as I slowly bow to the king. Dimitri follows suit, bowing as well. We all turn to look at the door as Jayce closes it behind him.

"I don't know who's taking this harder, Aurora or us. I hate seeing her cry; it's actually quite scary to see." My eyes widen, and I start to laugh, thinking about the past. "Remember Dimitri, that time Aurora got hurt and started crying? Then she shifted, and her Lycan destroyed half the house and part of the forest."

Dimitri starts laughing and shakes his head. "Yeah, or the time her Lycan forced the shift and at least a half dozen trees were taken down because her wolf couldn't handle the tears."

Nicodeamus smiles gently and nods slowly. "It seems like my daughter acted more like a dragon than a wolf. Hatchlings tend to be confused by emotions. Sadness turns to anger. Fear turns to anger. Pretty much everything turns to anger until they get older. " Nicodeamus starts laughing.

"I'm sorry, it's quite dangerous to raise a baby dragon or dragon hybrid without a dragon to temper its emotions. I was just thinking about all the craziness my daughter must have caused in her first hundred years." He's still laughing his ass off as he finds a place to sit down nearby.

"First hundred? Try two hundred plus, and we're still waiting for her to mellow out." I look to Dimitri and then over to Nicodeamus, who just nods along until he cants his head to the side.

"Hmm, must be because she's a hybrid. I'll have to ponder this further." Nicodeamus rises up to his full height and walks out of the house. I sit here wondering how many centuries that male has lived to know everything he does.

I draw in a steadying breath as I walk out of the front door to go for a walk. Elena stops me and pulls me around the corner with her. "Shhhh… don't alert the others." She's going all James Bond and shit on me and has us sneaking around the compound. It's gotta be a Lycan trait to be bat shit crazy. She leads me to a shed outback. Not creepy at all… no, not at all. I roll my eyes, following behind her towards the creepy shed.

I'm half expecting this to turn into a slasher movie where heads and body parts will be hanging from the ceiling. Nope, it's much worse! The two heads Aurora brought back are being boiled in a large cauldron in the middle of the room. I feel sick to my stomach seeing the Dire Alpha's head and his beta son bobbing around, floating and sinking in the cauldron's water. Random eyeballs float around in the cauldron, giving it a Halloween feel. Unfortunately, it's all real and not for Halloween. Clearly, Elena isn't fazed by what Aurora has done, but she can tell I'm disturbed by it.

"Death is but a doorway, Andre. Do not fear what cannot be controlled." She comes out carrying herbs and some bottles of an unknown liquid and dumps them in. She starts mixing it until it is boiling without a fire.

Okay, now I'm getting concerned. She leans forward and plucks several hairs from my head, and throws them into the mix. Okay, either I am about to be cursed, killed, or turned into a zombie. Maybe I shouldn't have watched all those horror movies with Aurora when she was growing up. Oh, shit, am I the reason she's the way she is?

My eyes shoot to the only escape route, then back to Elena. Can I make it out in time before she turns me into a zombie? "What are you so afraid of, Andre? I'm trying to figure out the magic my sister used to bind the two of you to Aurora."

Apparently, I've been panicking for nothing, but you must admit, it hadn't looked good for me. "Dimitri may be the better one to test. He was the one that the blade sliced. I'm bound to him by blood because of our jobs in the castle. My gift is an echo of what he got." Echo, side effect, a happy accident... however you want to call it. It's really disheartening to think my extended life span was a mistake or an accident.

I look down at the ground when Elena comes over and hugs me. She knows this whole thing is breaking me. I love that homicidal wolf like my own child. To leave her now, I can't bear to think about it. A single tear rolls down my cheek thinking about the possibility of passing away.

"I will do everything within my power to help you and Dimitri." She kisses my cheek gently and moves back towards her cauldrons. "The best I can figure out is that my sister used blood magic combined with black magic. I'll need Dimitri's hair to determine how far down the rabbit hole my sister went." Her eyes lock with mine, and I can see the faint glow of her wolf backing up her claims. They genuinely believe they can help us. I give her a slight bow and back out of the shack.

Aurora's mate Jayce is walking around with his head down and kicking a rock around. "Something bothering you, son?" His head snaps up and his wolf blazes to the surface, then fades slowly; he gives me a soft nod and motions towards the swings. I follow him, watching his body language. He looks dejected. I wonder why? Aurora isn't the type to ignore anyone for any reason. We reach the swings, and we choose the two right next to each other. Side-by-side, we begin to swing. "You gonna talk, or did ya just need someone to hang out with?" I ask playfully with a slight chuckle.

He laughs softly, then turns to look at me. "Sorry, I'm still dealing with leaving a man I've been with for the better half of fifty years for a female. Don't get me wrong, I'm thankful and blessed that I've found my mate." Jayce sighs deeply and draws in a slow, measured breath just before a single tear falls.

"Part of me, I feel like I'm betraying what I had before. The other part can't wait to start my forever with Aurora." He rubs at his eyes then looks back at me.

"I thought Aurora was going to murder me for kissing Sebastian back the way I did. I swear to the gods I saw my life flash before my eyes, and I pictured her ripping my head off or my spine out. That female is fucking lethal and then cool as a cucumber like nothing happened afterward." His eyes are wide, as if he is still in shock over it all.

I start laughing and honestly can't contain it. "I'm sorry, Jayce, I'd love to say you'll get used to Aurora's antics, but two hundred plus years later, I'm still not immune to her. She literally can go from serial killer to snuggle bunny in like point five seconds." I widen my eyes in mock horror then smirk.

"It scares the bloody hell out of me half the time. Gods help you if someone fucks with anyone she's claimed as hers, that's an instant death sentence." Mentally I'm ticking off the last ten deaths at her talons; sadly, I see her point in all of it. I finally hear Jayce laugh a little bit.

"Yeah, she's intense, to say the least. I need to sit and talk to her later." Jayce stops swinging and folds his hands in his lap.

"I don't want her to think I don't care; I'm just trying to get my head straight before I get intimate with her." Slowly he shakes his head left to right.

"The last thing we all need is for me to say the wrong thing at the wrong time, and heads start rolling, literally." He looks up at me, double-checking his logic.

Smart man, he's figured out our girl quite early on. "I have to ask you a personal question. I know Aurora only says what she means, but do you think she regrets accepting me?" He shrugs his shoulders. "I mean, I've spent more time in relationships with males than females." On a loud exhale, his shoulders lower and curl as if defeated.

"To be honest, Sebastian is fucking hot as all hell. I mean, I hope to get to ride that pony at some point. But will she kill one or both of us for being intimate?" Jayce slowly looks back up at me, his brows furrowed, hopeful I have the answer he's looking for.

I double blink as the crux of his problem just became blatantly apparent. He's obviously more attracted to males than females. "Okay, umm... she's used to being around a gay male." I point both index fingers at my face, wiggling them around.

"She's always been very accepting of my lifestyle and choices over the years. I tried dating, but I couldn't bring myself to be away from her for too long. What can I say? I'm an old mother-hen when it comes to her." I smile warmly, thinking about how blessed I've been over the years with her.

"She loves all of her mates equally. None is above the others no matter what they think." I cough out "Sebastian," and Jayce starts to laugh again. "All Aurora is going to care about is that everyone is happy and safe and that no one fucks with her wine and dark chocolate." Jayce raises an eyebrow when I mention her kryptonite to him. A slow, knowing nod is given, and I smile in reply to him. I just gave him the ultimate insider information that will win him instant brownie points with our alpha.

He bounces up from his swing and hugs the hell out of me, and kisses my forehead. "Oh, my gods, Andre, thank you so much!!! I'm going shopping. Don't wait up for me!" When motivated, a bitch power walks.

He takes off like someone set his tight ass on fire. Perhaps I just gave him something that the other guys can't give her. It's sad that I just lost his company, but a delight to watch him leave. My eyes roam the town square, and that male from earlier is watching me again. I wave to him, and he waves back. Hmm, perhaps I'm getting somewhere? He slowly starts to move towards me, and I feel my heart rate pick up. I'm trying my damnedest to fight my fight-or-flight instincts. He's probably the hottest guy I've seen in years. His eyes are forest green, and his hair looks charcoal black. The best part, he's got muscles for days. "Hi." Oh, my fucking gods, I am so freaking lame. What the actual fuck am I thinking? I know what I'm thinking. I'm thinking with my dick. You know, the thing in my pants I haven't used in forever.

The hunk smiles. "Hi to you too. I'm Darren." He extends his hand to me, and for a moment, my dumb ass just stares at it before placing my hand in his to give him a firm shake.

"Andre. The pleasure is all mine." I stand before him, and we're almost the same height—my tall, lithe frame to his I'll-end-your-fucking-world muscular build. I rest a hand on his firm shoulder and look deep into his eyes. Mine are boring compared to his, but I can easily get lost in his. Just as he leans in to kiss me, I hear catcalls coming from behind him. Damn it to all hell; the gods must hate me. Aurora and her other two mates are approaching.

She's smiling from ear to ear and has to rub it in that in the last two weeks, she's gotten more dick than I've gotten in the previous hundred years. "Hey, Dre! Darren, I see you've met Dre!" She's way too fucking chipper; it's scary to witness this side of her.

"I thought we would have lost you for the better half of the afternoon with these two young studs." I quirk a brow and look between the two of them. Immediately they both start posturing and puffing out their chests, trying to look all badass. Aurora smacks them both and starts laughing.

"Oh, trust me, they can handle me. I was more concerned where mate number three disappeared off to." Her eyes shift to that of her beast as she scans the area. Her nose twitches for a moment, and I know she picked up his scent. A soft smile crosses her lips briefly before continuing.

"He's so... I don't know how to explain it." A sigh escapes her lips as her steel-gray eyes stare at the ground.

"It's almost like he has a hard time adapting away from his boyfriend. I gave him the option to stay with him. I don't want him unhappy." Both of the boys' wolves surge to the surface, making their eyes glow as they sense and, perhaps, feel her distress. Aurora is sandwiched between the two of them within moments, and she visibly starts to calm down.

She sighs gently and rests her head on Dominik's chest. "I just don't want him unhappy, Andre. Please talk to him for me. I honestly don't know how to broach the subject."

"I talked to him a little today already... he sought me out." That gets her attention, and she pries herself away from her mates. She grasps both of my hands to drag me to the picnic bench to sit.

"You're partially correct. He is having a hard time adapting, but I think it's mainly because he's mostly dated males." Gently I kiss her cheek and rub my thumbs over the backs of her hands.

"He loves you, and he's grateful he's found his mate. From personal experience, it takes time to get over a breakup. He appreciates that you gave him a choice." Smiling confidently, I squeeze her hands tightly, trying to reassure her.

"Jayce knows in his heart he made the right decision. His mind just needs time to catch up with what his heart wants." I draw in a deep breath and watch Aurora. I can tell she's in a deep conversation with her Lycan and just nods slowly.

"I understand, Andre. Thank you for being the best momma bird a pup could ask for." She leans forward and kisses my cheek, hugging me tightly. Her mates slowly move off to give us time and space.

"I hope he understands I accept him fully. I don't mind him kissing or having sex with any of my other mates." Sebastian's head shoots up with that, and his eyes glow faintly.

"There are things only another male could give him. I know I'm strong, and I can be rough at times. But let's face facts, I don't have a schlong, and I'm not about to put a strap-on on to rail my mate from behind." Every male within hearing distance coughs, and their eyes bug out of their heads.

I cough and clear my throat, attempting to look as serious as possible. "Aurora, love, that was quite the visual you painted." She smiles and nods, proud of herself.

"Trust me, we fully understand the differences in the mechanics between the genders." Stifling my laughter, I shake my head at

Aurora. I swear you never know what's going to come flying out of that girl's mouth.

"You're absolutely right; there are things a male can do to another male that a female could never do on her own. But that would never replace your part of this whole bond." I can't help but smile at how far my baby girl has come.

"You are the glue that holds these boys together. It's fortunate for all of you so far that they have been all true matings. Trust me when I say that when a bond is forced, it's never the same or as strong as a true mate." Sebastian winces at my statement; I study him closely as he regains his composure. "Your poor mother, gods, rest her soul. Her only true mate was Nicodeamus. She had to force the bond with the other three males to make the political alliances."

I grit my teeth. "That fucking Lycan Alpha chose her other mates for her. She didn't have the choice as to who was in her bond." I release Aurora's hands abruptly and make fists trying to contain my anger over what happened.

"I was so thankful when I saw her Lycan reveal itself to Nicodeamus. The Lycan Alpha was furious, and it's why shortly after that, he forced the other males to be castrated—including Nicodeamus. He wanted to be the only male capable of being able to father children." I start to laugh.

"Little did he know that during one of his meetings, I snuck Nicodeamus in to be with your mom before the Shamans arrived to perform the castrations." I look down, thinking about those dark times, and I feel a hand land on my shoulder. The dragon king is standing right behind me. My eyes widen in fear because I didn't know if he had wanted Aurora to know the whole story, and I just blabbed everything.

"Relax, old friend. I've been dreading having to tell Aurora that story since we've been reunited. You have once again done me a great service." He gives me a gentle side hug and moves forward to stand before Aurora.

"Jayce is a smart man. He has a lot to sort out in his mind. Moving and relocating isn't easy for everyone." Nicodeamus walks over to his daughter and hugs her. He holds her as only a father can.

"Little one, he loves you so very much, never doubt that. Before your mom... I also had a male that I was considering bonding myself to." Nicodeamus slowly lowers his head on top of Aurora's and sighs softly.

"He was the most beautiful male I had ever seen; he and his dragon were lean and sleek and brilliant." Nicodeamus closes his eyes as he remembers the past.

"My brother, the alpha of our clan, called for me one day and told me I was being sent to the Lycan fortress. I argued with my brother as I had no interest in an arranged mating. After all, I already had someone I loved right at home with me." Nicodeamus opens his eyes and pins a returning Jayce with his stare, rooting him to his spot.

"I arrived at the Lycan Fortress and was escorted to the main hall. Your mom was already so defeated after her first couple of mates were forced matings. She was so sad she wouldn't even meet my eyes when I first entered. My dragon had other plans. He dropped the temperature in the room so swiftly that frost began to gather on the wine glass your mother was holding." Nicodeamus closes his eyes again and nuzzles the top of Aurora's head.

"Anca's eyes opened wide as the frost spread across her glass. That's the moment she looked up at me. She actually saw me. Her Lycan in all of its glory burst forth and made her presence known and ran to stand before me." He sighs wistfully.

"I only allowed my eyes to shift to that of my dragon, for the hall we were in wasn't large enough for me to fully shift in safely. I touched her face, and she nuzzled my cheek. I knew at that moment that she was mine." Nicodeamus hugs Aurora and kisses the top of her head, and backs away so she can look him in the eyes.

"It took a while before your mother, and I slept together and completed our bond. It took Andre running to tell us about the alpha's plans to castrate all the mates, other than Vladimir, to force my hand. Mentally I was ready; I knew what she was to me. Emotionally, that was a whole other demon to deal with. Emotionally I felt like I was betraying the male I had loved for many years." There was a hollowness to Nicodeamus's haunted gaze.

You can see the gears turning in Aurora's head as she takes in Nicodeamus's story. "So, what you're saying, Dad, is that just because he's not trying to bone the hell out of me doesn't mean that he doesn't love me. It just means that he has a few things to work through first." Aurora bites her bottom lip and searches her father's features.

"*Da*! That's exactly what I am saying. Give the lad some time. I'm sure when he's ready, he will make the first move. In the meantime, be supportive of him, love him, and show him affection." Nicodeamus smiles.

"Make quality time just for him because out of your mates, he's the most emotionally sensitive. With two potential alphas in your bond already, you need someone that isn't always trying to prove themselves." He smiles a smile that tells you of the years of wisdom he is speaking from. Nicodeamus gently hugs Aurora again and then pats me on the shoulder. He heads straight to Jayce, and they both walk off towards the main house.

I look between Aurora and her two mates as they move to join her. Her eyes search mine for a bit, then look between her two mates. "You guys know I'm all good with ya'll being together, right?" Sebastian and Dom nod and look at each other, then back to Aurora.

"Sebastian, I'm counting on you to make sure Jayce feels secure and comfortable. Dom, you're his brother and know him best. Any advice you can offer would be wonderful. I know it may be months before he's ready to mate with me, and I'm fine with that." Her eyes turn to me.

"Andre, take flight and find that stubborn bear of ours. We will not go in search of the next mate until my bond with Jayce is in place. We cannot venture forth without being able to sense everyone in the bond." Her hand rubs over her heart as she closes her eyes, clearly concentrating. "I feel him faintly, just barely a whisper. That's not strong enough to be venturing into new territory."

The guys nod, and so do I. We had our orders, and now it's time to put them into motion. My first mission: seek out the bear. Secondly, watch over all my new pups and make sure they all play nice. I start to walk away from the love fest behind me and strip as I go. Before my new admirer knows it, I shift into my eagle and begin my bear hunt.

CHAPTER 18

Dominik

I've always been my brother's keeper; it's not a task I take lightly. Jayce has always been the sensitive one between us. I was schooled in combat, where he was schooled in the art of negotiating and politics. For being twins, we're polar opposites. I'm a brute; I'm bulky and have a horrible temper, whereas Jayce has a toned, athletic build and is calm as all hell. I mean, seriously, it takes a lot to rattle his cage. Our faces are almost identical, except I have more green in my hazel eyes, and he has more gold. I always thought it was unfair because it seems like his wolf is showing more often than not.

I stand here listening to Aurora talking to Andre about Jayce, and my chest hurts thinking about how this is hurting her. The level of understanding she has for what he's going through is mind-blowing. I wish Jayce could hear what she's saying.

Then I remember I have my cell phone, so I start recording the conversation. He needs to know that she's seeking help to understand. Listening to her makes me love her more. How could you not? She defended my brother against me, of all people, when she first met us. Put me flat on my back, and sadly, she was right I... was being a dick.

Andre is a saint of a male having raised her; it couldn't have been comfortable with as jumpy as he always seems to be. Nico, her father, has arrived, and shit, I didn't know he is bi also. Am I the only one that hasn't fucked or been fucked by another male?

I'm kind of feeling like the odd man out here. Sebastian kissed my brother, and the way Aurora confirmed what I smelled... shit, it was hot. I didn't think two dudes kissing would ever be seen as hot by me, but it was. I almost was able to imagine myself in Jayce's place.

What the fuck am I thinking? Am I bisexual? Do I want to fuck my bond mates? I mean, anyone other than my brother because that would just be fucking weird. I know it's common among our culture for the dominant wolves to fuck the weaker ones to establish dominance. Hmm, I wonder if I could dominate Sebastian by fucking him stupid, then I will be viewed as an equal to him instead of a threat.

I start to turn to walk away and spot my brother reappearing with a brown paper bag in hand, looking suspicious. Nicodeamus roots Jayce to the spot with a glance as he tells his sad tale. I watch the emotions flitter over my brother's features, and he seems more at peace with the way Aurora responds to her dad. Nicodeamus moves to join Jayce, and they walk off together. What the actual fuck just happened? Did I miss a secret meeting or something? I must have. I return to Aurora's side, and she snuggles in closely and kisses my cheek.

"What can I do to help your brother? I mean, I don't want him to feel pressured, but I also don't want him to feel ignored or isolated." Her beautiful brows furrow as she ponders her predicament.

"The best thing I can suggest is to spend time with him. He likes to cook and bake, so maybe hang out in the kitchen with him. Tell him which foods are your favorite, and he'll be thrilled to cook for you." I beam with pride. I am always so very proud of how good of a cook my brother is. And if his cooking could bring them closer together, then that would be awesome.

Sebastian and I could definitely use the help. There have been times where we have come damn close to tapping out. Aurora is a beast in the bedroom, with an appetite that we're having problems keeping up with. I hope my brother gets with the program soon as I don't know how much longer Sebastian and I can last. She's got the drive to handle three mates, and when only two are in the game, it gets exhausting.

I decide to track Jayce and Nicodeamus to see what they're up to. It looks like my brother went on a mission. He's spreading all kinds of chocolates on the picnic table, along with a basket and fluffy stuffing for the basket. His eyes widen with shock when he sees me enter. "It's all good, brother, let me help you." I smile at him—he took what Andre told him to heart and bought Aurora chocolates.

"I hope it helps. I mean, I don't want Aurora to think I don't care for her. I want her to know that she's special, and I'm only hers." His eyes drop to his horde of sweets. A slow shake of his head is given before he starts stuffing the fluff in the basket. "I'm not sure how to date a female anymore. It's been almost a hundred years since I last slept with one." His eyes raise and search mine.

"Okay, not a problem; that's an easy one, and I'll do what I can to help. You know how you like being held and snuggled?" He nods emphatically. "Well, Aurora loves touch, especially her neck. It's super sensitive, and she'll soak her jeans if you kiss her just right. If you're looking to build up to sex but not have it, then offer to give her a massage, but don't touch her neck." I can tell he's taking mental notes, and his eyes are pulsing between human and wolf. "Maybe go hunt with her. She loves a good hunt, and it would be a good base layer for you two."

He raises his right eyebrow and tilts his head to the left. "Seriously, Dom! You know I'm not a great hunter. I don't want to look like a complete ass in front of her. You know it would be my luck Sebastian shows up and makes me look like a worthless pup." He already looks defeated, and he hasn't even tried yet.

"I'll get Dimitri to keep Sebastian busy so you can have some quality time with our girl. I promise it will be okay." I walk over and give my brother a heartfelt hug and kiss to his temple.

"Your present looks fantastic, now let's go find our queen so you can give it to her. I'll be right there with you, I promise." He smiles and nods, then starts to head towards Aurora's favorite tree on the property.

There she is, our future queen, hanging upside down from the lowest limb on the tree, just swinging back and forth. Her hair is so long the tips are touching the grass blades. "Keep that up, love, and your beautiful white hair will be stained green." Her eyes pop open, and she smiles at Jayce and me.

Curiosity is getting the better of her, so she drops down out of the tree. "Whatcha got there, cutie?" Slowly she moves towards us, like the apex predator she is—her steps, silent and deadly as she approaches Jayce and kisses the corner of his mouth.

Gently she snuggles into him, trying not to spook my poor brother. Jayce bands a single arm around her waist and touches his nose under her chin in submission. "I brought you a present, love. I hope you like it." He carefully backs up and offers her the present.

Up to this point, I believe my brother is the first of us to get her one. Aurora's eyes light up, and she bounces up and down before dragging Jayce over to a picnic table. Ever so gently, she sets the package down, afraid to break its contents. I've never watched her do anything so carefully in my time with her. Nico and Andre are on the hill to our left, watching with rapt attention.

Slowly the bow is untied, and the ribbon is laid out flat on the table. The first layer of the iridescent paper is gently pulled away and folded neatly. It's placed reverently next to the ribbon. Watching her closely, I see tears forming in Aurora's eyes; this single action has touched her heart so deeply. The following layers are peeled away in the same careful manner and placed on top of the first. Now she's down to the fluffy stuffing. Aurora looks completely baffled as to how to remove it without damaging anything. Her steel-grey eyes plead with Jayce for help, and he swoops in quickly to assist her. "Close your eyes, love."

Aurora obeys Jayce immediately. Everyone gathered is completely shocked, watching her immediate obedience to the omega of the pack. Jayce removes the fluff and sets it down beside the basket. Now all the different chocolates are exposed. "Open your eyes, love."

Aurora can't open her eyes fast enough. Those same eyes open so very wide in shock. It appears he's the first to render her speechless. Her eyes dart between him and the chocolates, then back again. "They're all for me?" Aurora's tone is so innocent you could almost forget the carnage she caused less than a week ago.

Jayce gives her a single nod, and she leaps into his arms, burying her face into his neck, sobbing and thanking him repeatedly. Poor Jayce doesn't know what to do. Honestly, he kind of looks frightened. I catch his attention and motion for him to hug her and hold her tight. Instantly he bands his arms tightly around her middle, holding her.

Aurora slowly lifts her head, and it's the happiest I've ever seen her. Her eyes search his face, questioning if he's okay. Jayce smiles like the big idiot he is and kisses her cheek gently. Aurora buries her face between his neck and shoulder again. He turns in my direction and locks eyes with me, mouthing *thank you*.

I give him a thumbs up and walk off towards Andre and Nicodeamus. As I approach, they hand out high fives all around at my arrival. "I thought that would never happen." I breathe a sigh of relief. I was starting to get frightened that he was going to be stuck in a holding pattern forever. Apparently, I wasn't the only one—Andre and Nicodeamus nod.

We watch my poor brother fumble through the gift exchange. He's finally hit by a stroke of genius, or should I say a text message. Andre shoots him a text suggesting he feeds Aurora some of the chocolate. He glances our way just briefly, and by the look on his face, my brother thankfully takes the hint. He sits on the tabletop, and Aurora lays her head in his lap as he feeds her piece by piece.

Possible disaster averted by our covert team of matchmakers. Now, if we can get Sebastian to stop being a fucktard, we'd all be in a better place. Speaking of the fucktard, I better have a talk with him so he doesn't piss in Jayce's cheerios.

I head out in search of the fucktard, and as usual, he's in the outdoor gym pumping iron as his mother talks to him about pack politics. "Got a minute Sebastian?" He puts the weights down and flexes a bit before walking over to me. I never realized how sexy muscles covered in sweat look. Now I understand why Aurora likes watching us work out. Sebastian is now in my personal space and way too fucking close just for a conversation.

I lock eyes with him and tilt my head to the side. "Like what you see?" Challenging him? Absolutely. Why the fuck not? I want to see what kind of wannabe alpha he is. I look over his shoulder, and his mom is long gone. Thankfully there is no one else around.

Without warning, he reaches down and cups my balls, and gives them a gentle squeeze. "What if I do? Are you wolf enough to stop me?" He puts a finger under my chin to keep my gaze locked with his. Slowly his eyes turn the ice-blue of his wolf, and his fingertip turns into a claw.

Its sharp point lightly digs into the soft skin under my jaw. I'm not about to show discomfort or fear. I reach down and cup his balls. His cock is hard as steel and pulsing under my hand. Obviously Sebastian likes being challenged. I back up a step and raise my chin in defiance.

"Maybe I am, maybe I'm not. There's only one way to find out, isn't there?" I'm very curious as to where this new desire to fuck or be fucked by Sebastian is coming from. In all actuality, the strongest bonds come from all the mates being mated to each other. I turn and start walking back towards the alpha house. Sebastian hot on my heels. He takes the bait: hook, line, and sinker. I don't need to turn around to know he is right there. I head into my room and begin to remove my shirt.

I start thinking of the way Aurora would strip slowly out of my button-downs. I stop in the middle of the room and turn around, locking Sebastian's eyes and start undoing the top button. His wolf surges to the forefront, watching me undress with rapt attention. Each button slowly reveals my muscular chest hidden beneath the soft fabric. I bite my lower lip hard, drawing blood— it's something that affects us males, and any blood play makes us rock fucking hard.

Sebastian's gasp is audible as my blood drips slowly onto my exposed chest. I reach the last button and ease the shirt off my shoulders, letting it fall to the floor at my feet. My hands go to my favorite black jeans. Claws burst free of my fingertips as I pop the belt buckle open. Sebastian strips down at a record pace, trying to get ahead of my agonizingly slow progress. His massive, veiny cock springs free of his once restrictive briefs. He's already dripping precum down his thick, pulsing shaft. This is getting more and more interesting by the minute. My jeans hit the floor, and I'm bare before him.

What he has in length, I have in girth. I do not lack in any sense; I'm just thick and throbbing at the thought of being able to dominate Sebastian. But the look in his eyes tells me he has other ideas.

"Turn around, Dominik. Hands on the mattress and feet by the posts," Sebastian growls out his commands, and fuck, my cock is leaking a small river thinking about what he may do. I slowly obey. After all, I don't want to make it too easy on him. A loud crack is heard, and my left ass cheek is burning from his hand's impact on my flesh. It's moments like this that I'm thankful I love pain. I don't turn to look at Sebastian as I hear him freeing a belt from the discarded pants, and then the sound of a second belt is freed. Smart male using the leather belts to bind my ankles to the bedposts.

I feel his sharp claws run up the backs of both of my thighs as I stand there, curious as to what he has in store for me. His clawed hands grip the meat of my ass hard, probably drawing blood. His lips are so close to my neck; I feel his hot breath caressing me.

"Someone's just as turned on as I am. I can smell your need, Dom." Sebastian's hands slide around my waist and down my V until he grips my rock-hard cock. He gives me a few firm tugs as he thrusts his wet cock between my ass cheeks. I can't help the moan that escapes my lips. I'm trying to fuck his hand as he's thrusting from behind.

Suddenly he pulls away quickly, and instantly I miss his heat and his hands upon me. I look over my shoulder to him, and he's grabbed a tube of lube from god knows were. That shit is going to be fucking ice cold. "Lean on your forearms on the mattress Dom. I'm going to get you ready for me because I can't promise I'll be gentle once I'm in you."

I do as he commands and slowly lower down onto my forearms. I'm so fucking close to orgasming; it's not even funny at this point. I understand entirely why Aurora fully submits to Sebastian... the man is a sex god, and he fucking knows it. I feel his lube covered fingers slowly rubbing around the tight pucker of my asshole. The tingles he's producing causes my cock to jump against the mattress. "Grab your cock, Dom. I want to know you're stroking yourself while I play with your ass."

I apparently don't move fast enough for him because he chooses that moment to bite my ass cheek. I hiss from the sting of it and rise up higher on one forearm to grip my cock with my right hand. I angle myself so he can watch my hand gliding over my length in the mirror on the wall. A grumbling growl of appreciation escapes him as he presses his first finger past my sphincter. My hips thrust forward of their own accord in response to his invasion.

"Damn, that feels good. Give me more." I'm breathy like Aurora gets when you tease her too much; I can't help it. I'm stroking my cock painstakingly slow, making sure to give Sebastian a good show. My moans are becoming deeper and longer. I feel that familiar tingle at the base of my spine, and my balls draw up tight.

Sebastian stands once he's satisfied that I'm loose enough. I feel the cold squirt of lube on my asshole again; this time, there's the pressure of the head of his cock pressing down on me. I breathe in slowly and push back against him until he pops past the muscular barrier. Sebastian gives me a few shallow thrusts before he buries himself to the hilt deep within me. I'm so full, almost to the point of bursting.

The burn hurts, yet feels so fucking good. His hand comes up and grips my throat tightly, and pulls my body back against his. I now know precisely how our girl feels at this moment. The adrenaline high is so fucking worth it. Sebastian pulls almost all the way out before he slams back home as hard as he can. I'm not going to fucking last long.

He must sense how close I am because he starts to fuck me as hard and as fast as he can. The echoes of our slapping flesh bounce off the walls. Our grunts and moans echo off the walls... I stroke my cock in time with his thrusts keeping up with his punishing pace. I scream out my orgasm as ribbons of my seed shoot out over my comforter. Sebastian's movements become erratic as he gets close too.

I arch my back, changing his penetration, and that does it for him; he howls deeply as he cums. Without warning, he sinks his canines into my shoulder, biting hard and deep, marking me as his. I feel the feather-light tether snap into place as he slowly releases my shoulder. He licks my wounds clean then frees me from his grasp and the bed.

I stretch my body out before walking to the bathroom to retrieve two wet towels to clean ourselves up with. We sit on the bed side by side in silence. It's not awkward or anything; we know what needs to happen next. It's his turn, and I'm looking forward to it. My cock starts to swell again, so soon after that killer orgasm, so I reach over to stroke Sebastian's soft cock.

Wouldn't you know, that's the moment my brother decides to walk in. My shoulder is still bleeding, and Sebastian and I are both naked in different states of arousal. The look of shock on my brother's face is priceless. His tears, though, gut me. "Jayce? What's wrong?" I stand slowly, walking over to him, and place my hand on his shoulder.

Jayce's bottom lip quivers, and he smiles at me. "I love you, Dom. I don't know what to say. I never thought I'd see the day you would ever let another male touch you." His eyes drink in Sebastian's prone hard form sprawled out on the bed. "So, how are we finishing the bond?" His innocent eyes bounce between Sebastian and me.

"That's easy," Sebastian says as he moves off the bed and stands before me.

His index finger rests under my chin and raises my head so I can look in his eyes. "I take your brother right here, where I had you moments ago. You take me while I take your brother. That's two matings done, and only one left." He removes his finger, then moves to Jayce and kisses him deeply.

His hands roam all over my brother's body. He is much gentler than he was with me. I'm honestly fascinated watching him move and position my brother on his back on the bed. Carefully I squeeze the lube in Sebastian's outstretched hand. And gently, he prepares my brother for his intrusion. My hand grips my thick cock, and I stroke it slowly, coating it with the lube before I move to start grinding myself against Sebastian's tight ass.

The baritone rumble coming from Sebastian makes my cock leak. My index finger begins to massage his tight sphincter trying to get it to relax. Ever so slowly, I press my index finger and middle finger in as deep as I could go. Rhythmically I begin to scissor my fingers to loosen up his rectum. Jayce gasps the minute Sebastian enters him, and he remains still. Now's my chance.

Without warning, I press the head of my thick cock into him. Watching his muscles tense and his head bow backward. I've got him now. I do a few short thrusts letting him adjust to me before I drive it home. Sebastian's claws tear through the comforter as he moans deeply. My thrusts are slow and controlled, drawing out every inch before pushing it back in deep. We find our rhythm, thrusting and drawing back. One almost out while the other is seated deep in the other. Our fucking seems to last forever.

Jayce is the lucky one; he fucking came at least twice already. Me, I'm holding off as long as I can, enjoying this level of control over Sebastian. I start to lick and nip Sebastian's shoulder, and his thrusts start to become erratic. Swiftly he lunges forward and bites Jayce on the shoulder, completing the first half of their bond. Soon as Sebastian stands up, I start pounding the hell out of him, driving my cock as hard and as deep into him as I can. I show no mercy, just like he did to me earlier. I feel the tightening of my testicles and that telltale sign of my impending release. My hand shoots forward, and I tightly grip Sebastian's throat and pull him back against me. My other arm wraps around his straining abdomen while he whimpers from my erratic thrusts. One final thrust and I'm buried deep within him as my mouth latches onto his shoulder, biting deep into his flesh as my seed fills his ass.

Several flashes of light slowly disrupt my post-orgasmic bliss. Slowly I release Sebastian and lick his wound clean as more flashes of light go off, and I hear Jayce giggle on the other side of Sebastian. Okay, that has my attention. I turn and look towards the door to find our mate with several wet towels in one hand and her phone in the other. "Really, love?"

Her smile is so broad and bright; I can almost forgive the incriminating evidence she now has on her phone. "Okay, I thought Sebastian kissing Jayce was hot... This will fucking inspire so many damn wet dreams, it's not even funny!" Aurora passes out the wet towels as we withdraw from each other. Sebastian looks about as uncomfortable as I feel right now, and well, Jayce honestly is fucking glowing. Aurora climbs onto the bed and lays her head on Jayce's shoulder, and snuggles in close.

"Hey, baby." Aurora kisses Jayce's chest and watches Sebastian, and I clean up. "So? This is a thing now?" She asks while smiling like the cat that swallowed the fucking canary.

Sebastian stops wiping his flaccid cock off and stares at Aurora. "You ever want to be the wolf in the middle... pick your two, and I'm game, doll." And just like that, cocky Sebastian is back in full effect. I shake my head at him, then move to the other side of the bed and sit next to my brother.

"Elena suggested that all three of us should be mated to each other as well. It will provide the strongest bond and give each other immunity for the war ahead." Aurora nods, taking in all that Sebastian is telling her. Carefully he leans forward and kisses her, then Jayce. He turns towards me next. And roughly grips the back of my neck, kissing me deeply. I can't help the soft grumble that escapes my lips. Sebastian saunters off, clothes in hand, buck naked.

My gaze then falls on Aurora and Jayce, who are snuggled up tightly on the bed. Perhaps my brother is finally making progress. "I'm going to hit the shower. You two are more than welcome to stay here tonight if you like." Aurora smiles and keeps stroking Jayce's abs tracing every bump and line. I can see her wolf swirling to the surface, then her struggle to suppress her. Traveling my gaze to Jayce, his wolf is also on the surface. Who knows, maybe he'll take the next step with her soon. I mean, it's killing me knowing my brother is struggling with this.

My shower time sets a new world record for speed in every division. Returning to my bedroom, I find Aurora in the middle of the California king bed and Jayce on her other side. Both of them are snuggled under the covers, giggling at the rom-com they've decided to watch. I honestly couldn't care less what is on the t.v. at the moment, two of the most influential people in my life are in my bed. The bed looks so inviting, but first, I have a plan. I gently kiss both Aurora and Jayce on the forehead and head down to the kitchen.

What movie night doesn't have popcorn, right? After making the massive bowl of extra cheesy popcorn, I return to my room. You would think I discovered cold fusion the way Aurora and Jayce are acting. They hoot, holler, and bounce all over the bed, demanding the bowl of popcorn. Reluctantly I give Aurora the bowl and wink at my brother. He is consciously putting forth the effort to spend quality time with our mate and it is paying off. He is more relaxed, and most importantly, Aurora looks very happy with her current situation. Once we all get settled in bed, we watch several movies until Aurora falls asleep between us. Leaning back in bed, looking down at our sleeping Aurora, I sigh. This is a good night for all of us.

CHAPTER 19

Sebastian

What a night! Two out of three complete matings are done with the guys. At some point today, I have to catch up with Jayce and finish my mating with him. I'm not looking forward to letting the omega fuck me. Still, I'll do anything for Aurora—especially to secure her safety and my place in the pack. I lay here in my bed, staring at the ceiling. We've made progress on all fronts.

Under the threat of a painful death at the hand of the dragon king, I was ordered to leave Jayce alone if he's near Aurora. We need him to complete his bond with her for so many reasons. The main one is the strength of the pack bond. The second one, I honestly think my dick may fall off eventually. Aurora has a sex drive strong enough to handle three virile mates.

Unfortunately, there are only two of us in the game while the third tries to dislodge his head from his ass. I'm guessing Aurora spent the night with Dom since she's not in bed with me. Reluctantly I get out of bed and dress for the day. Slow steps carry me down the hallway past Dom's door. A few moments later, Dom steps out and silently attempts to close his door. "What's up, Dom?" I motion towards his door.

Quickly he moves towards me and drags me down the hallway. "Shh, Aurora, and Jayce are still sleeping. I'm hoping they fuck when they wake up." Decent idea, letting nature take its course without interruption.

"Brilliant idea, hopefully her pheromones override his reluctance." I give him a brotherly slap on his shoulder as we move downstairs for breakfast. From the smell of it, Nina, my mother's friend, is already making breakfast for us. I honestly don't think I'll ever get used to others doing things for me. But here we are... we have servants now all because Aurora is the lost princess.

Nicodeamus is sitting at the head of the table, drawing on parchment. This can't be a good way to start the day. Coffee and battle plans are apparently how he rolls, though. "Sit, boys, we have much to discuss." He motions to the chairs near him. It isn't a request; it's an order. We take our seats next to the king and fill our cups with coffee. "I hate to be the bearer of bad news, but I have reports of Strigoi attacking not far from here. I believe they will attack tonight." On the parchment before him, he has the town drawn out. He's even got individual buildings marked.

"What are the x's on the map for?" Dom beats me to it, damn it. He already seems to be more in favor than I am because of his prior relationship with Nicodeamus.

"The x's are buildings with bomb shelters in the basements. If we send the females, children, and the mated males down there, it will be safer. The five of us, as well as Dimitri, will take a stand in the center of town." I lean over to get a better look at his map.

"Where will Andre be?" I assume he will be the early warning device, but I can't swear to it. "Are we using him as an advanced warning system?"

Nicodeamus finally smiles at me and pats my shoulder. "Exactly my thoughts, son. Eagles have the best eyesight of all the shifters. He can watch for the attack and call out when he spots them. We all nod in acknowledgment of the plan. Several hours are spent with some of the pack elders going over evacuation routes to the buildings. Once the courses are planned, a pack meeting is called in the great hall.

Aurora and I stand before the masses, getting ready to address them. The twins are off to the side but up here with us. Aurora winks at me, then closes her eyes, and her voice booms in my mind, calling the pack to order.

Damn, now that's an impressive alpha power to have. I spot Nicodeamus and her guardians at the back of the hall. Nicodeamus, the proud father, gives her an approving nod. I guess she tapped into his ability for the force she used.

My people! We are about to be attacked by the Strigoi! Everyone here has a copy of the piece of the plan which they are a part of. Please initiate the plan the moment you hear Andre's screech from above. That will be our only warning. Run, hide, follow the plan. We need everyone to survive this attack. I have a team set up for defense. Do not come out until you hear Sebastian or me in your head. She moves to the edge of the platform and looks out over the crowd.

I have to admit, my mate is powerful and commanding. I'm sure her mother would be proud. Nicodeamus wipes a stray tear from his cheek. Aww, a proud daddy moment, indeed. Andre's eyes keep darting out the door, watching the sun. His head turns to Dimitri, and in a blink, Andre shifts to his eagle and is resting on the glove on Dimitri's right hand.

Aurora catches Andre's shift and draws in a deep breath. Her eyes lock with mine, then the twins. Her command echoes in our minds for us alone. A single, short nod is given to Dimitri and Andre, and out the door they go. I remain at Aurora's side for a moment longer. "It's time; go get ready, the sun is starting to set. We don't want to be caught unprepared."

She looks at Nicodeamus. "Father, the town square is yours. Four of the five safe houses are there. I will join you shortly. After all, they are coming for me." Aurora fucking smirks; she's actually enjoying the idea of the impending battle. Wow, do we have our hands full with this one. I step outside with the twins. We're heading towards the one building set back and away from the town center. Our theory is because Aurora is staying in the center of town, the Strigoi will focus their attack there. As the plan stands now, I'm supposed to be on top of the building between the center of town and the twins.

The sun is slowly setting on the horizon—the sky burning bright with shades of yellow-orange fading to a pinkish-purple. The wind has shifted, blowing in from the southwest. The faint hint of death lingers in the air. If I were a betting man, I would bet the Strigoi are holed up in the caverns about two miles from here. I text the group about what I'm scenting, and they agree with me that it is more than likely where they are hiding.

Andre starts his lazy circles in that direction, trying not to look conspicuous. Aurora climbs up to stand on the rooftop with me as she keeps her eyes locked on Andre. "He sees movement in the cave. You're right, Bash. They are in there. Odds are they have a second hiding place we aren't aware of."

I move back a bit and update the others and watch the horizon. "Aurora, tell Andre to check out the knoll over there to the east where that one lone cedar is. I think I saw movement over there, I'm just not positive." Aurora gives me a nod and looks back to Andre, and he changes course quickly as it's getting way too close to full sunset for him to delay. Andre's screech fills the air as he raises the alarm. Aurora shifts almost immediately and howls, sending all the wolves into action. Her father's dragon takes up most of the town square as he starts coating the ground with ice to slow the invasion.

Aurora takes a running leap as the last person enters the building the twins are guarding. Her talons grip the wood as she starts to freeze the building. Nico sees what his daughter is doing and starts coating his safe houses in a thick layer of ice as well. In the distance, the mob can be spotted moving steadily towards the town.

My eyes narrow as I search in both directions. The dead heads have planned a smart two-front attack. Aurora finishes icing her building and looks towards where her father is. Two quick, well-timed leaps, and she's on the ground again, pacing by her father's side, waiting for the fight to begin. She's not fun to be around when she's made to wait for too long. I watch her flexing her taloned fingers, already itching to rip something apart.

It doesn't take too long for the first wave of the assault to blow past the twins and head right for Aurora, as we predicted. Now that we are one hundred percent sure they are only after her, we all convene in the center of town. Aurora and Nicodeamus's fighting prowess is on full display as they weave in and out, dancing around each other.

You would think they have fought together for the last hundred years. The fluid movements executed by the two of them are almost hypnotizing. Then you remember you're in the middle of a battle, and there's Strigoi to kill. I'd love to say we made short work of them, but that would be a lie.

Each wave seems to be followed by another and yet another after that one. Nico and Aurora show no signs of stopping, but the twins are starting to fatigue. Three hours straight we have been fighting, ripping off heads and limbs as we go. Aurora, I've just noticed, has a pile of fucking skulls again! What is her obsession with collecting heads?

One of the twins falters and falls before Aurora. She lets loose such a deathly bellow it's frightening. Nicodeamus sees the Dire Wolf down and unmoving, his taloned hand reaches out, scoops him up, and tucks him under his wing. Aurora nods to her father and begins again, ripping heads off.

Out of what seems to be thin air, an arrow shoots Aurora in the shoulder. She growls and falls to one knee while Nicodeamus starts covering everything with ice. I've never seen him this angry before. I rush over to Aurora and sniff the arrow. A wolf shifter shot her... what the actual fuck?

She's starting to lose consciousness. Whatever is on this arrow is either killing her or sedating her. I grip the shaft as close to her skin as I can and rip it out quickly. It's now as I hold my mate in her human form that I wonder why the attack stopped. I look up to find Dimitri and the remaining twin standing in front of us. Nico turned the town into a winter wonderland.

Sliding down one of the ice walls comes my cousin, Michael. Oddly, he's here; I haven't seen him in years, and yet on the night of the attack, he's here? Something doesn't add up. I see my mother stepping out of her home, and I give her a quick shake of my head to stop her. Thankfully she obeys and remains on the porch. I shift back to my human form, so do Dimitri and Jayce. One mystery solved, Dom is the wolf under Nicodeamus's wing. I hand Aurora over to Jayce and motion to my mother. He and Dimitri move quickly with her away from us. "Long time no see, Mike. What brings you back?"

I'm already suspicious of him as something seems very off with the way he's watching Jayce walk away with Aurora. "You know, cuz, a little bit of this, a little bit of that." He won't make eye contact with me for long, so I reach back and place a hand on Nico. *Can you hear me?* I wait, hoping he can; otherwise, this is going to suck.

I can, young prince. Oh, thank the gods...

I think my cousin shot Aurora. Please take Dom and guard my mother's home. I'll handle Michael. Nico's head comes down even with my shoulder, and he snorts frost.

Consider it done. Bring Aurora his head and heart. With that said, he lumbers over to my mother's cabin and wraps his body most of the way around it, watching Michael and me.

"That was freaky. I mean, that Ice Dragon walking around the place." Michael looks nervous, his eyes continuously looking back to see where Nicodeamus has gone.

"So, Mike, did you ever get that ink on your arm finished? I see some color poking out of the sleeve." I'm hoping I'm wrong, but Mike was always getting string slapped when he would shoot. I pray that telltale welt isn't on his arm; otherwise, I will have no choice but to take my cousin's head.

"Hell yeah, it's done!" He unbuttons his sleeve and rolls it up. He turns his arm so I can see the back of his forearm, not the soft inside. I grip his forearm and turn his arm over. There, sitting plain as day, is the welt, the motherfucking welt. My eyes lock with his, and he knows that I know what he's done. "I can explain. Honest, I can."

He backs away quickly and bumps into the solid mass of Dimitri's chest. Mike knows he's in deep shit now. Dimitri grabs him by the back of his neck and lifts him off the ground. "What do you want me to do with him, Sebastian? Break his neck? Rip his head off? Or torture him for the next month… slowly." Dimitri's bear is making its presence known. Fur is rippling over his arms and face. He is very unstable and furious.

"I'll handle it, big guy. Go protect our girl." I watch Dimitri come back to his senses, and he drops Mike on his ass. My wolf is demanding blood. This fucker hurt our mate—possibly killed her —he will not walk out of here.

"What the fuck were you thinking? What was worth betraying your own kind for!" My words are growled out and barely human as my body starts shifting on its own accord.

"I was paid to kill the white-haired female because she's a threat to our kind. Tomas said he would keep attacking the pack until she's dead. She must die! I can't let my mom and sisters die because of one female," he growls, but his wolf isn't an alpha; he isn't even wolf enough to be considered a beta.

My Lycan looms over him as he pisses himself out of fear. His begging for his life falls on deaf ears. Mike makes the fatal mistake of running from me. Oh yeah, my wolf is quite happy he fucked up to that level. We chase him and play wolf and fawn with him. We track him for the better half of an hour. Finally, he shifts and turns to face me.

His Lycan isn't even half the size of mine. His hand raises, and his claws flex as he swings for me. I strike. My claws dig deep and rip into his chest and grip his heart. I can feel the rhythmic contractions of the smooth muscle in my grip. I close my clawed hand a little tighter, and his eyes bulge out of his head. The blood vessels in his eyes begin to rupture as my grip increases. His arms drop; he knows death is imminent for him, and I am the angel who will send his ass to hell.

With a quick flick of my wrist, I sever all the arteries that hold his heart in place. I have his quivering, bleeding heart in my hand right in front of his face. Several seconds pass before his body drops like a ton of bricks before me. I now understand the feeling of holding the final moments of someone's life in my hands. I know why my love, my mate, said she needs to feel something other than being a monster. I look at my cousin's heart in my hand and then back to his blood-covered corpse. Nicodeamus steps up to me and scares the fuck out of me. I shift back to my human form and stare at him. "Seriously?"

"Yes, you were deep in thought, my child. You did well; I am proud of you." Nicodeamus gives me that fatherly smile, and for once, I'm not freaked the fuck out by him.

My eyes fall next to the literal silver platter he is holding. Okay then. I place the heart on the platter then proceed to cut my cousin's head free from his body. Once I finish, I put the head next to the heart and arrange them to be aesthetically pleasing. Gently I take the platter from Nico and begin to head back to the house. My mother is famous for her rose bushes, and thankfully they are in full bloom.

Carefully I place the platter on the deck and pick a half dozen roses to decorate my offering. I stare at my handiwork and start questioning my sanity. What the actual fuck am I doing? I'm bringing my injured mate a severed head and a heart on a platter lined with roses. I look from my presentation then back to Nico.

The fucking dragon just gives me a single thumbs up with his only hand. Daddy dearest is just as fucked in the head as the rest of us.

Fear grips my heart as I ascend the stairs. The house is quiet; this can't be good. I run through the lists of gods and goddesses that favor the wolves, begging them to make sure Aurora is okay. I make it back to the guest room, and my heart almost fucking stops.

She's so fucking pale it looks almost as if all the blood has drained from her body. Her ruby lips shine so brightly against her now alabaster skin. Tears break free and roll down my cheeks. I can't breathe; I'm gasping for air and having a borderline panic attack. Dimitri comes up to me and takes the tray away.

"Mom! Please, tell me she's okay?" I blubber like an idiot looking at my ghostly-white mate. Jayce is snuggled up so tightly against her, and his eyes are bloodshot from crying.

"Sit down, boy. Nicodeamus, I need your blood to help Aurora." Mom is like a brigadier general ordering us around like peons. She is calm and commanding as she begins setting up a makeshift hospital in her home. Alexis had arrived at some point and is setting up for the transfusion. Thank fuck we have a nurse in the pack; otherwise, I think my beloved would be doomed.

Nicodeamus sits in the chair as directed and stretches his arm out. "Take it all if you have to. You must save my baby!" Even Nicodeamus is crying, looking at his near lifeless daughter. Alexis moves quickly, setting up to take at least three pints of blood from him. She has a pole set up next to him with saline to help replace the blood volume he is about to lose.

"Mom? What's wrong with Aurora?" My heart is in my throat as I lean on the counter next to Nico. I rest my hand on his shoulder as we both look at my mother for answers.

"It's quite simple; they tried to poison her. The arrowhead is made of silver, and the toxin it's coated with is a blend of aconite and nightshade. They didn't know of Aurora's true sire; otherwise, they would have known this combination wouldn't kill her." Elena moves to adjust the saline drip for Aurora, making sure to hydrate her to help flush out the toxin.

"I'm going to flood Aurora's system with her father's blood to try to reverse what damage the toxins did to her body. I'm positive it's the quickest way to heal her safely." Elena doesn't look up to regard anyone as she prepares everything for the tricky transfusion she will attempt.

I watch how carefully Alexis moves towards my mother with the first pint of blood. Together they hook Aurora up and start the drip. Jayce won't move for anything. He is far too frightened to leave her side. At this point, I'm too afraid to close my eyes or even go to relieve myself. "How long before we know if it's helping her, Mom?" My voice quivers like a scared, tear-filled child. The love of my life is before me, fighting for her life, and I can't do a fucking thing to help her. I'm so fucking grateful that her father lived and is with us. Without him, she'd be dead.

"Have faith, son. Alexis is a nurse and specializes in hematology. The first signs of a positive response will be the return of color. While this pint infuses, we need to drain a pint, which will make her body start to produce more red blood cells and platelets." She sighs softly.

"It's pretty much going to be a rinse and repeat the process with the three pints. Tomorrow if we need to, we'll take two pints from you, Sebastian, to help wake up her wolf. Then the tough part will be that you are going to have to force her shift, so her wolf finishes healing her." Say what? I stand there, blinking as Dominik comes flying through the door.

Dom immediately drops to his knees when he sees the state our mate is in. His tear-filled eyes seek out my eyes and then his brother's. My mother pulls him out of the room to catch him up quickly. When he returns, he thanks Nico for protecting his fallen body and hugs it out with him. Jayce calls Dom over and switches out with him, and runs out of the room. I watch Jayce leave, then look at Dom. "Bathroom run." Ah, that explains the swift departure.

I swear to the gods above, Jayce just broke the land speed record for taking a piss. He rushes back into the room and tugs on Dom's arm to get him out of bed. Dom reluctantly leaves Aurora's side and walks over to me. "Makes me want to cry. It takes Aurora almost dying for my brother to get over his shit." Dom bites his bottom lip and sighs; a single tear rolls down his cheek, and I draw him in for a tight hug.

Honestly, I don't know if I'm hugging him to comfort him or to comfort myself. "I feel so fucking powerless, Bash. I'd trade places with her if I could."

Nicodeamus's head whips up at that exact moment. His eyes burn liquid mercury as he stares at Dom. "Did you not hear what was done? You would be dead, leaving that poor girl behind without her mate. A severed bond feels like you died right along with them." Nicodeamus's voice cracks with emotion.

"I fell from the fucking sky when her mother died. I didn't want to live without her. If it weren't for the fact that I felt my child's life, I probably would have mourned myself to death."

Nicodeamus looks away at that moment; the pain from the loss of his mate still evident on his face. Over two hundred years later, and it looks like it was just yesterday to him.

Seeing the depth of Nicodeamus's loss really puts how lucky we truly are into perspective. I kiss Dom's temple, then lean down, and side-hug Nicodeamus and kiss the top of his head. We are all suffering together. Unfortunately, Nicodeamus is in hell all over again. My eyes remain locked on the pint, and Aurora's color is slowly improving, so that is a blessing. I exhale a bit louder than I thought, and everyone looks at me. "Her color is coming back." Everyone's eyes shoot to Aurora, and tentative smiles break out across the room.

My mother enters the room, passing out food and drinks. "Eat! She'll kick your collective asses if you don't take care of yourselves. That means you too, M'lord." She winks at Nicodeamus and hands him a burger as well.

Only Jayce doesn't budge; he is still too frightened to move. When I finish my food, I move over to him and sit on the edge of the bed. "Please eat. She needs us all strong for her. I'll lay with her until you're done eating, okay?"

Jayce slowly sits up and nods. He's so broken up he's practically gone mute. Ever so carefully, he slides out of bed. He reaches over and readjusts Aurora's pillow and her blankets before he motions for me to slide in where he was. Once I am situated, he adjusts my pillow and pulls the covers up. "She needs to stay warm. Keep her warm for me." He whispers when he speaks— his voice quivering with emotion. Tears well up, threatening to overflow as his eyes turn bloodshot again. Jayce's cheeks flush as he attempts to hold back the feelings that threaten to break free. Out of the males, he is the one most in touch with his emotions.

To see him fight against his nature hurts my heart. "I will guard her 'til my dying breath and then some. I swear to you I will keep her warm and safe." I allow a few rogue tears to flow down my cheeks, and Jayce smiles at me. He then leans in, kissing my lips softly, whispering his thanks before walking over and hugging his brother. As soon as he is in Dom's arms, the dam breaks, and all the tears and sorrow flow freely.

My heart starts aching for him, and that's when I feel it. Aurora's arm moves slightly. "Guys!! I think she just moved!" Everyone crowds around the bed, watching Aurora. She's midway through the second pint of her father's blood when she starts to twitch a little.

Anyway, you look at it; it is a step in the right direction. Any positive is a bonus at this point. Jayce moves closer to the side where the transfusion is running and slips two fingers into her hand. Without warning, her hand snaps shut, gripping him tightly. His eyes widen, and a moment later, he starts bawling like a baby, saying she had just grabbed his fingers. I decide to expose her hand on my side and try it myself. Gently placing two fingers in her cupped hand, moments pass when she slowly closes her fingers around mine. Greatest moment ever! We look to Dom, and he moves to her ankle and places his hand there. Within moments she wiggles her toes on that foot.

"Okay, boys, back the fuck off and let me check her!" Holy fuck, my mom can still be scary even at her old age. Jayce and I hold up our hands that were being gripped by Aurora, and my mother smiles. She leans over and forces Aurora's eye open, and shines a light to test pupil reaction.

My mother is shocked to find the silver orbs of Aurora's wolf looking back at her. Aurora's pupils react very sluggishly, but at least they respond this time. "She's improving. We need to keep round the clock watch on her. One in the bed, one awake. Switch out every four hours to give each other a break. So, to spell it out for her mates, one awake, two asleep. If you all need a break, get Nicodeamus or me."

Mom leaves quickly after that, and we all look at each other. "Jayce, why don't you sleep beside her first? I'll take the first watch. We can switch about midnight and so on if that's okay?" I look between Dom and Jayce, and they both nod. It takes several attempts for Jayce and me to get our fingers free. Once free, he scoots in where I was, and I make sure that he and Aurora are comfortable.

The first watch isn't bad at all. I discover that both twins snore quite loudly. I also discovered that Dom laughs if he farts in his sleep. When it is my turn to slide in, I defer to Dom since he hasn't had the chance to lay next to her yet. It kills me to give up my chance, but to be a good alpha means putting others before yourself. I move to the recliner and lie back. I keep my eyes on them for as long as I can.

The warmth of the morning sun is on my face when I wake up. Fuck, I slept through my watch. I wake up with a start, ready to launch out of the chair, when a firm hand lands on my shoulder. I look back and see Nico. "Shhh, all is well, son. The twins weren't handling her being ill very well, so I took over for the last eight hours to let them both sleep beside her. You wouldn't wake up when it was your turn." Well, that explains that. I nod slowly and examine Aurora. Her color has fully returned, but she still isn't waking up.

"Sebastian, get in the chair; it's time to draw blood from you." My mom is way too fucking happy about stabbing me this early in the morning. Dimitri, my savior, comes in carrying a mug and a pot of coffee.

"Thank the gods that Dimitri brought coffee. I don't think I can handle getting stabbed without it." Mother allows me long enough to get my coffee made before she sticks my happy ass in the chair to start draining me dry. I watch my lifeblood drain into the bag and hope and pray that this finally wakes sleeping beauty up. It's been two days since she fell in battle, and it feels like forever. We are starting to look worse for wear as the days tick on. Hell, I sound like it's been a month instead of two days.

Jayce won't leave Aurora's side for anything, except maybe for a bathroom break. I guess since he can't feel her through the bond, he's twice as leery as the rest of us that can feel her. I can almost bet that once this is over, that bond gets put in place the moment Aurora is able. I watch him as he sits there, brushing her hair, talking to her as if she's awake. Then again, no one knows for sure how much someone who's in a sleep-like state actually hears. Bag one gets taken away, and bag two gets hooked up.

"Ow, what the fuck!" My eyes dart to Alexis as she starts the I.V in what is my free arm.

She mouths *sorry* but continues to do her job. I can see her looking me over from head to toe. Her arousal is palatable in the air. Something makes my wolf stir for a moment. Just as quickly as it happens, it passes, and I refocus on what's going on.

Lord fucking help Alexis if Aurora wakes up right now. "You know I'm a mated wolf, right, Alexis?" That catches her off guard and gets my mother's attention. Mom comes over and takes one sniff of Alexis and boots her ass out of the room immediately.

"Fucking vultures," Elena grumbles as she walks back into the room. Dom and Dimitri both spit their coffee and look at me. All I can do is shrug. Mom approaches me, leans down, placing a kiss on my temple.

"You know Aurora is more than likely going to hunt her ass down and kill her?" Slowly I nod, then turn to stare at my mate.

"I hope she wakes up soon. I don't know how much more we can take, Mom." Jayce is still in his own little world, giving Aurora a sponge bath in bed. Me? I feel so fucking helpless. I've put myself on self-imposed guard duty. Every night Dimitri and I take turns standing guard while the twins keep Aurora warm at night. It's not that I don't want to sleep next to her; my wolf would do better in close quarters.

Aurora's color is improving more with the first bag of my blood, and I can see how happy Jayce is looking. He gently leans over and kisses her lips like a prince from a fairy tale. Aurora's left-hand shoots up, gripping the back of Jayce's head, holding him in place. The rumble of her wolf echoes throughout the room. We all gasp and stop what we are doing. It's eerily quiet. We all practically hold our breath, waiting. Just as quickly as her hand rose, it falls, and she is silent again. She's fighting, and that's the most important thing.

CHAPTER 20
Jayce

I feel so guilty. I fought hard but not hard enough. Aurora ended up shot and fell in battle, and I blame myself because I'm the weakest link. As much as Dom, Sebastian, and the others try to convince me it's not my fault, I still blame myself. I'm over-analyzing every move made around Aurora. I won't let her be harmed again. I wish I were more dominant—being an omega fucking sucks. I'm not as strong as my brother, who's a potential alpha. I'm not even in the same orbit as Aurora or Sebastian.

It does get quite interesting to watch when Sebastian would get too full of himself and Aurora would knock him down a peg. Aurora's dad, Nicodeamus, has been fabulous with me. He worries about if I'm taking care of myself while I tend to his daughter. That's what a father is supposed to be like. Not like the monster Dom and I had for a father. I was so happy when Aurora and Nicodeamus killed him. Dare I say best day ever? For the first time in years, I saw Alex smile, like really smile.

There was a noticeable weight lifted off of Dom's shoulders as well. After all, he was next in line for the political mating. Ugh, the bitch he was supposed to get was a hag. I hope my brother realizes just how blessed we are. Sadly, it took my mate almost dying for me to see how truly wonderful she is.

When Aurora wakes up, everything is going to change. No more being a chicken shit and hiding. Instead, I'm going to face my feelings. I love her with all that I am. I will lay beside her all day and all night for as long as I can. The guys have been incredible, letting me stay and not enforcing the rotation rule with me.

At the end of day one—yesterday—her father's blood had brought back a lot of color to her skin. We are so thankful that Elena knows what she's doing when it comes to poisons. Pint after pint, her color has improved, and at one point, her hands moved. I keep talking to her, and the guys look at me like I'm nuts.

Elena gives me that motherly smile and touches my shoulder. "Don't worry, prince, she'll wake up." She gently runs her fingers through my hair in a soothing manner.

"Keep talking to her; she needs to know you're waiting for her. Right now, her wolf is in protection mode, making sure she heals right." Elena leans over and kisses my temple, and hugs me.

"I'll get you dry shampoo and a brush for her hair. And I'll show you how to use it, so she wakes up not feeling gross." Elena makes a final check of everything and leaves to go procure the goods.

I wave for Sebastian to trade out with me; I need to stretch my legs and hit the men's room. I don't think I've ever pissed so fast in my life as I had since last night. My chest fucking hurts being away from Aurora for too long. My wolf feels like he's trying to rip free of my body to get back to her. I can't blame him; I feel exactly the same way. It's never easy for an omega to deal with the alpha being injured. We tend to go into nurture mode and mother the hell out of them until they recover.

Elena returns with all the hair care and skin care products she could find. The boys and I all watch as she explains what each is for and how to use it. We all want to help with her care; some of us are just more in tune with our nurturing side than the others. I can see how uncomfortable Sebastian is with everything, and I snicker out loud. The boys only really hung around for the bed-bath portion of the care instructions. Figures, right? I smile and copy everything that Elena showed me. I feel like I'm really making a difference in how Aurora feels.

We slept peacefully last night, and I wasn't bothered. Sebastian and Dimitri were like sentries watching over us as we slept. Kind of creepy, but with everything that's happened, it's a necessary evil at this point. I wake up to them prepping Sebastian for his donation and fresh coffee. I sit up and start fussing with Aurora's hair and cleaning up her face, making sure she is ready for the day. I made sure I explained to her what was going on with Sebastian.

My hands shoot to cover Aurora's nose when I smell Alexis's arousal. Thankfully Sebastian and Elena handled it before I said something. Slowly I begin Aurora's bed bath, making sure every inch of her body is cleaned and dried. The first bag of Sebastian's blood is hooked to her IV and is flowing into her.

I can already see tiny differences in her color and skin texture. I can't help myself. I cover her up and lightly touch her face before I lean over and kiss her gently. I miss her so much. Without any warning, her hand grips the back of my head, holding my lips firmly to hers. The rumble from her wolf makes me hard in a second as she holds me in place. I surrender to her completely in this very moment. My heart is pounding in my chest; I feel as if this kiss has gone on forever.

She manages to nip my bottom lip, drawing blood. I feel her suck at my bleeding lip, and flick her tongue over the wound before her hand and teeth release me. I'm panting from the intensity and the passion I felt. I can't bring myself to look at the others just yet. I know in my heart this was her way of telling me that she's going to be okay, and I just have to be patient.

Slowly I turn and look at the guys. I can't help the lovesick puppy look I have on my face—the single most significant moment of my life. I return to giving her the sponge bath and whistle while I work. Sebastian comes to sit next to her once all three pints are taken from him.

"Love, I found and killed the person that shot you. I took their head and heart to give to you as a gift." Sebastian's eyes drop to Aurora's hand, and he picks it up, holding it.

"If you can hear me, baby, please squeeze my hand. I beg you." I feel so much sympathy for Sebastian. He's an alpha without his mate. Alphas usually don't do well when they are separated from their mate for any reason. I can see Aurora's fingers twitch in his hand then close slowly. Part of me is pleased as punch that she reacted stronger to me.

But on the other hand, I feel horrible that he's not receiving just as strong of a reaction from her. There are no words of comfort in moments like this. We tend to beat ourselves up when bad things happen.

An audible sigh escapes Aurora's lips, and she moves her entire body, adjusting her position. Dimitri runs off, yelling down the hallway for Elena. Aurora is fighting so hard to wake up. Her eyelids flutter, and her eyes move rapidly. "Come on, baby; you can do it. Please open your eyes." I can't help but prompt her. I can't resist urging her to return to us.

One eye pops open first, then the other. She blinks them rapidly and yawns. "Did we win?" she croaks, her voice scratchy from lack of use. Of course, Aurora worries about victory at a moment like this.

"Yes, love, we won. You were shot by a poisoned arrow. If it wasn't for Mom taking pints of blood from your dad and me, I don't think you would have lived." Sebastian's voice cracks, mentioning her near-death experience. His eyes well up with tears, and he lets them run down his face.

Dom and I share the same side of the bed as we observe Aurora. Her eyes lock with each of us in turn until she gets to me. "Thank you, Jayce, for keeping me clean and telling me about the day. Thank you for keeping me warm at night." She reaches out and grabs my hand. "Thank you for remembering to treat me like I was awake and here." Tears roll down her cheeks as she smiles at me. She truly appreciates all that I have done for her.

"Anytime, my love, anything for you... anything you want, it's yours." I mean every word. I lift her hand and kiss the back of it, looking into her eyes as I do.

"Jayce, when I'm stronger, I want you in my bed, just the two of us. We need to finish our bond. I love you so very much." She makes the motion with her lips like she wants a kiss. Who am I to deny her? I lean forward and let her control the kiss. It starts sweet and tender until she bites my lip again and licks my wound. I can't help but smile. I am the happiest wolf on the planet at this point.

I reluctantly move out of the way for the others and let everyone in to show our girl some love. I feel so relieved and scared at the same time. I am scared because as soon as she heals, it's going down! Or should I say I'm going down? Crap, most incredible, and worst day ever. Performance anxiety? Absolutely. My eyes catch the movement of Sebastian leaving the room quickly. I wonder what the cheeky bastard is up to.

Sebastian returns, carrying something with a towel over the top of it. Nico strolls in right beside him with his hand on the edge of the towel. "My love, I present to you the head and heart of the man that attempted to kill you." Sebastian drops to one knee next to the bed and holds the covered platter out to Aurora. Nico removes the towel with a practiced flourish. The smile that creeps across Aurora's face is worth witnessing this disturbing scene. Who in their right fucking mind gives a head and heart as a present?

It fucking must be a Lycan and dragon thing because Aurora is elated. Nico beams with pride and Sebastian is smiling. Meanwhile, Dom and I are looking at each other like *what the fuck just happened?* We're confused as all hell by this display, but it makes Aurora happy, so it's worth it.

"Elena? Mom?" Aurora calling Elena *Mom* brings tears to the old lady's eyes. She moves forward and sits on the opposite side of the bed as her son.

"Yes, sweetheart?" Aurora rests her hand on Elena's. "Can you please prepare the skull to hang with the others? It deserves a place of honor in our home." Elena nods and motions for a Lycan male to enter the room and take the tray from Sebastian.

"Aurora, I took the liberty of taking your skull pile and sent them to be cleaned as well," Elena states plainly. Well fuck... The look all three of us give Elena and Aurora is one of shock. Has Sebastian's mom finally wholly lost her shit? How is it that this skull hoarding is now a thing?

Nicodeamus clears his throat. "It's a dragon thing to horde the skulls of your enemies. The more skulls, the stronger the dragon. I didn't think my baby would have that instinct." He sniffles and wipes his eyes with a handkerchief. "I'm so proud right now, I can't handle it. Please excuse me." Aurora waves everyone off, and her father comes to sit before her; she holds him tightly as they both cry together.

Perhaps her odd behavior isn't so odd after all. She's merely following the instinct of her dragon side. That explains a lot. Well, maybe not, but it makes a little more sense. "Daddy, will you show me how to make a menacing display of my trophies?" Seriously? I must be in the twilight zone. Nicodeamus nods and smiles before getting up and leaving the room.

"Guys, I'm famished. Can I have steak and pasta and something cold to drink?" Everyone scrambles about while I move and sit beside Aurora again. I'm not letting this girl out of my sight until the bond is dead solid. I pull Aurora into my lap and nuzzle her neck. Fucking instincts, of all the times for them to kick in, now isn't it. Aurora giggles and snuggles in closer, holding on for dear life.

"You're a good fighter, Jayce. You held off a lot of Strigoi after your brother had fallen. I'm very proud of you." She kisses my cheek gently and rests her head on my shoulder.

Everything is right in the world other than my mate collecting skulls. It's something I'm going to have to adapt to and overcome. Gently I run my fingers through her hair and carefully massage her scalp. A soft sigh escapes her lips as she relaxes into the massage. With a giggle and a flop, she ends up with her head in my lap, looking up at me. Those stormy grey eyes shine with love and happiness. Deftly I seek out the knots in her hair and remove them with my fingers. Gently I move my fingers and start massaging her temples and forehead. The sounds she's making—lord save me—go straight to my cock.

I'm praying she won't notice my erection, but let's face it, she is right there, inches from it. Her eyebrow raises, and she looks right at it. "Someone's happy to see me."

That devilish smile has Dom stopping in his tracks in the doorway and raising his eyebrow at me. I wave at him to enter, which may or may not have been my brightest idea. I would sit here suffering from the boner from hell until I knew she was fed and strong enough. Fucking bastard has a mind of his own at times. After helping Aurora sit up, Dom and I set up the table for her and watch her eat. I never in a million years thought I would take pleasure in watching someone else eat. But here I am, watching our mate eat like it is the most beautiful sight.

Dom elbows me, and I follow him out the door. "Sebastian and I are going to patrol the grounds tonight. Dimitri is going to remain as his bear on the porch and Andre on the roof. You'll have the house to yourself." Dom grips my shoulders tight then pulls me in for a hug to end all hugs.

"She knows you love her. It's time to show her how much. Let her in Jayce, let her love you back." He raises a knowing eyebrow at me.

"And don't give me that *I'm an omega* bullshit. You're a great warrior when you have to be. You're a far better man than I am; you can understand emotions. That's a gift I wish I had." Dom smiles at me, and in his way, I received a pep talk. Now, if someone had a roadmap to a woman's G-Spot, that would be awesome. One last snicker from Dom before he starts to turn and walks off.

"Don't worry about what to do. Aurora is dominant; she'll submit when she wants to, but most times, it's hold on for the ride of your life." Dom gives me his usual wise-ass two-finger salute before heading off down the hallway.

What the actual fuck have I gotten myself into? I run down the hall to my room, take a quick shower and trim my mustache and beard. Once I am pleased with my appearance, I pick out a nice silk shirt and my favorite slacks. My suit jacket is perfectly tailored to me. I stand before the mirror and do a last-minute check; I fucking love the way this suit looks on me.

Reaching into the top drawer of my dresser, I retrieve the necklace I had bought Aurora while I was in town. Carefully I pull it out of its satchel and stare at it. The pendant is an exact copy of the paw print Dom and I have tattooed on our wrists. One can only hope she appreciates it. Gently I place it in my right coat pocket before I head back to see my mate.

Lightly I knock on her door and wait. Man, I've never been this nervous in my entire life. The clicking of the knob turning draws me out of my inner monologue quite quickly. Aurora stands there, hair in a messy bun with a nightshirt that aptly says *Fuck off*. I smile and lean in to kiss her gently, but the princess has other plans. Aurora grabs onto my lapels and drags me into the room, and locks the door behind her.

Mercury orbs gaze back at me, and in this moment, I know what a rabbit feels like when we hunt them. Slowly her gaze moves over my body inch by inch; I swear to the gods that I can feel her eyes caress me. A gentle smile graces her lips as she moves in closer. Ever so lightly, her fingertips glide over the soft material of my jacket. Her hands stop at my waistline before she steps back and makes the turn around motion with her finger.

I'm quick to comply with her silent command. I'd do anything for my mate, absolutely anything. Her smile lights up the room and puts my soul at ease. "You look very handsome, Jayce. A well-cut suit on a man is like a tiny lace thong on a woman. Very much appreciated."

Her eyes bounce back and forth between human and wolf; apparently, I have the attention of both. "Allow me," she says softly as she reaches forward and slowly unbuttons my suit jacket. I gently toe off my dress shoes because fuck if I'm going to be fumbling with them later.

Slowly she exhales and reaches up, placing her hands on my shoulders and slides my jacket off. I don't know who's getting more turned on here, me because I'm being stripped, or her. It's quite evident she's getting worked up. The scent of her arousal is filling the room and engulfing me in her scent, almost strangling me.

Her hands gently hold my jacket as she moves to lay it over the arm of the chair. When she returns, her eyes remain locked with mine as she undoes my tie. Fuck, this is the single hottest thing I have ever witnessed or been apart of. I'm literally terrified to speak; I don't want to break the spell. She slips my tie off and lays it on top of my jacket before she returns and works on my silk shirt buttons.

She stands on her tippy toes and lightly presses her lips against mine, and whispers, "do not move a muscle." I feel my cock harden and pulsate, straining against my boxer briefs. For the first time in history, I'm afraid of blowing my load too early. After what seems like an eternity, she has my shirt open, and with feather-light touches she caresses my skin.

Aurora keeps her eyes locked with mine as her fingers roam over my chest and abs. Holy fuck, she's tracing every single cut and ripple of muscle I have. Silently I thank my brother for forcing me to work out with him. Every pain-filled workout is now made worth it seeing the appreciation in her eyes. Aurora moves behind me and grips the collar of my shirt, and pulls it off. Again, I feel her soft touches moving over every bump and ridge of corded muscle. My eyes close of their own volition. I can't help the shuddering breath that escapes my lips when she kisses my left pec right over my heart.

"Can I call this mine?" She speaks so softly; her breath tickles my skin.

I open my eyes to see this dominant female looking so unsure of herself. I can't have that. I reach down and take her hand in mine and place it over my heart. "It's always been waiting for you, my love. It was yours long before I knew your name. I just hope to be wolf enough to deserve yours in return." Tears threaten to break loose from my eyes as I finally speak my heart to her.

Aurora's eyes well up with tears, and she begins to softly cry. I bend down and gently kiss away her tears. Lingering on the last one, I press my forehead against hers. "You've always been wolf enough for me, Jayce. I love you for you. You are the kindest, most thoughtful mate a female could ask for. I am grateful I was blessed with you."

Her hands come to grip my belt, and it comes off super-fast. That confidence she lacked just a moment ago is now back in full force. I can't help but laugh at her antics as my pants hit the floor.

She steps back and cocks her head to the side, and smiles. "I've found a huge difference between you and Dom. *Yours* is definitely bigger." She bites her bottom lip as she grabs hold of my boxer briefs. One finger shifts, and her talon slices through the cotton like a hot knife through butter. Mercury orbs lock on the sight of my rigid leaking cock.

Just for good measure, I give my cock a slow, measured stroke. Her eyes follow my hand as it glides up and down my length. Now I've got her. I reach forward and use my claws to slice the nightshirt free from her. She looks a little shocked, but it's worth it. There it is, the fabled black lace thong she favors. I drop to my knees before her and grip the lace with my teeth. My hands rest on my thighs as I slowly begin to pull the thong down.

To be continued.... ***HUNT...***

Epilogue - Tomas

Moldavia, Romania

I pace back and forth within the castle walls. The calls and emails I've been receiving are quite disturbing and concern me immensely. Apparently, I failed in killing off the Marelup line. To make matters worse, it's a female child that was born. I summon Bane Kraus, the alpha of the Ice Dragons, and Ellis, the Polar Bear clan's beta. In theory, if that Marelup bitch is following tradition, these are the last two clan's she'll need a mate from.

Lucian from the Dire Wolf clan called me a week ago about the missive he received from the shaman's sister. The fucking bitches hid the last heir to the fucking throne from me. I throw my chalice of blood and watch it smash against the wall. The white marble is painted red as I watch the life essence run down the length of the wall. Shaking my head, me and my fucking temper, that was a good tasting AB positive.

My eyes scan through the last several messages from Johan the beta. He is frightened by the Marelup bitch. Somehow, she was able to kill a Wendigo—whatever the fuck that is. Damn new world abominations. In his last text, he said he and his father would kill her if she survived the battles she had left. The arrogance of Vlad was the downfall of his people, and now his child will be tortured.

Honestly, I can't wait to sink my fangs into her neck and drain her dry over a series of days. Her stupid father secured his breeding right by neutering the other mates. Heh, I had to laugh to myself. A purebred Lycan female was weak and frail, so this should be easy. Perhaps the other shifters in the new world are more vulnerable as well. I walk out onto the balcony of what used to be the north tower. Slowly I look over what remains of the castle. Most of it is in ruins from the attack over two hundred years ago. Some sections, like this one, I've made my slaves repair. What's left of the Lycan forces, as well as the Dire forces that enslaved my people are now my slaves. I felt it was only fitting. They started as slaves and are now slaves once more.

Bane enters my domain, and I see his white dragon making slow, lazy loops in the air before he lands in the courtyard. I'm still waiting on Ellis to arrive. Fucking bears are slow as molasses in winter. Returning to my desk, I roll out the area's map, extending into Bane's territory and over into the Polar Bears'. There is only one path for the bitch to take, and that's to cross the land bridge. I sit here calculating the distance from the Lycan compound in North America to the land bridge. Unless she flies, it will take the better half of a week to two weeks, depending on the weather.

In mid-thought, Bane bursts through my doors and enters my office—the fucker didn't even knock. Maybe I should put dragons back on the menu because of his insolence. "Glad you could make it," I mutter under my breath. *It took you long enough,* I say to myself. I force a smile, though I know my grin is one you see in nightmares. Unlike Vlad the Impaler, we Strigoi don't have retractable fangs. Instead, it's rows of needle-like teeth that leave hundreds of puncture wounds; the better to bleed you with.

"Why am I here, leach?" Dragons are always so fucking dramatic. He seems put out by being summoned. His boots clop on the floor as he moves towards my desk. Every little thing about him irritates the fucking hell out of me.

I make a graceful sweep across the map. Each of the three territories are marked clearly, including the Dire Wolf and the Lycan's compound. "What the fuck, man? I thought the last of the wolves were here, under your control.?" He moves quickly away from the table to the balcony. He glares at me, and I can see that fabled dragon temper flaring. Blackened slits bleed through the green of his eyes, making his dragon's presence evident.

"It gets worse. Anca's daughter survived that night. She's now collecting mates. There's no answer from Lucian or Johan, so I'm figuring they were killed off or failed and are hiding. Either way, it doesn't bode well for anyone involved." I lean over the map, watching the dragon alpha process the information given to him. He pulls his phone out and starts typing out a message.

"I just alerted my son to be watching for any communication from the Lycan's about a visit. He said nothing yet. So perhaps the problem sorted itself out, and no one survived the battle in the Dire compound." He shrugs his shoulder like this is one big fucking joke.

"So that's your answer to this problem? Just wait for the message stating she's on the way?" I am getting more and more irritated with the giant fucking lizard. I swear to the nine hells that he is so fucking stupid even a rock would know better than him.

"Yes, that's my fucking answer. Are you daft? Think of it this way; if she follows protocol, she'll reach out to me to meet my sons. Then we know exactly when she's on her way. No wasted resources. We can set the trap when we can estimate her travel time to the land bridge."

He takes my ruler and starts measuring mileage. "Depending on how fast she drives and what route she takes, she should get to the ice shelf in eight days. Once she hits the ice shelf, it's on foot from there. Besides, how hard is it going to be to spot a pack of black wolves on snow?"

He has a point, and I hate admitting he's right. I'm stressing over nothing. "Okay, so now we wait for her to reach out. Ellis, the beta from the Polar Bear clan, should be here in a few moments. They'll lead the initial attack on the ice bridge. Your people will be the last line of defense." I draw a line from Wales, Alaska, to Diomede Island over to Naukan, Siberia. Next, I draw a diagonal line from Uelen, Siberia to Naukan, Siberia, and put a pewter dragon on the line I drew. I make my lines as Bane watches and nods along.

Ellis chooses this time to knock on the door frame. I wave my hand at him to enter, not wanting to lose my concentration. "Just in time, Ellis. I need you and your bears on Diomede Island when I call you. You'll be waiting to ambush a pack of black wolves and Lycan's trying to cross the land bridge. There will be a single female with them. Bring her to me alive, everyone else you can do with as you please."

Ellis nods slowly before adjusting his hat. "So basically, the bears are doing all the heavy lifting while you two sit up in your ivory tower?" He crosses his muscular arms over his chest as his eyes lock with mine. Have to hand it to the bear; he's got more balls than brains. He kind of looks like the bald guy from that police show—chiseled features, chocolate skin, and well-defined muscles. I always found it odd how a white bear had black skin, but hey, how can I judge when I'm a walking nightmare creature?

"No, not exactly. Lycans and Dire Wolves aren't built for the conditions. I think mother nature will do most of the damage for you. I mainly need you to recover the female." I smile—just this once, I do so without showing any teeth. I don't want to frighten the help too severely now.

"What's so important about this female? I mean, Polar Bear females are small and weak. Unless you're looking to breed her, I can't see the value. Just saying." Ellis shrugs his shoulders because, quite honestly, he doesn't give a fuck what the blood-suckers want. Little does Bane know that his son is working against him behind the scenes, and Ellis was doing the same behind the back of his alpha. Neither alpha deserved the title, mostly since they sold out to this reject from the old movie Nosferatu.

I twitch when Ellis speaks back to me. I know I need the Polar Bears because they could stay out on the ice for weeks without any problem. Dragons could only hold that position for a short time, and well, the Strigoi would freeze solid if on the tundra for too long.

So, there is only one solid tactical choice... the Polar Bears. "Gather your forces, and let me know what supplies you'll need to pull your mission off." I move behind my desk and pull out two burner phones. I toss one to Ellis and the other to Bane. "These will only ring if it's me. No one else has these numbers. They also have GPS trackers implanted in them in case you fall in battle."

Ellis and Bane nod their understanding. Then in typical Bane manner, he runs and leaps off the balcony and takes flight, heading home. Ellis shakes his head and walks out of the office.

Ellis

I reach into my pocket and turn on the mapping program on my phone. This was not only a bullshit meeting; it was a recon mission for the resistance. I took a significant risk attempting to map and double-cross the Strigoi, but it was worth it. When I finally reach outside the castle gates, I hop on my dirt bike and take off.

Riding as fast as I can to put as much distance between the Strigoi and me. I get about a hundred miles outside of dragon territory when I pull over and wait near what used to be a factory. The steel skeleton of the factory remains—the brick and mortar long since fallen. Mother Russia can be a real bitch when it comes to weather. Only the strong survive.

After what seems like forever, the outline of Alaric's dragon can be seen on the horizon. "It's about bloody time."

Alaric shifts and pulls a cloak from the bag his dragon carried. "Ellis, my man, how did the meeting go?" We exchange a proper bro hug—complete with the typical manly side hug and the exaggerated claps on the back.

"Bro, this situation is so beyond fucked up, it's not even funny." I start pacing back and forth.

"Your dad was there planning on attacking the lost Lycan Princess when she crosses the land bridge. That's wrong on so many levels." I grab a stick and begin to draw the sketch that the

Strigoi had drawn in the snow to give Alaric a clue as to what's going down.

"Hmm, looks like the leach put some thought into this. Then again, Tomas has had over two hundred years to plan his defenses. Don't worry, I'll post my team on the front line. We'll protect her and her pack when they come across." Alaric grabs a metal rod and points to the spot he intends to hold.

"You and your team can bring up the rear. We'll attack those loyal to my father together." Alaric has a coldness to him beyond that of being the son of the Ice Dragon alpha. You can tell that he has hit the point where he is tired of the injustice.

"You think we can take them? I mean, I know dragons are fucking tough, but it's dragon versus dragon, man. We bears can't take a direct hit from your ice blast." I watch Alaric closely as he paces when he then suddenly stops.

"Rumors are floating about that the princess is a hybrid; dragon and Lycan, first of her kind. If that's true, the ice blast won't phase her." He stops and looks up at me for a moment before continuing.

"Also, if it's true, she will make a perfect political alliance to have. I know a non-true mating won't yield children, but having the last Marelup heir as my mate would be impressive." Alaric seriously ponders the implications of this pairing, nodding slowly as if deciding for himself.

I shake my head in disagreement. "Not cool, bro. I know she needs a dragon mate, but you have brothers that may be a true mate to her. At least give her a chance to have a true mate. I know she also needs a bear; she can check out my entire clan for all I care as long as she's happy in the end." I cross my thick arms over my barrel chest and puff myself up a bit. I know head-to-head I wouldn't be able to beat Alaric, but fuck, I'm not some chicken shit.

I believe in being fair and not being a selfish fuck like the prince before me. "Seriously, bro, everyone deserves to be happy. Not all of us get forced into mating because of a passed down title."

Alaric's eyes flare to life at the mention of his title. He fucking hates being the damn Prince. "Yeah, it's a shit ton of fun while my father sucks Strigoi dick to keep his dirty dealings hidden. Yeah, it's fucking awesome that my people have no faith in the monarchy because of my father's shit. My father is a fucking puppet for the Strigoi" Alaric roars into the frozen wasteland before him. His rage is tangible in the air.

Surprisingly, there is a slight edge of pain to the scent. His eyes turn to mine. "We need to make this right. We need to take down the Strigoi, my father, and any other leader tainted by their poison. I know by now, your alpha was informed of the mission. Choose as many as you can that you trust." Alaric rests his hands on my shoulders and presses his forehead to mine. "Don't die."

I smirk and draw Alaric in for a tight hug. "Yo, you go from plotting domination to getting emotional and shit on me. Shit, I think I have whiplash. But seriously, be careful on your side of this shitting mess. It is far more dangerous than mine."

Alaric can't help but laugh. "Yeah, I know I'm all over the fucking place, man. There's so much to do and not enough time." Alaric's phone starts to ring.

His eyes fall to the caller ID. It's Alexander from the Dire Wolf compound. "Hey man, what's up?" Alaric puts the phone on speaker. "I've got Ellis here with me; speak freely."

"You sure it's safe to talk? What I have to tell you is super important." Alexander sounds more nervous than usual. There's a quiver to his voice that speaks volumes of what he is dealing with.

"What happened, Alex? Talk to me. Did your father kill your boyfriend like he's been threatening the last hundred years?" Alaric is getting agitated; he hates that Lucian treats his son like shit because he is gay.

"No, he's dead. Aurora and Nicodeamus killed him after Aurora survived the gladiator pit. That's why I was calling. We're preparing for war here." He swallows hard.

"She's building an army. A horde, so to speak. She's going to be heading your way the minute the twins complete their mating to her. She's fucking terrifying. Her wolf is bigger than any Lycan I've ever seen." Alaric and I stare at each other, jaws dropped in shock and total awe.

Once I can compose myself enough to piece together a complete thought, I'm the first to ask, "Hold up. How many rounds did she fight through before she got to Lucian?"

"Technically three. Though the last round really didn't count as it was her father she went up against. He bathed her in his blue-white flame and healed her. She was covered in fucking fire!" he practically screams.

"She walked out and kissed her father's maw, and then they proceeded to fuck shit up. It was the scariest and most exciting thing ever to happen here." He dramatically pauses for a few moments then starts up again.

"Then she left me as pack master to train a team of assassins. Seriously, what the fuck happened? I still don't get it. She came through here like a force of nature," Alex states.

Alaric begins to pace with the phone. "The dragon king lives, which means my father's claim to the throne is shit. You say she survived two rounds before her father and then his flames? Those flames he used were no joke. I'm curious, what color is her fur?" His eyes lock with mine at that exact moment. If his suspicions are correct, her fur definitely won't be black.

"We've been calling her Snow White. Her hair and fur are as white as freshly fallen snow. Her eyes are pools of mercury like her father's. She has the shifted form of a Lycan, with some dragon scales on her arms, like gauntlets near her talons, muzzle, and around her eyes. She's also got a disturbing obsession with collecting skulls. Just a heads up."

Alaric starts cracking up and pointing to himself after the skull comment.

I shake my head at Alaric's antics. "Apparently, Romeo over here has a skull collection too. It must be a dragon thing; skulls are fucking creepy. It's not Día De Los Muertos up in this mother-fucker. Crazy ass fucking dragons. Either way, thanks for the heads up, man. If you know when they are heading out, shoot us a text with a smiley face emoji and nothing else, so we'll know what's up."

I shake my head at Alaric, laughing hard enough to have tears in his eyes. "This is what I have to deal with. Peace out, Alex, keep in touch, and stay safe." I hang up the phone and stare at Alaric, waiting for him to compose himself. "Time to move, lover boy, we've got to set our plans in motion."

"Stay safe, brother. See you soon." Alaric turns then runs and leaps into the air shifting into his dragon. Great white wings carry him higher and faster; now he's even more inspired to fight, knowing that now there is a chance at victory. I return to my dirt bike and start it up. The ride home will be a long journey, but at least I will have something worth thinking about—an unknown princess and an impending war. Life was about to get real interesting real fast.

Thank you to all of my loyal fans that have followed me into this new version of Aurora's story. It means the world to me that YOU took the time to revisit her journey with me. Instead of writing full length stories for Aurora and the guys I'll be doing holiday Novella's. Each Novella you'll see Aurora and the kids as each new set pops up.

Moving forward I have a Nephilim Series I have been working on in the background. As well as a new Wolf shifter series and a Alien Mermaid series.

Keep your eyes peeled in my readers group Serenity's Den on Facebook.

Also by Serenity Rayne

The Aurora Markup Saga Hunt

The Aurora Marelup Saga - Fight

The Aurora Marelup Saga - Attack

The Aurora Marelup Saga - Welcome Home

The Dark Angel Chronicles

Made in United States
Troutdale, OR
03/12/2024

18392382R00139